Shira's Children

The Flight

Written by: Don Clayton

Illustrations: Clayton L. Peden

I0553721

Published by: Lite Works Publishing

Copyright © 2009 by: Don Clayton

Printed by: Lulu Press

ISBN 978-0-578-01927-7

Printed in the U.S.A.

To
Wesley, Trevor, and Magan,
whose love for a good story has inspired me!

Contents

Prologue

T his story begins on a clear night in the kingdom of Arielana; a lone horseman rides from the Delthyna castle. The evening is well spent when he turns onto the King's Highway and prepares for more than three hours of hard riding. The horse obediently quickens in answer to his prodding and spurring. With nostrils flaring, the animal's steaming hot breath is visible even though it is a mild midsummer night.

Across the country's rich farming valleys to his destination the horseman flies, while farmers in the cottages and cabins, long since retired for the night, are totally unaware to his troubled plight. The fate of a life long friend and his family depend on the safe delivery of the message he carries. He had struggled between the oaths to his country, which he had taken when he became a soldier, and the life of his companion since childhood. The enduring love for his friend had won over. He travels at break-neck speed driven by the decision he has made. The lone rider is determined to give the family of this life long friend as much time as possible to escape; they are going to need it.

Behind him, a band of the king's finest is preparing to ride. Desperately trying to put as much distance between him and this band, he is hoping to divert the intended fate of his friend this night, a fate that was chosen for him by the evil fiend: Devlin Rekaso. Behind him, Devlin's army of minions is now mounting up to ride to do his bidding. This hoard will carry out their orders without question. Many of the soldiers are the rider's friends. Nevertheless, they submit to their senior officer, their commander in arms, this Devlin, commissioned by the king himself. They have only been informed that an enemy of the kingdom must be defeated this very night. Asking no questions, they ride on, focused only on accomplishing the objective given them by their leader. They are just following orders, as loyal soldiers must.

The man in flight is an informant, planted deep within the

ranks of Devlin's men, the men that were once the king's loyal subjects. He is a very shrewd spy and well trusted, even though he reports Devlin's every move to a small group of rebels. These rebels know Devlin's true nature, and his evil intentions, even though the king does not.

The message bearer hastily reined his horse up the way to 'The Old Traveler's Inn'. Arriving at the three-story inn, he dismounted hurriedly, leaving his horse in the lane. He quickly approached the door and began pounding on it with the bottom of his fist. Presently, a dim light from an upstairs window became visible. It flickered and slowly disappeared as the candle was carried from the room, through the hall and down the steps. The bearer hurried, thinking it might be a late, weary traveler needing a place to rest for the night. The light reappeared in the windows of the lower level. The metal latch clanked and the heavy door creaked as it opened.

A drowsy eyed man stood before the lone traveler. The strong, slender gentleman was clothed in a nightshirt that reached his ankles. A neatly trimmed beard accented a face that was well weathered by years of toil. His eyes sharpened when he recognized the old familiar face, but his countenance changed quickly to concern. The visitor's serious expression told him something was not right!

Spencer Windmere had spent the day as any other, doing much of the same activities, business as usual around the inn. Although this day had started as so many before it, it would end as no other. For the life of the humble inn keeper and his three beloved children would never be as it was, all because of the message the lone rider carried.

"Marcus, my dear friend, whatever brings you here at this hour can *not* be good."

"Spencer, the time has come. … Devlin rides tonight!"

Up and Away

R oyce! … Royce!"
       Royce Windmere barely opened his eyes then slowly closed them again, his body not willing to give up its pleasant sleep.

"Royce, you have to wake up, *now*!" The father put his hands on his son's shoulders to bring him into awareness.

Royce rubbed his eyes. "What?" The candle flickered in the eyes of his father. Through the dim light he could see that something was causing his father much alarm.

"I need you to listen to me. You must take your sisters to the chalet in the mountain country," Spencer spoke with an urgency that his son had rarely heard.

"What? Chalet?"

"Royce, listen to me! We haven't much time! In the Hestia foothills is a chalet. You will go there. Stay there until I come for you. I have hidden provisions there, enough to last until I can come to get you. Do you hear me?"

Royce nodded and sat up.

"You must care for Wyn and Keli, keep them safe. Do you understand?"

The thought of caring for his two younger sisters did not set well. He was old enough to stay here and help his father, to stay and fight if need be. He cared not to baby-sit two girls, but he was not sure whether he dare say so to his father. "Yes, Father! What…what's happened?"

"Good. I do not have time to explain now, but I will when I get there. Do not travel the road; keep to the cover of the forests, stay out of the open spaces. Do not let anyone know of your business and trust no one! … I mean *no* one! Do you understand this?"

Royce nodded uneasily.

"Go straight north into the Black Forest."

"The Black Forest?" Royce interrupted. "But…"

"Yes." Spencer wrinkled his brow. "It will be far safer than engaging the rebels. … Now, listen close; this is important. Go north until you find the river. Follow it until you find a fork. A ridge splits the river. Follow that ridge; it will lead you to the valley just west of Mount Hestia. There you will find the chalet. With God's protection, you should reach it in five days. Be sure to stay out of sight. Make certain no one can follow you, cover your tracks like I have taught you. I will join you as soon as I can."

"But Father, let me stay. I…I can help."

"No! … No, it's too dangerous! I need *you* to protect Wyn and Keli. You take care of them with all that is in you. … I can *not* afford to lose them also." He paused for only a second. Royce knew why. It had been just more than a year, but he could still see his mother in his mind just as if it had been yesterday. His father still loved her so. He could see it in his eyes, even in the dim candlelight.

"I will not fail you, Father," his voice now had a boldness that did not sound like his own.

"I know you will not." He paused again to collect his thoughts. "Now, we must move quickly before they get here."

"Who, Father?" Royce climbed from his bed.

"Some very evil men. Some you know very well and some you don't. That is why you must trust no one! When I have lost them in the lower plains, I will join you, but only when it is safe. Now, go get your sisters and bring Sherwin! Get your necessities, and all that I have told you to gather. I will meet the four of you in the stables. I will have your horses ready."

There was so much he needed to ask his father, so much he needed to know. He opened his mouth to speak, but his father stopped him short.

"I will explain it all later. Now go!"

His father disappeared out the door and down the stairs. Royce went to wake the girls.

Something really terrible must have happened! He was scared, but he was not the only one, so was his father. Royce had seen it in his face and heard it in his voice. His father would never ask of such except under the gravest of circumstances. By the fear in his voice Royce knew that it tore at him to ask of such a difficult task. The decision had been a grim one to make. This would be no pleasure trip, this he knew for sure.

Royce had never been to Mount Hestia, nor had he ever heard of the chalet. He *had* been in the Black Forest a time or two, but only the edge. Even then he had seen why they called it the Black Forest; it was very disquieting to look upon. Still, if his father said to go, he would go! He would do it or he would die trying. His father certainly had great confidence in his ability; he feared maybe a little too much. If only his own certainty was just as strong. He hoped his fear had not shown to his father, though he was sure it had.

He slipped down the hall of the inn, using the back stairs to get to the upper level.

Rumors of people getting run from their homes, robbed and terrorized were going around, but Royce had never seen any of this. He had thought they were just rumors. What he had noticed was a difference in his father. A usual jovial person, he *had* seemed preoccupied lately. Royce was not sure why. These were indeed dark times.

He did not know if there were any guests sleeping at the inn or not. Just in case, he was very careful. Keeping a sharp eye out, he darted from shadow to shadow until he reached the girl's chamber.

Even though Wyn was younger than he was by two years, she was already as tall. She was sweet as a lamb most of the time, but could be ferocious as a lion if crossed. She had a mind of her own and most of the time it was already made up. He dreaded waking her at one in the morning. She would drill him for every detail, and he did not have any, nor did he have time for it. He shook her gently but urgently, if that is possible. "Wyn, wake up. We have to go. Now!"

His urgent voice woke her so quickly that Royce wondered if she had even been asleep. "What's going on? Where's Father? What did he say?"

"He's in the stables. He'll tell us everything. Right now we must be going."

Keli, on the other hand, was not a problem. "Keli. … Keli, I need you to get up. We are going on a trip."

"Really!" Keli aroused in an instant, her usual merry self. To her, this would be an exciting adventure into the forest on horseback. Being ten years old, she did not always understand all that was going on, but to her it did not matter, she could be happy in any situation. She could will herself to be. Royce almost envied her for that. Though she was three years younger than Wyn, she seemed to have no fear. The more daring and dangerous, the more excitement it generated in her. He wished he had some of her courage now.

She popped right up. Her dark brown hair fell into her face, which she immediately attended to. She instinctively shed her sleeping gown and put on her riding dress. Then she left to recover the pantry items, just as instructed to, if ever this day should happen. Their father had told them that they may be going on a trip soon and to have things prepared. When and if that time came, they may have to leave quickly. That time had come. He also had told them to tell no one about it, which did seem a little unusual. Nevertheless, Keli had gathered the necessary food items and hid them in her wardrobe. She could be ready in just a few short minutes.

Wyn's job was to gather nonfood essentials, such as cooking utensils, medicines, first aid supplies, a few blankets, etc. She also went to gather her stash, but at a slower pace. Though she did not complain, doubt and fear filled her mind. This was not quite the type of departure she had expected. She knew this moment might someday come, but she had prayed that it never would. Although no one had told her so, she sensed immediate danger in starting a long trip in the middle of the night. Something was wrong—very wrong.

Royce tried to be as quiet as he could and told the girls to do the same. If they could escape without even the staff having any knowledge of it, then they would not be able to disclose any vital information that would endanger them. He climbed the stairs to the highest level of the inn to a small room that his father had prepared for Sherwin to sleep. To his surprise, Sherwin was not there. The bed did not seem to have been slept in. He headed back down the steps wondering how was he to bring him if he could not find him.

From his father's personal chambers he collected a sword, a couple small daggers, a bow and quiver full of arrows. His father had showed him earlier where they were kept. He made a mental note to retrieve an axe or a hatchet and some rope from the tool room in the stables. He and the two girls met at the back door of the cook's kitchen with their packs and the items they had collected in hand.

"Why do we need all the weapons?" Wyn asked, eyeing what Royce had collected. "Where are we going?"

"We have to be prepared." He handed her the bow and the arrows. "Do you know how to use this?"

"Of course!" she sneered.

She did not hide the sarcasm in her voice. She took the bow in hand and fit the quiver over her left shoulder. He did not know for sure if she knew how to use it or not, but there was no time for a lesson now. He handed one of the daggers to Keli and told her to strap it around her waist. She obeyed without question.

They packed the supplies to the stables where they found their father waiting with eight horses, saddled, bridled and ready to ride. Royce eyed the eight horses.

"Good, you're here!" He put his hand to his mouth as to quiet them before they started in with the questions. He took his two daughters in his arms and hugged them tightly. "My dear sweet girls, did anyone see you?"

"No, I don't think so," Royce said as he took a hatchet from the tack room and started packing the supplies onto the horses. His father interrupted his work.

"I need you to take Sherwin with you," his father said.

"What?" Royce looked up at him in dismay.

Sherwin had come to live with them not many days earlier. He was a skinny boy, about ten years old. That was a guess, but no one seemed to know for sure how old he really was, even him. He was supposed to be kitchen help, but he did not even know how to scrub a pot. Royce wondered why his father would want him to take Sherwin, an almost total stranger.

His father could see the question in his eyes. "I know he will slow you down some, but he may be able to help you along the way. There is nowhere else for him to go, and we cannot leave him here. Everyone is to leave. We took no guest in last night and the staff is not here. When the men get here, they will find the inn empty. I expect you to take care of him the same as you would the girls."

"I will, Father."

"Good."

Wyn had detected her father's word that said they were going separate ways. "What do you mean? Are we not going together?"

"Wyn, I cannot risk it. You and Royce are going north."

Even though the lamplight was dim, the worried look on their father's face shone as if it were daylight. They had never seen him this way, and this disturbed the Windmere children.

Spencer began his final check of the saddles while he spoke. "You will go north. I will go south. I will take the extra horses and leave a trail that will be easy for them to follow. I will make them think we have fled to the coast. Then you will be able to get to the chalet unseen. Once there, you should be safe, until I can get there."

Safe? Royce thought. *How could we be safe without Father!*

"The chalet? Father, what is it? What has happened?" Wyn pulled back a little.

A serious expression took hold of their father's face, and he stopped working with the horses. "Listen to me. Listen carefully. The rebels are on the move. We have an informant that tells us that they are planning to attack the inn at dawn."

"Oh, no! Why, Father? The inn is all you have. It's all you have worked for all your life," Wyn objected.

"No! It's not all I have. I'm not worried about the inn, the inn they can have. I'm trying to protect something far more important."

"What's that, Father?" Keli was about to cry.

"You and Wyn and Royce … and Sherwin."

Royce thought it odd that his father was including Sherwin. Sherwin had not been with them much more than a week.

Spencer continued, "I can't tell you everything now. There is not time. I will explain it all to you when I come. Right now you must ride. You must ride as hard as you can. You must leave at once. Be brave, my children."

"Father, we must stay together!" Wyn insisted.

"That is not possible, Wyn. But you must go for now. You will all just have to trust me. Do as Royce tells you; he knows how to get you there. … God be with you. I love you dearly."

Spencer had carefully chosen the four best horses and separated them from the others. They were the strongest he had, those he knew to have speed and endurance.

Royce had started once again to pack the supplies. "But…" He tried hard not to let his fear show, but his eyes watered, and he quickly wiped them dry.

"Royce, we will all be together again very soon. I promise." His father gave him a forced smile then he leaned close to Royce and almost whispered, barely able to keep his voice from cracking, "I know you will take good care of my girls…but you must also do the same for Sherwin. Promise me you will value his life as your own."

"His life?" Royce turned to look at Sherwin.

"Promise me!" he repeated.

"I will," Royce suspiciously agreed.

Spencer hugged all three of his children at the same time. "Mount up!" Then he helped the children onto the horses.

Sherwin attempted to do the same. He stuck the wrong foot in the stirrup.   Realizing this would cause him to face the rear end of his horse; he tried to correct it on the way up. He found himself standing on his knees in the saddle. Spencer patiently supported the boy as he turned himself aright. He plopped down into the saddle causing the horse to jump. Spencer put the reigns in his hands and instructed him to hold tight.

Keli giggled, and then quickly put her hand over her mouth, but Sherwin did not act as if he heard. Royce just watched and shook his head. Was this what he was going to have to deal with the whole journey?

His father straightened and then spoke louder, "Now go! And let no one keep you from your task! … God speed and be careful! … I love …you." Spencer Windermere gave a small wave as he watched as his precious children begin to fade into the miserable night. "Dear God of all living, give my children safe passage! They must not fail." Then he was fully in tears, something he had not done in a year.

Walking the animals from the backcourt, the four eased their horses through the front gate and looked back; their father gave one last wave and disappeared. They urged their horses to a quickened pace as they turned onto the open highway. Their adventure had begun.

Children, What Children?

As the moon rose, it was nearly full, illuminating the countryside quite clearly. It was a gracious help for the nighttime travelers. It was clear enough to make long shadows on the shoulders of the road.

No one spoke. All were lost in their troubled thoughts. The only sound was that of the horse's hooves clattering on the hard packed roadway.

Royce watched his shadow as it rippled over the uneven rocks along the edges of the road. He was deep in thought; he was confused and bewildered. Father had explained very little in his haste. They had been sent from their home in the middle of the night. Not completely sure where they were going was bad enough, but he did not even know why. Why would the rebels attack the inn? They had nothing of any real value! There were many other estates that would prove more lucrative if it were valuables they were after. They had very little copper, no silver, no gold and no gems. What could they possibly be looking for?

The last few days with their father had been very strange. More often than usual he had said he loved them. He had told them that no matter what may happen, to do exactly as he instructed with out question. He had overheard him tell the girls that if anything were to happen to him they were to follow Royce's lead, also without question (something that would be nearly impossible for Wyn). His father had known something was brewing, but why did he not tell him more? Father had suggested several times that they may soon be required to take a trip, but this is not at all what he expected. Many times they had gone with their father on some very pleasurable excursions. Though Royce loved those times of travel, this would not be one of those times. They had never been separated from their father like this before. None of the other expeditions had required them to leave in the middle of the night under cover of darkness. They had never had to fend for themselves, going to a place they had never been. How would they find their way? How would they protect themselves? When would they return? No, this was not to be one of those pleasurable trips.

In five hours, the sun would rise on the old inn, but it would be empty, something that had not happened in all the years since it was built. Sixteen years earlier, Spencer Windmere and his new bride had started with nothing. Virtually penniless, they started building a home for themselves, and for the family that would follow. Work was not something that Spencer feared. He had not only built a home for his family, but it became a profitable business and somewhat of a comfortable living. It was no palace, but it had been their home for all these years. Royce could remember living nowhere else. It had been a loving home, a caring home, a safe home, until now! Now they were being forced from it with very little explanation! Would they ever be able to return?

Royce wondered what the rebels would do when they got to the inn. All would be quiet when they surrounded it at daybreak. All would be silent until they smashed down the door. They would think nothing of destroying their beloved home. They would probably search ever room, ransack the place, but they would find no one. Hopefully, they left no clue to let them know where they had gone.

The escape was nearly flawless. No one saw the children leave. Few were awake at this hour in the small community of Recidell. The highways were deserted. With all the fear and unrest in the kingdom, people did not travel much any more. If they did, they never traveled alone, and for sure, not at night. No one would know where the children had gone.

A league and a half from the inn, the four met the only other travelers they would see all night. A faint glow began to appear in the road ahead. Royce studied the glow trying to figure what it was, but Sherwin knew right away.

"Riders! Get off the road! Quick!" It was the only words Sherwin had spoken the whole evening.

The light had warned them just early enough for them to scramble off the highway without being seen. Scarcely had they hidden the horses between some boulders and shrubs before the barrage was upon them. They climbed upon the rocks and peered over the ledge to watch as the heated riders passed beneath them. It was good that they had hidden themselves, for these men rode hard and looked none too friendly. They numbered at least thirty, maybe forty. Prepared for battle, each carried a sword or a spear, some carried both. All wore mail armor and had shields. Many of them also held torches, which was a stroke of luck for the children. The band passed by with no knowledge of the four watching them from the ledge above. Leading the group was a man the children knew well.

"It's Uncle Dev…!" Keli started to rise, but Sherwin stopped her. He pulled her back down quite abruptly.

"Stay down!" he spoke in a loud whisper but was not likely to be heard over the thunderous noise of the horses. He said nothing else until the horsemen were well beyond the next rise. "That was the king's Elite, not the highwaymen."

The Elite were rarely seen in their sleepy little town, a lone rider now and then, but not this barrage. The three siblings looked at Sherwin. He was not one to talk much; in fact he almost never spoke unless spoken to. Even then he would answer in as few words as possible. It surprised them all for him to speak in such a manner.

"How would you know that?" Royce quizzed.

"They were all bretagne!" Sherwin answered.

When he did talk, Sherwin would almost always say things that made no sense at all. Maybe for this reason he was so quiet. Royce was not quite sure that all his candles were burning. Royce and Wyn looked at each other, but neither replied to his statement.

Keli turned, looked confusingly at him, and whispered back, "That was Uncle Devlin. He has come to help Father. Right?"

"I do not think so," Sherwin said.

"What do you mean, you don't think so? Of course he has come to help," Wyn said forcefully, she looked confused at Sherwin.

"Devlin is your uncle?" Sherwin looked surprised.

"No, not really," Royce said uneasily. "He's a man Father used to work for. We have known him for years, no relation really. How do you know Devlin?"

"All know Devlin," Sherwin replied darkly.

"Well, Father said not to trust anyone," Royce told them.

"Well, surely he didn't mean Uncle Devlin?" Wyn defended.

"He is not *really* our uncle!" Royce repeated.

"He's always been like an uncle to me," Keli spoke as she looked in the direction the riders had gone.

Wyn looked hard at Sherwin and then at Royce, but did not say anything further.

"Let's go!" Royce spoke again only after he felt sure it was safe. "We are leaving the highway."

"What?" Wyn questioned.

"It is too dangerous to follow the road!" Royce was angry with himself already, knowing that he had almost led them into trouble. His father *had* told him not to go by the highway.

"Where are you going?" Wyn asked.

"To the chalet in the mountains, as Father said."

"Where is this chalet?"

"In the shadows of Mount Hestia. Father instructed us to go there and wait. He said he would meet us there."

"Mount Hestia? Do you know how far that is? It is eight or nine days hard ride!" Wyn looked shocked. "I hope you know what you are doing."

"I do. We are taking the short way. We will be there in five days through the Black Forest. Now let's go," he said the words with much more confidence than he felt.

"The Black Forest?" Wyn grabbed Royce's shoulder and pulled him about quite roughly. "No sane person goes in there. Nobody goes through the Black Forest!" Wyn's voice was near panic.

"We do! Father's orders!" Royce said firmly. He pulled loose.

He started for the horses hoping that would end the conversation—it did. Wyn said nothing more, but the look on her face caused Royce's doubt to grow even more.

They rode away from the highway hoping to avoid any more royal confrontations. Any attempt to track the children from that point would prove difficult. The rocky knoll would leave few tracks, but it was not to be that way for long, the knoll gave way to an enormous farming valley. Unfortunately, by first morning light the four were still many leagues from the Black Forest. The rising of the sun and the wide-open fields would make it difficult to stay hidden.

As they rode, Keli hummed a tune, one that Royce was very familiar with, though he could not think of what it was. That was Keli's way; she was always happy wherever she went. She always looked on the bright side of any situation, good or bad. Very few things escaped her attention, and she was interested in everything, especially nature and animals.

Royce knew Wyn, on the other hand, would be miserable. When she was at home she rarely ventured out, especially since they had lost their mother. He was sure she was more interested in pretty dresses and social events, though she had had little opportunity to attend any. Yes, Wyn would be very ill prepared for this trip, or so he thought. She did surprise him in that she was even able to manage a horse as well as she did.

Sherwin just rode and kept quiet.

***

When the sun finally rose, it appeared to be a big, red flaming ball that seemed to come right up out of the earth. The early scattered clouds also appeared to be afire, reflecting the sun's light into burnt oranges and deep reds. The travelers paused in the middle of a wide field to notice the glorious morning that had just dawned. The Ole Traveler's Inn had been surrounded by such a thick grove of trees that they were rarely able to see such a glorious sunrise.

"Oh!" The sight definitely moved Wyn. "I don't know when I've ever seen such a magnificent sunrise."

"When have you *ever* seen the sunrise?" Royce's words took the smile from Wyn's face, and he was sorry he had said them.

"I've seen it," Wyn snapped "…a few times."

"It *is* beautiful!" added Keli. "Isn't it, Sherwin?"

"Yes, my lady." Sherwin did not seem too impressed by the glorious sight.

After they traveled on for most of the morning, Royce estimated they had covered at least three leagues before sunrise, but maybe half that in the hours since. He was sure that was not fast enough. The early sun did insure them of their northerly direction. Nevertheless, crossing the freshly cut hay fields, they could be spotted like a fly in the milk. A small grove of trees offered them a little welcomed protection. Royce stopped his horse and dismounted.

"Why are we stopping here?" Wyn looked about her with an uneasy feeling.

"To give the horses some water. They have been carrying us for hours, they must be thirsty." He petted his horse on the side of the neck and led him to a brook that meandered through the small wood. "There you go Ole Murdoch, have some water." Then Royce hollered over his shoulder, "Sherwin, dismount and refill the water bottles."

"Yes, my lord." Sherwin began to obey immediately.

"Don't call him that!" Wyn retorted. "Sherwin, you are not our servant. We are equals. Everyone can fill their own water bottles." The last statement was more directed at Royce than anyone else.

She gave him a glance that caused him to withhold what he was about to say in reply. Hunger was beginning to set in, so Wyn handed each a small bread cake.

Royce tried to bite into his. "These things are hard as stone!" he barked.

"Don't complain!" Wyn barked back. "They have been dried, makes them keep longer!"

Keli quickly jumped to the ground and patted her horses on the side. "Sweet lady," she whispered.

"She is not a she, she's a he," Royce corrected with a little smile. He patted Ole Murdoch, and then began checking the saddle as the horse got his fill of the cool spring water.

"Well, he's still sweet." Though it was a bit of a stretch for her, Keli rubbed the back of her horse's left ear right under the mane. "What's his name?"

"Butch," Royce answered.

"Oh, no! What kind of a name is that for such a majestic animal? He must have a better name than that." Keli's imaginative mind began working. "I'll call his name…"

"How about '*Tempest*'?" Wyn had also dismounted, though she did not want to. She would have rather kept going. "Because that is what it feels like to me."

"That's not a sweet name for a horse," Keli disagreed.

"Stormy, then!" Wyn was rubbing her back.

"That's no better." Keli did not appreciate the suggestions. "What about Dante'? I have always loved the name Dante'."

"Keli." Royce sometimes wished she could just be satisfied. "He already has a name. … It's Butch."

"Okay, I'll just call him Bishop, that's sounds important. That way he won't notice the change as much. Not as good as Dante', but…"

"Dante' is a good name. It means ever… last… ing," Sherwin's voice trailed off when he realized he had gained the attention of the whole party. This attention made him very uncomfortable. He then turned away and pulled his horse forward to the stream for a drink.

The other three looked at each other, and then Keli broke the silence. "Then I will call him Dante'."

Royce shrugged his shoulders and nodded. If it makes her happy, he could live with it. It was definitely not worth an argument. He continued to check the rest of the saddles.

"What is Sherwin's horse called?" Keli wanted to know.

"Victor," he replied.

"Now that is a good horse name. Don't you think Sherwin?"

He just nodded back over his shoulder.

"Victor! Now that is a name a horse deserves. Sounds like: Victory! Not Butch." Keli shook her head. "That sounds like a meat cutter. Or a mistake … Botch!"

"What's my horse's name?" Wyn asked.

"Whirlwind," Royce said meekly.

"That figures." She rolled her eyes.

"Wyn, you're just not used to riding for so long," Royce chuckled. "You will get use to it."

"At least you're not wearing a dress!" She glared at him, still rubbing her back.

Keli laughed out, thinking what that would look like.

This was true. Royce tried to think of something to say to ease the situation. "You will get used to it…eventually." That was the best he could come up with.

"I don't want to get use to it!" she cried. "This whole situation is… is unacceptable! I just want it to be over!"

She walked a few steps away. Royce decided to leave it alone. He was feeling a bit sore too, but he was not about to admit it, particularly to her. He did feel for Wyn and Keli. He tried to consider how much harder it would be to ride a horse in a dress.

***

Crossing the cornfields they could stay virtually hidden among the stalks, for the corn would soon be tasseling, but in the hay fields and the pastures they looked very conspicuous. Royce decided that if they were going to be seen, riding the road would arouse much less suspicion. It made sense, but it did not prove to be a wise decision. As soon as they had started down a tree-lined lane, they received exactly what they did not want—attention.

"Halt!" They heard a shout from behind them.

Royce turned to see two men dressed in military mail armor with spears and swords. They were mounted atop two horses and displaying the realm's colors. These were not farmers wondering why they had crossed their land as he first hoped, but two highwaymen. He was not about to stay and see what they wanted.

"Get up!" he hollered to his horse. He told the other three to do the same.

Each spurred their horse to a full gallop.

The men hollered again, "Halt! ...Halt by order of the highwaymen!" They pursued after them.

The chase was on. Down the sandy road they flew, dust boiling up from each hoof as it pounded the ground. Knowing that they would have little chance of out running them, Royce looked for someway to lose them. Then he saw what he was looking for, the Black Forest! They were near! If they could get into the trees, maybe they could lose them.

"This way!" he hollered back to the others.

Royce left the road again and directed his horse out across a wide hay field. The other three followed. Unfortunately, so did the highwaymen. He urged his horse to go faster, checking often to make sure Wyn and Keli were still with him. He was not sure if it was that his sisters could ride that well or it was the fact that the horses were trying to out do each other, but they were staying close, pulling along side as if almost to pass him. Even Sherwin was holding close, not looking like a novice now, but riding like an expert. It would not have been enough if they had far to go; the men were gaining. If they could reach the Black Forest, then just maybe they would have a chance to escape. With a last burst of speed they entered the woods.

Royce did not really expect the highwaymen to stop at the edge of the forest, but he was hoping. Nevertheless, that is exactly what they did.

"I'm not following them in there!" The first man shouted to the other as he pulled his horse to a stop.

"Why not?" said the second.

"That's the Black Forest! Half of those that go in never come out! The ones that did had been missing for weeks!"

"What are you going to tell Devlin? How do we tell him that we let four children get away?"

"Children? What children?" The first man stared at the second.

"The four riders, they were children!"

"Did you see any children? I didn't see any children!"

"Are you blind, I....?" The second man stared blankly until he grasped what the first had meant. "No ... No, I didn't see any children either!"

The two highwaymen turned their horses in the opposite direction and trotted back the way they had come.

Into the Black Forest

The children did not slow their horses until they were deep into the Black Forest. Only after being absolutely sure that the men did not follow them, they relaxed.

"Why were they chasing us?" Wyn wanted to know.

No one had an answer for her.

"The important thing is that they did not follow us into the Black Forest!" Royce was gloating a little in his victory.

"Proving that they are much wiser than we!" Wyn said sarcastically.

Royce frowned, so much for his victory. "It got us away, did it not?"

"Temporarily!" Wyn complained.

"Let's just ride!"

"This saddle was not designed for a lady."

"Don't worry, you'll get used to it," Royce's words were no comfort to her, he knew, especially when they generated such a look from her.

"I don't want to be here long enough to get used to it. I don't like it here! ... It's creepy," Wyn complained some more.

"One can see why they call this the Black Forest," said Royce.

"Yeah, I've heard the guests tell stories about this place; it's supposed to be full of ghosts and goblins and all kinds of suchlike!" Keli cupped her hand over her cheeks. "Oh, my!"

"Cut it out, Keli." Wyn glared at Keli. "These woods are not safe. We could be in real danger. Who knows what we will find in here? There could be wild animals. ... I just want to go home, where we were safe."

"We will, just as soon as Father takes care of the revolt, but for now we may be safer here. Father thinks so anyway," Royce said it to reassure himself just as much as Wyn. He too, wanted desperately to go back home; back to the life they had before, but he had no idea when that would be.

"But what if he can't? What if he can't put down the rebels? What if they have grown too strong?" Her grief showed severely in her eyes.

"Don't talk like that!" Royce pulled his horse to a stop and put his hand on her shoulder, but she pulled away. "Father is a wise man, a brave man. He knows a lot of people that are still true to the king. I know he will make everything right." Royce tried to smile again. "We just have to keep the faith... in him... and the Father above."

Wyn wiped her eyes, for she knew she could be brave, but right now, she found it extremely hard.

The deeper they entered the mystifying woodland, the thicker the trees became. The trees produced such a thick, impenetrable canopy that the sun was completely blocked out. They found the woods harder on the horses than in the fields. The ground was uneven and obstructed by fallen logs and debris. Without a beaten path to follow, the traveling was more difficult than Royce had expected.

They rode in single file, continuing on the best they could. Keli lagged behind. She was almost always last; for she had to stop and take note of the all the new and interesting wonders she was passing through. Suddenly, Keli heard a slapping sound followed by an "ugh". She looked up in front of her just in time to see Sherwin rolling head over heels off the back of his horse. As the horse passed by a huge beech tree, apparently the end of a limb had caught in the horse's bridle. When it pulled loose, it swung back into place with a snap, stinging his cheek. The force was not nearly enough to knock poor Sherwin off his horse, but the surprise of it caught him completely off guard. His reaction caused him to do a complete somersault off the horse's rump and land squarely upright on his feet on the ground. The horse did little more than jump and then turned to look at his unseated rider. For a second, the horse and rider seemed to gaze at each other in bewilderment. Sherwin checked himself for any damage. His cheek stung a little, and his pride—a whole lot.

After watching the whole event take place in front of her, she could not hold back her words, "Interesting dismount!" She tried, but could not contain her laughter. Sherwin did not appreciate the humor of the situation, and he let her know by glaring at her. Keli stopped laughing at once and tried to wipe the smile off her face when she saw his pride had taken a hit.

Sherwin quickly remembered his place and softened his glare. "Sorry, my lady." He climbed back on his horse and continued.

Royce hollered back for the two of them to stay close, and they urged their horses to go a little faster.

Keli coaxed her horse up to the side of Sherwin's. "Are you hurt?"

"No, my lady."

"I'm sorry I laughed…"

"Yes, my lady"

"But it was funny."

"Yes, my lady." Sherwin looked at her, but he did not smile, in fact, Keli had never seen him smile, ever!

"Forgiven?" Keli could not stand for anybody to be angry with her, especially when it was her fault. If she could get Sherwin to smile, all would be well. Keli wondered what made him so sad. He would just have to cheer up. Keli decided this would be her quest during their expedition, getting Sherwin to smile.

"Forgiven," he consented.

It was the most words that she had heard him utter the whole day. True, Sherwin did not like to talk much, but if he stayed around Keli he was going to have to change that. She would make sure of it. They rode on in silence for a short while, but Keli just could not stay quiet for long.

"What did you call the horseman on the highway last night? …Britain's?"

"Not the horsemen, the horses. 'Bretagne'!"

"Bretagne? I never heard it. What is it?"

"It's a bred of horse. They are known for their great strength and their comfortable gait. Usually they are only owned by the very rich. It is what the highwaymen use. The common man cannot afford one."

"How do you know so much? You're only a staff boy."

Sherwin looked down.

"Oh… I'm sorry. I didn't mean it that way. You haven't always been a peasant, have you?"

"No, my lady."

Keli caught the sadness in his words. "We haven't always been runaways either."

"You two are going to have to keep up!" Royce hollered again. "We will never get there if we don't get a move on!"

Keli and Sherwin hurried to catch up.

***

By nightfall they had still not come upon the river, though they had covered several leagues that day. Royce could not help but to second-guess his memory. Was he going the right way? Shouldn't he have found the river by now? How could he not find something as big as a river? Was he really going to be able to do this?

Finding a level spot in the rough terrain, Royce announced, "We will camp here tonight." He dismounted.

"What? Here?" Wyn was shocked at the idea of spending the night in the Black Forest.

"What else would you suggest," Royce answered roughly, "a room in the inn?"

She said no more but glared at him in deep disgust.

A particularly thick evergreen proved to be a great place to bed down for the night. The ground was a bit softer on the pine needles, and possibly they would stay dry, protected from the morning dew. Though they had not seen any sign of people for a long while, that night Royce decided against building a fire for fear that it might still attract attention. They tied a rope between two near-by trees and secured the horses. Wyn poured water for them into a hollowed place on a stone while Keli scurried the area for grasses, leaves and any plants that a horse could eat. Then the travelers had a supper of dried fruits. They ate ravenously. Aside from Wyn's little bread cakes, it was the only thing they had had in nearly twenty-four hours.

The Black Forest was just that—black. It was dark in the daylight, at night it was nothing but black as pitch. The moon rose a few hours after sunset. Then it gave an eerie glow to the trees among the foggy night air.

Royce had just as soon the moon not rise. He remembered what Keli had said about ghosts and goblins and suchlike. Trying to put that out of his mind, he attempted to look at the stars, the few he could see through the canopy of leaves. Sleep did not come easily. The crickets and tree frogs had begun their night long concert right after dark. They seemed ten times louder than the children had ever heard them before. The ground was hard, unlike their soft beds in the inn.

For the longest time Wyn kept whispering, "What was that?" or "Did you hear that?" every time she heard the slightest noise.

Despite all of this, they did get some much-needed sleep, but only because of sheer exhaustion.

Royce said a silent prayer before he drifted off. "Please, Lord, keep Father safe."

*

It was already light when Royce woke the next morning. He found it difficult to move, for every joint in his body ached. The hard ground had taken its toll. He heard footsteps. It took some effort but he forced an eye open. He looked around; someone was already up. Wyn came walking into the camp. "Who missed the sunrise this morning?"

"Where have you been?" he grunted.

"Preparing to move on! We need to get going! The quicker we get out of these woods the better!"

Royce did not like being told what to do by his sister, but he did not reply because he knew she was right.

"Look what I found!" Keli had also gotten up before Royce. She came running into the camp holding up something wrapped in her handkerchief. She opened the cloth revealing a good bit of nuts and wild blue berries.

"Good job, Keli!" Wyn praised.

She beamed with pride.

Royce got up and looked around the camp. "Where's Sherwin?"

"He said he was going to ready the horses," Wyn answered calmly.

A terrible though struck him as he looking at the rope that now hung empty between the two trees. He spoke again, a little louder, "And where are the horses?"

"I... ah." Wyn also looked at the empty rope.

"Oh, no! Father said to trust no one! I can't believe I have been so stupid," Royce yelled.

"Royce, calm down, he didn't mean Sherwin. He is just a boy."

"Just a boy? When I get my hands... Sherwin! ... SHERWIN!"

"Yes, my lord?" Sherwin came up the embankment leading all four horses back into camp.

"I said not to call him that!" Wyn corrected

Royce shot a negative glance at her then turned on Sherwin.

"Where have you been?"

"Watering the horses. There's a good spring at the foot of the hill."

Royce burned with embarrassment. "Okay, just… just let me know the next time."

"I would have, but you were asleep, my lord."

"Don't call him that!" Wyn strongly corrected again. "You are not a slave."

"Yes, my lady," Sherwin replied sheepishly

"And don't call *me* that, either!"

"Yes, my… Yes."

"Okay! Let's eat." Wyn softened a bit, hoping that would be the last time she would hear 'my lord' or 'my lady' from Sherwin.

After a prayer of thanks, the four quietly enjoyed the breakfast that Keli had collected from the forest.

"Royce." Keli looked at him, apparently pondering something. "How big do birds get?"

"I don't know. Some can get quite big. Hawks and eagles can get a wingspan equal to a man's outstretched arms. I hear that a condor could get bigger than that. Why?"

"Well, while I was out I just saw the biggest bird. It flew over while I was picking the berries. It had to be much bigger than me! …At least…I think it was a bird. It looked very strange."

"What else could it be, a flying horse? Now that would be handy." Royce chuckled.

"Yes, wouldn't it?" Keli said quietly.

"It could be a leviathan!" Sherwin spoke softly.

"It could be a what?" Wyn questioned.

He had spoken without thinking. Now all eyes were on him again. "Have you not heard the stories of the great beast that rules over the Black Forest?"

"No. What stories?" Keli was intrigued.

"Leviathan is a legend that supposedly lives in these black woods. It's a furious beast that towers two or three times higher than a man. They say he is as big as a cabin. They also say he can fly, and that he carries with him the fire of a thousand candles."

"Really?" Keli cried with excitement. She loved such stories. "Tell me more!"

"No," Wyn interjected. "He is lying. He is just making up wild stories trying to scare you. There is no such beast! Sherwin, please hold your tongue. We have enough to think on as it is."

"Yes, my la…" he stopped short when Wyn gave him the look. "Forgive me, but I never lie. I said it was a legend. I was just repeating the stories I have heard others tell, nothing more."

After eating, they bridled, saddled and packed the horses and once again took up their trek, heading north. Maybe today, with luck, they would find the river. Then it would be on to the mountain chalet.

The deeper they went into the forest, the rougher the landscape became. The slopes became higher and steeper. The trees grew closer and thicker. They had to duck often because of the low limbs. The under brush also was growing thicker and harder to pass through. Obviously these woods were never traveled. It became impossible to always head north because of the obstacles. They wound their way back and forth, but still they pressed on all morning, hoping to find the river.

Royce gave his horse a pat just under the mane. He glanced at his two sisters and Sherwin. "Try to keep up! We have a long way to go!"

"It would be easier if you slowed a little. We are not used to such a hard pace." Wyn was right a usual, but Royce did not want to slow down.

"You said the quicker we get out of this forest the better."

"Yes, but I want to be alive when we do!"

"There's a greater chance of that if we go faster!"

"What?"

Though Wyn was younger than Royce she still could be quite overbearing. It had been that way since they had lost their mother the year before. She, being the oldest girl, just stepped up and took the responsibilities that their mother had carried. She felt that the cooking, the sewing, the mending, and all the things that her mother had been doing was now her responsibility. Many times, Royce thought she carried it a little too far. She tried to tell him what to do just as Mother would, and he resented it.

Keli, on the other hand, was always happy and carefree. Though she and Wyn were sisters, their characters were as different as daylight and dark. She had the courage of a lion, but the nature of a shepherd. She loved all living creatures, and they seemed to love her. She was absolutely enjoying the trip thus far. Anytime there was any wildlife she would be the first to spot it. Then she would point it out to all the others so that they could enjoy it as much as she.

They had a long way to go, but Royce had no way of knowing how far. He did know one thing; he had to push the others if they were ever to reach their destination. Nevertheless, questions kept filtering into his head. Once they had found the river, it would be confirmed their direction was right. He thought they should have reached it long before now. In all his travels throughout the country with his father, he had always depended on his father to guide. Now, he was in charge, and he found out what a responsibility it was. It did not help that Wyn thought he was just being stubborn and bossy. Maybe he was. It was not that he wanted to be, however, what other choice did he have? He had to push hard and appear to be confident, though thoughts of doubt clouded his mind. The task seemed much simpler when his father had described it, but now that they were here in the middle of unfamiliar territory, confusion nagged at him. What if he could not find the way? What if they were going the wrong direction? They could be lost out in the Black Forest for a long time, maybe forever. The kingdom seemed to stretch on and on endlessly. He had no map to guide his way, there were not many that included the Black Forest, and very few of those that did were accurate. All he had to guide him were his father's words.

Still studying on this, Royce rode through a break in the brush. He came out of the trees into what he thought was going to be a clearing. His horse reared! He pulled back on the reigns and gripped the front edge of the saddle to keep from being thrown to the ground!

"Whoa! … Whoa." His horse settled and backed a few steps. He looked in front of him. "Whoooaa," he said in a long, drawn-out tone. He took a moment for his heart to catch up with him.

There before him was a rock cliff that dropped off several hundred spans. He could see above the treetops to the next ridge, it seemed ever so far. The forestland had given way to an enormously deep gorge.

"Careful!" he warned his sisters and Sherwin, but they had already seen what had disturbed Royce's horse and began to dismount.

"How beautiful!" Keli whispered. "I have never seen anything like it in my life! Do you think so, Sherwin?"

"Yes, my lady," Sherwin replied in his usual monotone way.

Beauty was not the word Royce would have used to describe what he saw. Maybe it was in a grand sort of way, but all he could see was a hindrance. How would they get down? How would they cross? And where was the river? It was the first time he had been able to see this far ahead, but he saw no river! No. This was not beauty; this was a major problem!

When given this task, Royce considered failure unthinkable, but he must have gone wrong somewhere. He replayed in his mind the route that brought them this far. He ran it over again and again, searching for anything he may have missed, for anywhere he may have made a wrong turn. The last moments with his father had been disturbing, but he was sure he had followed his instructions exactly. Although, it *had* been one o'clock the morning, nobody could think straight at that hour. *Given the stress of having to flee for your life, how could I have remembered every detail?* he thought inwardly.

Tragedy Strikes

For several minutes, the four stared in silence out over the canyon carved deep into the earth. If it were not for the fact that they had to cross this great expanse, it would have been an awe-inspiring sight.

Wyn was the first to break the silence, "Just continue going north, we'll find the river." She was not being supportive, she was being sarcastic.

"It is down there … somewhere. It has to be!" Royce said, quite annoyed.

"I think we will have to go back."

"Go back where, to the inn? We can't do that," Royce spoke a little harsher than he meant to.

"Well, it is obvious we can't go forward!"

"We have too. Father would not have sent us this way if we couldn't get through!"

"Unless you can sprout wings, we have no choice! We can't get down from here. Maybe Father didn't know there was a canyon. Maybe he has never been this way. Maybe he has never been this far into the Black Forest! Or…maybe…we are lost!"

"We are not lost," Royce answered quickly. "Father knows the way. We did just as he said." That statement was not completely true. Royce knew it. His father had told him to go straight north and to not follow the road. The night they had fled from home, the first hour of travel, he *had* followed the road. The road did head north, but veered to the east. Maybe it had veered more than he thought. Maybe it was just enough to throw them off the right path.

"Just what do you suggest?" Wyn was waiting for his decision.

"Had we left the road sooner, we would have come upon the canyon farther west. I say we head west and look for a way down."

"And I say we go back and start again."

"No. We have no time for that. That would put us three days behind. If we go west it will put us where we should have been, had we left the road sooner."

"Okay…I hope you know what you're doing, for our sakes," she did not sound very confident.

Royce was aggravated, a little at Wyn for having so little faith in him, a lot at himself for not having gone straight north from the start. His father had told him not to travel the road, but it had been so much easier than across the country. His disobedience almost caused them to get caught by the Elite, and then by two of the highwaymen. Now, he may have made it harder on all of them in the long run.

Following the cliff edge proved to be undoubtedly too dangerous. The trees and underbrush were so thick in places that it over hung the cliff edge, preventing the horses from passing safely. If they fell back into the woods the way would be much easier, but they might miss a passage down the cliff. Royce made the decision for the girls to take the horses back into the woods and travel west for a half a league or so, and then they were to make their way back to the canyon rim. Royce would walk the cliff edge and search for any possible way to the bottom. This decision did not set well with Wyn; for she voiced several times that they should stay together. Royce would not give in but insisted that they do as he instructed. She reluctantly agreed.

For a while they kept in contact by occasionally hollering to one another, but their voices eventually became so faint they gave that up. Hiking the rim was trouble. The underbrush tore at his pants legs, limbs slapped him in the face, and the rocks were sometimes extremely difficult to climb over. However, he checked every inlet, every crevice for any possible way down. Twice, he found places he was sure he could have climbed down himself, but he needed a slope gentle and easy enough to get the four horses down.

Two hours later he heard familiar voices. He came to a clearing in the trees where his sisters and Sherwin sat waiting with the horses. There beyond them was a cut into the rock cliff with a gentle sloping bottom. The ground looked as if at one time it had been a road, but had long since been abandoned.

In any event, Wyn sat smiling. "What happened to your pants?"

"Don't ask!" He looked at the tear in his trousers. He was happy they had found a passage, but at the same time quite aggravated for leading them astray. He did not want to discuss it. "Let's go!" he said crossly.

The girls smiled at each other. "Right behind you, oh fearless leader," Wyn snickered.

"I don't need that right now, Wyn!" He turned away, grit his teeth and grabbed Ole Murdoch's reigns.

Again, Wyn had been right, and he had been wrong. Another bad decision, he had been so sure he could do this. He had believed he could do this. His father had believed he could do this. He so wanted to make his father proud. But so far, all he had done was make mistakes.

They mounted up and descended into the gorge. Royce led the way. Wyn followed him. Sherwin followed her. That left Keli to bring up the rear, humming her little song. It was that same familiar song again; yet, still Royce could not remember what it was or where he had heard it.

The path into the canyon was easier than the way they had been following, though it narrowed so in several places they had to keep single file. It looked as if it had been traveled frequently in years past. The path hugged closely to the rocky wall. The wall grew taller as it wound down into the deep ravine. The cliff rose higher and higher on their right, and the embankment dropped off steep on their left. At times, the rocks extended out over their heads. The temperature cooled as they descended into the canyon, a very welcome change. Soon, they entered again into the cover of the trees. The sheer cliff gave way to a steep slope. Royce felt sure that the river would be somewhere below him in the gorge. If they work their way down and across the lower area they were bound to find it.

Unknown to the four travelers, they were not alone. Sinister eyes watched their every move with great interest. From the top of a rock shelf a huge panther crouched as the horses passed below. It did not move a muscle but waited patiently as it zeroed in on a target. As was its hunting instinct, it waited to attack the last to pass by. The last to pass under was Keli atop her sweet Dante'.

The panther sprang with a loud screech. As it did, Dante' reared up on his hind legs. The cat landed on the neck of the horse and dug in with its claws and teeth. Keli was knocked off the back of the horse. Dante' and the panther tumbled over the embankment to a rock ledge below. Even after the fall, the panther was still attacking the poor horse without mercy.

Royce, hearing the commotion, grabbed the sword from its sheath and jumped to the ground.

"Stay with the horses!" he ordered Wyn.

Royce, not seeing Keli, assumed that she must have gone over the edge with Dante' and the cat. Not taking time to think, Royce, swinging the sword, wildly screaming, jumped down to the ledge where the two were still struggling. His abrupt movement startled the panther; it jumped back a few feet. The horse lay motionless. The big cat paused to collect its poise and stared for a second to size up its adversary. It was not about to give up its prize without a fight. Royce braced himself with the sword ready. For a short time they stood in silence, looking at each other.

The panther crouched low, his eyes black and evil, his teeth showing. A low growl emitted from deep within its throat. It sprang at him suddenly. He sidestepped, swinging the sword with all his might. The sword barely lanced the big cat's shoulder. It landed, spun around and attacked again. Straight back at him it came, this time he had no chance to ready his sword. The cat pounced with its full force. Royce braced himself for the inevitable. Right before it hit, its body went limp. Its sharp teeth did not bite in, nor did its claws rip into his body. The force of the animal's momentum knocked Royce to the ground with its body landing on top of him. The sword, knocked from his hand, bounced loosely on the rocks. He landed hard, the wind was knocked out of him, but he was not hurt, at least, not seriously.

Royce pushed the panther aside and sat up. It seemed to be dead. He was out of breath, and his heart was pounding in his chest as he tried to figure out what had happened. He looked at the panther now lying lifeless on the ground beside him. There, protruding out of the side of its rib cage was an arrow. He looked up to see Wyn standing motionless twenty feet from him. She was trembling. Her left outstretched arm still held the bow, the right hand still up by her shoulder where it had released the arrow. She had killed the attacker with one shot. Now she froze, as the realization of what she had just done caught up with her, she looked as if she were in a trance. A cold icy stare on her face showed no sign of emotion whatsoever.

Royce got to his feet, looked at the panther then at Wyn. The other horses were nowhere to be seen, nor was Sherwin.

"I told you to stay with the horses!"

She snapped out of her trance and looked at him angrily. "If I had, you would be dead by now!"

This was true; she had saved his life. The two stared at each other. The recognition of what Wyn had just done sank in. Royce glanced back at the panther. A sob broke into his train of thought.

"Keli!" Royce wheeled around in search of his little sister. She was kneeling on the ground, stroking Dante's head. The horse was lying flat on the ground, unmoving, except for his breathing. His side was rising and falling under great distress. The wounds on his neck and throat were extremely bad. Royce knew there was no hope. Even if they were back at the stables, with their father's knowledge of animals and medicines, he would not stand a chance. Viewing his sister and the horse, he felt completely helpless. She did not look up at Royce as he walked over to her. He could see the tears streaming down the side of her face. "Oh, no. Royce. No."

Royce just stood there as Wyn rounded him and knelt down on the other side of Keli and put her arm around her. "Keli, are you okay? Are you hurt?"

She shook her head no, still sobbing. She was fine physically, but her heart was breaking.

How could he have been so unaware of the dangers in the Black Forest? Royce had not even considered the possibility of a panther attack. Was there something he could have done? Now they had lost a horse. Dante' would not go any farther. What could he say to Keli? He had never had to comfort someone before, but he knew what a loss felt like. He knew what it was like to lose something or someone dear. He remembered his anger, his pain when he lost his mother. One day his mother was there, and the next she was gone! No warning, no chance to say goodbye, nothing, she was just gone.

He stood beside Keli but kept silent for a bit, trying to think of something to say to her. Words never came easily for him. "Keli … I'm sorry... There is nothing we can do for him now. We must go."

"And just...leave him here?"

"Yes," his answer was cold, he knew it, and immediately he was sorry. Could he at least have put a little sympathy in his voice?

"We can't just leave him!" She was fully crying now.

Wyn shot Royce a disapproving glance, then a caring one to Keli. "Keli, Dante' was a fine horse. He was trying to carry you to safety, and he was doing a valiant job. But he didn't carry you this far for you to give up and stay here. It's not safe here. He meant for you to carry on. He would want you to go on. I know it's hard, but you must carry on, with ... without him."

Royce was ashamed. Why could he not have thought of

words of that nature? Words that would have helped, comforted, strengthened, instead he had showed little compassion.

Keli shook her head in agreement but still did not rise.

After several minutes, Sherwin came slipping and sliding down the embankment. He looked at the panther for a moment then knelt down beside the fallen horse. He laid his hand on Dante's head and closed his eyes, raising his own head upward. Sherwin spoke slowly but precisely while the three others watched in silence.

"Our dear, everlasting Dante', our fallen comrade, it is because of your sacrifice this day that Keli is able to carry on her quest. You have forfeited your own life for the saving of hers, and for this, those who knew you should forever hold you in high esteem. I would that I held a sword in my hand, for I would now dub thee a knight! We do honor you this day!" Sherwin then turned to Keli and continued, "Keli, Dante' will truly be everlasting, for we will never forget the life he has unselfishly surrendered today so that another could continue. As we remember this, to us, he will forever be 'everlasting'."

Royce and Wyn stared at Sherwin, wondering at the speech they had just heard, had it come from a ten year old staff boy or a man twenty years his elder. In any event, Keli had stopped sobbing. She stood up to leave but still looked back at her sweet, majestic animal.

After she walked by Sherwin, he helped her back up the embankment.

"From whom do you suppose he heard that?" Royce asked Wyn, breaking the silence.

Wyn spoke in a low and forbidding way, "Ease up, Royce!"

"Hey. I'm the one that almost got killed."

"You almost got killed because of your rash behavior! You don't attack a panther, not when it's on the hunt! You almost sacrificed yourself for a horse!"

"I thought Keli was down here!"

"The panther attacked the horse, not Keli. Keli was up on the path, safe! Pay attention to what's going on around you or you are going to..." she did not finish but turned to follow Keli and Sherwin.

Royce was angry. It seemed that she had more sympathy for the horse than she did for him. Although, deep down he knew she was right, again! He had put himself in harms way for no reason. It was only because of Wyn that he had lived to walk away. His pride had taken a hit, and so had his confidence. Would he be able to get

them to the chalet safely or not? Not if he continued to be so careless.
He looked at poor Dante'. Now, he had to do something that would
be harder than anything he had ever done before.

"I can *not* leave him here to suffer."

Wyn stopped and turned. Their eyes met for a moment, she
knew exactly what he meant, but she could not bear to stay and watch.

"Oh, Royce!" This time her words were sad and sympathetic.
Her eyes dropped from Royce to the panting Dante'. Nodding her
head once, she turned and hurried up the embankment following the
others.

He lingered for a long while after she left. He was not sure
where the strength had come from, but he did it. He felt guilty,
ashamed, and almost evil! He had never done anything like this
before; he had never had to. Why did it have to be Dante'?

"Sorry!" he whispered. A tear was on his own cheek, he was
glad Wyn had not stayed to see it.

He retrieved the arrow from the panther, for they had so
precious few. He had to force himself to look one last time upon dear
old Dante', 'The Everlasting'. He untied the pack of supplies from
the horse's back, swung it over his back, and then hurried to catch up
with the others.

***

An hour later they managed to catch up with the horses.
Luckily, they had run straight down the old abandoned pathway. An
uneasy gloom fell over the travelers the rest of the day. Royce's eyes
scanned every ledge, every cliff, as they passed. Any movement or
any sound alerted his attention. He began to realize the Black Forest
was much more treacherous than ever he had imagined.

Wyn said nothing after the panther attack. No doubt she was
hurt. After saving him, all he could do was berate her for not doing
what she was told. She had made an amazing shot at a moving target
under great pressure. A knight with years of training would have had
difficulty making that shot. She proved herself braver than he had
ever thought possible. Why couldn't he just be grateful and say it.
Why couldn't he just praise her, tell her how extremely well she had
done. It was his pride that kept him from doing so. His pride had
taken another hit. It was he that was supposed to be protecting her,
and not the other way around. What would his father say had he seen
the event?

The extra supplies that Dante' had carried were now mounted

on back of Wyn's horse. Keli now rode in front of Royce on his horse. She said nothing, but she still sobbed now and again. He knew she was hurting. How could he ease her pain? Then he remembered something his father had told him a year ago.

"Keli, I know you are sad, but God will make it up to you. The Lord gives and the Lord takes away. Blessed is the name of the Lord. Father says that nothing bad ever happens without some good coming from it."

"But…why did He have to take Dante'? What good could come of that?"

"Well I… I… We don't know now, but we will someday. You just have to believe that God knows what He is doing."

"Do you think it is as Sherwin says? Did he give up his life to protect me?"

"I'm not sure, but if he did, I'm glad he did. He was sure a fine horse."

Royce did not hear her sob again after that.

* * *

They found a small clearing at the bottom of the bluffs in which to set up camp. This night, not having a fire was not even considered. The chance of someone seeing the firelight this far into the forest was not likely.

Royce found some wood and dry sticks and chopped them into little pieces. He collected dry leaves and pine needles; anything that he thought would ignite easily. Putting a good size log down first for a base, he sprinkled the leaves on top and bunched them together. After choosing a straight stick that was good and dry, he smoothed the bark with his hatchet. Setting it down against the base log he began spinning it between the palms of his hands. As the stick spun, it moved around on the log. This would never do. He took his knife and carved a small hollow just big enough to accept the end of the stick. This would hold it in place while it was spinning. However, after working some time, all that he accomplished was a little warmth on the log.

"Would you like some help?" Wyn asked. She walked up and dropped one of the supply packs on the ground. "What Father does is…"

"I can do this!" Royce barked at her, but did not look up. *She is probably laughing at me*, he thought. "Why don't you go somewhere? Comb your hair or something."

"Fine!" she barked back. She did not leave, but sat down across from him and began to unpack the food.

Royce went back to his work. He was sure she was laughing at him now. Several bleeding fingers and a fair amount of time later, there was no fire, no glowing coal, not even a spark. He threw the stick down in aggravation and sat down hard on the ground.

"May I try?" Wyn asked.

"Be my guest!" Royce answered, his disgust showing in his voice. He felt quite sure she could do no better.

Wyn picked up the hatchet and cut a live poplar sapling about the diameter of a large coin. Cutting it approximately arms length, she came back to the spot where Royce had set up the log.

"That thing is green; it will never start a fire."

She did not reply. Instead she retrieved a length of cord from her pack. She tied one end to the pole and formed a loop on the other end, carefully measuring the cord distance to be just shorter than the pole. Royce's interest was now peaked, but he said nothing. She braced herself, pushed the pole down hard against the ground to form it into an arc and hooked the loop of the cord over the end of the pole. The result was a contraption that looked much like her bow. She took a stick and hollowed a place in the side of it. She spit into the hollow (something he had never seen her do before in all his life). She took the stick that Royce had discarded and sharpened one end to a point. She wrapped the cord once around it and placed it between the hollow on the log and the stick she had spit into. Holding it there with one hand, she began moving the bow shaped pole back and forth with the other. The cord caused the pointed stick to spin rapidly. The bottom end of the stick began to heat; a tiny stream of smoke began to rise from the log.

Bam! Royce's pride took another hit! This time he swallowed it. He was hurt, but not to the point he could not help. He knew how badly they needed the fire. When he saw the smoke, he jumped up and asked if he could try the contraption. She allowed him to take it while she fed the spark with the dry leaves and pine needles. It was hard work, but they kept at it, working together. Neither of them spoke a word to the other but fully concentrated on their work. A small flicker appeared; both were overjoyed. For a split second, the dissention between them was forgotten. They had succeeded in building a fire. They grinned at each other.

It had taken a while, but eventually the fire was burning big and bright. It had a cheering effect on everyone. Its warmth was welcomed, as was its security.

Royce watched as Wyn silently began extending something over the fire on the end of a stick. "I didn't know you had to cook this meat. Hasn't it been cooked already?"

"You didn't know I could start a fire, either! This meat is as hard as those cakes. I'm just trying to soften it."

"Then try boiling it!"

"Just go take care of the horses!" she snapped.

She did not appreciate the suggestion. Apparently, she was still quite angry with him. He left the fire, stomping hard enough to let her know he did not care for her tone of voice. As he went to unpack the blankets, he thought about Wyn. Why was *he* so angry with his sister? She was only doing what she did for the good of everyone, but it seemed as if everything came so easy for her while he had to struggle. Maybe he did need to start paying attention to what was going on around him.

Sherwin collected the firewood for the night, while Keli attended to feeding the horses. When that was done they both brushed them. Royce overheard them speaking as he unpacked the bedding.

"I know you're going to miss Dante'." Unusual, but Sherwin was now the one doing all the talking. "I know I do. He was a great horse. I bet you've been good friends for a long time."

"Yes, the very best," Keli smiled, "for two whole days."

Royce smiled; he knew she was beginning to heal. Now if he could only heal things with Wyn. He carried the blankets back to the campfire.

"I… ah… about today." Why did he find this so hard? "I'm…sorry," there, he had said it! He looked at Wyn.

She stopped tending to the supper but did not look up.

"Why would Father send us into a place that is so dangerous? Keli could have been killed! You could have!" A look of confusion showed on her face.

Before he answered, he checked to see if Keli could hear the conversation. She and Sherwin were now investigating a tree frog that had begun to sing out loudly in a nearby tree. He leaned closer to Wyn so Keli would not hear.

"Because it was far more dangerous if we had stayed. They say the rebels have been doing their worst across the land. I know

Father has been trying to stop them. Father could not fight the rebels and protect us at the same time. They could and would use us to compromise father's ability to stand against them. The night we left, Father had received a tip that the rebels were on their way and had planned an attack on the inn. That is why we had to flee in such a hurry. Do you understand?"

Wyn nodded but still did not look up. "But...Father could be in grave danger."

"He is a wise man, and he is dedicated to the kingdom. Father can take care of himself. We just have to learn to do the same for our selves... and each other... I want to thank you... for what you did... today."

"You really scared me." Wyn then looked up at Royce. He saw that she was almost crying. Only one other time had he seen her do that.

"*You* were scared? ... What do you think *I* was feeling?"

Wyn halfway smiled.

"Where did you learn how to shoot a bow like that? I've never even seen Father shoot like that."

"Father didn't teach me. Mother did."

Royce stared at her in silence, deep in thought.

"But that shot was just pure luck."

"Lucky for me!"

"I had to do something."

"And you did it well. I'm sorry I put you in that situation. I will try not to let it happen again."

A loud thump caused the two to jump. Royce instinctively grabbed his sword and whirled around to see what had made the sound. As he peered into the darkness, he could see Sherwin getting up from the ground.

"Sorry my..." he said. "Sorry." Keli sat giggling, still up on the first limb. They had followed the tree frog up the tree. Apparently, Sherwin had slipped.

He got up and dusted himself off. It was obvious he was okay physically, but Royce was not so sure about him otherwise.

Royce then noticed Wyn standing beside him with her bow and an arrow at the ready. He shook his head. Both could not suppress a little chuckle.

That night he prayed for the Lord to watch over his father, but he also prayed that maybe he could send them a little help too.

The First Encounter

The morning came, only without its usual, bright cheering sun. The skies looked as if they were on fire. Even deep in the canyon with the trees blocking most of the heavens, it gave a strange orange glow to the whole forest.

Keli again rose early, hoping to find some more nuts or berries for breakfast. In the lower levels of the canyon, these things did not grow as plenteously as they did on the upper rim. She searched for a good while before realizing how far she had strayed from camp. This did not bother her, for she knew exactly were the camp was and how to get back. However, something else did. She stopped. Fear gripped her. She heard footsteps. Not as a man would make, but the sound of a dog… or… several dogs… or… Wolves!

Her eyes scanned the surrounding area. In the distance, she could see movement. The gray creatures, she was not sure how many, were beginning to circle. Suddenly, one of them howled into the air, and the others joined in. She ran. They followed. She glanced over her shoulder several times; the wolves were gaining. She knew she would be nowhere near camp before they caught her. What could she do? Climb a tree? The trees were tall and slender with no lower branches, not suitable for climbing. However, she could climb a rock. She scrambled up onto a large boulder. The wolves ran up and surrounded the huge rock.

"Don't panic," she told herself. "Maybe they will go away."

The rock proved to be only a temporary refuge, for the angry, snarling creatures began to climb up onto the edges of the rock. "Okay, now panic." She was not going to go without a fight. She found several loose pieces of rock and threw them at the wolves. Though they hit them hard, it did not deter them much. "Help! Somebody, help me!" she hollered, but she knew there was no one to hear. When she was out of stones, she picked up a broken stick that was lying close and began swinging it wildly at her attackers. Twice, she succeeded in knocking one of wolves back to the ground, but they

did not give up easily. The third time she swung the stick, the wolf
bit down on it, jerking it from her hand. The wolf and the stick
tumbled to the ground. Now she had no weapon of defense. When
they attacked again, all she could do was kick at them. They snapped
and bit into her leather boot. She fell back on the rock, grabbing at
anything to keep from being pulled off the boulder. She remembered
something. The dagger that Royce had given her was strapped to her
waist. She reached and pulled it from its holder, but she did not have
a chance to use it.

Suddenly, a deafening roar came from behind her, a sound
which she had never heard in her life. It echoed through the canyon.
The wolves broke off the attack and scattered in all directions. What
had caused the wolves to scatter in such a manner, she wondered, but
for only a second. Then she knew. She stood up and heard the sound
of heavy breathing, kind of like Dante' made after running a long
while, only much louder, heavier and slower.

She turned to look; she froze. There standing behind her was
a creature, the likes of which she had never seen in her life.

***

Wyn and Royce had just aroused that morning when a sound
of something alerted them.

"What was that?" Wyn obviously had never heard a wolf's
howl before.

"A wolf howling!" Royce had heard that sound before, he did
not know when or where, but he knew what it was and what it meant.

"Where is Keli?" Wyn's voice was urgent.

The blanket that she had used during the night was folded
neatly on a rock beside the campfire, which had long since gone out.

"Let's go!" he answered, without a second thought.

Royce retrieved the sword, which he had placed beside his
blanket the night before. He began running in the direction that he
thought the sound had come from. Wyn followed with the bow in
hand. Sherwin watched them run from the camp with their weapons.
He quickly looked back and forth, picked up a stick about two feet
long and ran after them.

It was hard to tell for sure if they were going the right way
with the echoes from the canyon walls. The panther attack was still
on Royce's mind. He ran a little faster. Before they had gone far they
heard another sound, a frightening, horrible, evil sound. It was loud
enough to echo back and forth between the canyon walls for several

seconds. It was a sound that one could never describe, but would have to hear for himself to grasp how evil. It's the kind of sound that sends icy chills down your back. The sound, even though you do not know what it is, you do know it means something is terribly wrong. Royce and Wyn looked at each other, terror showing on each of their faces.

"What was that?" this time Royce said it. He had never heard such a sound in all his life.

Wyn replied with only the look of terror.

***

Keli's heart nearly leaped out of her chest. The great creature looked at her at eye level, even though it stood on the ground and she on the rock. Its head (nearly as big as she) was the shape of a serpent, but had two small horns protruding out of each side. Its body was like that of a lizard, having four legs and a tail. It sat back on its tail and lifted its front legs into the air as a dog when it is begging for a bit of food. Its claws looked sharp and spiked. Its skin was covered with scales, gray and black in color. Beginning at the head, two rows of fins made their way down its neck. They grew larger across the back, and then diminished to nothing at the end of the tail. On each side of its body, attached at the shoulders, were wings that were stretched up and out into the air. They were shaped similar to that of a bat, only much bigger.

The creature stood staring at Keli for a good while. This thing had chased away the wolves, but why? Just to have her for itself? Its green slotted eyes seem to pierce right through to her very soul, but not as viewing a meal as her terrified heart first thought. It just looked at her as one creature regarding another. She stared back. As she did, her fear began to slowly melt, for it became obvious it did not mean her any harm. As a matter of fact, it had just meant to save her from the wolves. Keli understood this by its softened eyes. It slowly moved its huge head closer to get a smell of her. She winced, stepped back and closed her eyes for a moment. She felt something cool touch her forehead. She opened her eyes and then shut them again tightly, for inches from her was a humungous nose and mouth. It pulled back. After a moment, Keli opened her eyes again.

As she raised her hand to wipe her forehead, it raised its claw. She put her hand down; it put its claws down. The huge animal, whatever it was, backed away, cocked its head to the side as if listening for something, then spread its wings and took to the air. The wind it generated nearly knocked Keli from the rock. She bent down to brace herself. It rose straight up through the trees and out into the sky. She watched it until it disappeared out of sight.

***

After running a little more than the distance of an arrow's flight, Wyn spotted Keli nearly a league away. "This way!" she hollered, as she bolted across the flat woods.

Wyn must have eagle eyes, Royce thought as he tried to see what Wyn was seeing. The trees being tall and slender, with very little underbrush on the ground, made it quite easy for Wyn to see a great distance, but Royce's eyes were not as sharp. A feeling of relief swept over him as he finally caught sight of her. She was standing on a huge boulder, staring into the heavens. She did not move. Even as they approached, she did not look down at them.

"Keli...what are you doing? ... What are you looking at?" Wyn asked, breathing hard. Both she and Royce tried to see what she was staring at. Both saw nothing.

"You're white as a sheet! Are you well?" Wyn climbed up to her.

"I'm fine." Her throat was so dry she found it difficult to speak. Still she did not tell them of the creature that she saw, she was sure they would not have believed her, nor was she sure she even believed it herself.

"I thought you would have learned not to go off by yourself...after yesterday!" Royce said.

As they helped her off the rock, Wyn put her hand on Keli's forehead, still thinking something may be wrong with her. "What were you doing out here by yourself?"

"Looking for berries for breakfast," she answered.

"Well, you won't find them staring into the trees." Royce chuckled, happy to find her unharmed.

Royce noticed some tracks on the ground. After investigating, a concerned look came over him. He spoke seriously, "We had better hurry and get back to camp to check the horses. These tracks are wolf tracks."

Sherwin caught up with them just as they started back to the camp. He fell in beside Keli as they walked. "Did you hear that awful sound?"

"Yes!" she whispered in reply.

"Did it scare you?" Sherwin whispered back.

"Yes!"

"Me too! What do you think it was?"

"I think it was your leviathan!"

"My leviathan?"

***

The terrain was much flatter in the lower levels of the canyon. Traveling was easy. The enormous trees hindered the sunlight so completely that there was very little undergrowth to obstruct their way.

"Rain is coming," Sherwin said out of the blue, after riding a short while.

"Really?" Keli questioned. "How can you tell?"

"Morning sky is red," was all he said.

What could that possibly mean? Royce thought as he lightly tapped the reins against the side of his horse's neck.

An hour later, Royce would find out what he meant. He led the way through the canyon in the direction he hoped was north. All the while, the clouds were rolling in quite heavily from the west, now preventing the sun completely. With them came a feeling of depression. Without the sun, it was becoming increasingly harder to know if they were traveling in the right direction. It was growing ever darker. It seemed as if Sherwin was going to be right after all. No doubt, rain was on the way, and by the look of the sky it meant to be a storm.

No one spoke most of the morning. Royce was growing ever worried about the weather. The clouds grew heavier as the day progressed. Wyn was wishing to be anywhere but here. Keli's mind was on the strange creature she had encountered that morning. As ferocious as it first appeared, it had certainly a gentle gaze in its eyes. It seemed to be sad, almost lonely. She felt as if the great creature was longing for friendship. If it was leviathan, the vicious creature Sherwin had described, why had it not harmed her? The beast could have left her to the wolves or devoured her itself, but it did not. Instead it saved her and seemed to ask for nothing in return. Could a creature with such a ferocious exterior do such a kindly deed?

***

"The river!" Keli said a few hours later. She was the first to see it. "It is the most beautiful thing I have ever seen."

Despite the somber mood they had felt all morning, all the children were overjoyed to find the river, and the day was not half spent. It was a beautiful sight, mainly because they had been looking for it for so long. It was a wide, gentle, slow moving waterway that looked deep. Huge boulders lined each side forming tall, treacherous banks. The water was blue and clear. It was a glorious sight for sure, for this meant that they were headed the right way and making progress. Now that they had a landmark to follow, they knew that they were on the right path. All they had to do now was follow the river to the chalet. Once there, they would be safely away from the rebels, away from the Black Forest, and far from all the dangers they posed!

"The River Terranera," Sherwin said quietly.

"Terranera?" Keli questioned.

"That is what it is referred to by the maps in the king's library."

"Nice!" Wyn rolled her eyes, ignoring his comment. "Now, which way do we go, up stream or down?"

Her question interrupted Royce's revelry and posed a new problem. A simple inquiry to Wyn, who thought no more of it than asking the time of day, but it filled Royce's mind with a new doubt. His father had said to follow the river, whether to follow upstream or down, he had not said.

"I don't know," he said quietly.

"What?" Wyn and Keli both looked at Royce curiously.

"Father said, follow the river. I can't remember if… No. He didn't say…up or down stream," he spoke slowly. "Follow the fork that splits the river."

"Don't rivers run together to reach the sea?" Keli commented.

Something that she said struck a memory deep within. It did for Wyn too, for she began to sing:

"From far and wide, from mount and peak"
"Each the other is what we seek."
"Be not afraid to join together,"
"The greatest tempest shall we weather."

"Every turn, every bend, o'er every fall"
"Follow your heart, we'll o'er come it all."
"A greater journey for you and me,"
"We'll travel together to reach the sea.

"That's the song! That's the song Keli's been humming since we left the inn," Royce exclaimed. "Where have I heard that before?"

Wyn spoke softly, "Don't you remember?" She searched Royce's bewildered face. "Mother used to sing that when we were little, only all the time. I can't believe you don't remember."

"I remember. But that song is not about a river. Is it?"

"It could be. She *did* love the water, the sea, and a river, a stream…the rain!" Wyn glanced up at the sky.

"She would love to see this now, wouldn't she?" Royce had forgotten that about his mother.

"Yes." A faint smile was on Wyn's face.

"If she were here now, what would she say?" Royce wondered out loud.

"Probably, '*follow your heart*'."

"Heart? Is heart going to get us to the chalet?" He looked toward the river again. "Let's think this through. Okay. We are looking for a fork in the river. Do we look upstream or downstream?"

"I never saw a river that forked going down stream. Have you?" Keli asked.

"No, they don't. Not usually. Rivers run together to reach the sea. Good point, Keli. Water flows down from mountains."

"From mount and peak," Wyn repeated again. "Each the other is what they seek."

"It *is* about a river! The Mount Hestia! Water would be

flowing down from a mountain to the sea. We're looking for a mountain. Then it's up stream we go."

"Hey! You were right about going west to get off the canyon rim," Wyn stated.

He *was* right about that. Wyn even admitted it. Confidence! It felt particularly reassuring coming from Wyn. He had followed his heart without even knowing it, and it turned out to be right. Maybe he could do this after all.

They turned the horses upstream. Wyn began to sing that song their mother had taught her many years before. Keli joined in. The sound of their voices blended so pretty that Royce's spirit was brightened. This time he would not be bothered over what that song was.

The joyful song temporarily lifted all of their spirits, but did nothing about the weather. The clouds darkened ever more behind them. Royce remembered the comment Sherwin had made about the red sky being a sign that rain was coming. How did he know these things? Apparently he was right; this looked like it would be a brutal storm.

Boom! The thunder was so loud and so sudden, that Royce felt the vibrations in his chest. The wind began to roar in the treetops. The rain followed soon after. With no shelter and no place to hide, they were soaked to the skin in minutes.

Crack! A tree limb fell from a nearby tree and landed dangerously close. The horses jumped and pranced around in confusion. They were more frightened than their riders. They needed to find a place to weather the storm, some place safe, but the area offered no such comforts. The afternoon wore away but the rain did not, not until near evening. After traveling a great distance up the river, the banks became rockier and harder to maneuver. Eventually, they found a large boulder with strong outcropping. It was big enough to supply some shelter from the driving rain. It was a welcome sight to the four, wet, miserable travelers.

Even though they found some dry twigs and leaves under the overhanging rock, it would take an extremely long time to get a fire going. Royce set to work. If it had not been for Wyn sharing the knowledge of how to build a fire, it would have been impossible. Despite the damp, rainy conditions, he was able to get a fire kindled, though not as easily as the night before. It took nearly an hour.

Darkness would soon fall on the canyon. In his concentration,

Royce had not noticed the rain had stopped. He was also not aware that Wyn had left the camp. When he finally got the blaze aglow, he looked up from his work to see only Keli and Sherwin watching.

"Good job, Royce!" She was thoroughly enjoying the growing flame and the warmth.

"Where's Wyn?" He rose up looking around.

"She said she was going down to the river's edge," Keli replied casually.

"What?" He picked up the sword (now he would go nowhere without it) and started for the river. "Take care of the horses, Keli, stay close to the fire, and don't let it go out!"

"We have, we will, and we won't!" she could say no more before he was gone.

Royce hurried to the edge of the rock ledge and peered over. He scanned the riverbank for his sister. Eventually, he spotted her at the water's edge far below. She was standing knee deep in the water among the protected shallows of the rocks. She seemed to be working with something, although he could not see what from this distance. Curiosity getting the best of him, he tried to position himself to get a closer look. He climbed down and around the large rocks. When he saw her again, she had come out of the water. She picked up something from the rivers edge and started up the bank. Royce ran down and met her at the top of the bank. He offered her a hand up.

"Fish?" Royce greeted excitedly.

"Supper!" Wyn answered. She handed him one of the fish as he pulled her up onto the flat.

"How?"

"One bow, one arrow, and a lot of patience."

"Amazing," was all Royce could say.

"We have to do what we have to do, and we have to eat." Wyn smiled as they made their way back to the camp. "By the way, you're doing the cooking tonight."

Royce stopped walking when he heard that. He almost replied with a comment about cooking being women's work, but he caught himself. Instead, he changed it to something about she might be sorry if he did.

"Don't you ruin my fish; I worked hard to get them!" she replied. She was serious.

Wyn had surprised Royce. Was this the same girl that used to follow him around the inn a few short years ago pestering him unmercifully? When had she grown up? When had she developed such a will to survive? When had she become so fearless and self-sufficient? When had she learned to fish?

The fish cooked over the open campfire was not the way Cookie would have prepared it had they been back at the inn. It was not the way Wyn would have prepared it. Royce did not know how to cook, but he did the best he could. It *was* edible, it *did* fill their stomachs, and they were thankful for it. They were not sure of whether it was because they had provided it for themselves or that it was just fresh, whatever the reason, it tasted better than the dried meat! Each had their fill.

After supper, Royce leaned back against a stone and picked his teeth with a fish bone. "Best salmon I have ever eaten." All knew there was no way it could have been the best, though no one disagreed with him.

Wyn did argue with him on another point. "It's trout," she corrected, with a shake of her head.

How was it that Wyn could use a bow and arrow? When did she learn to hunt and fish? When had she learned to do all these things? How did she know that was trout? Had Father taught her this? He never knew she was even remotely interested in such things, but he supposed that one becomes very interested when survival depends on it. It seemed that there was a lot more to Wyn than he had ever known. For the first time, he began to appreciate having Wyn around. She was no longer the pest that he remembered her to be.

They sat around the fire absorbing all it had to offer, its light, its warmth but most of all its security. Eventually, their clothes began to dry. The blankets had been hung close to the fire to dry. They would smell like smoke, but maybe they would be able to get a nights rest. The four sat for the longest time quietly listening to nothing but the crackling of the fire and the chorus of the crickets. Somewhere in the canyon a faint sound of a hoot owl broke the silence. Equally as faint came the howl of a wolf. Presently, another answered from a different direction.

Wyn looked up from the fire, obviously a little nervous. Keli scooted closer to Royce, who pitched another log on the fire and checked that he had his sword near.

"We'll just keep the fire going all night."

"Good idea!" Wyn agreed.

The silence returned. Their thoughts dwelt on the eerie night and the distant sounds in the dark.

Suddenly, Keli diverted their attention. "I wonder where Father is tonight."

All three of the siblings instantly brought their father to the forefront of their thoughts and there was silence again, for a short while. Wyn broke it this time.

"You know, we may be going all this way for nothing. Have you thought that if Devlin met up with Father, they may have already put down the rebels by now?"

"Wyn, I'd like to think that." Royce took a deep breath and let it out slowly.

"Put no faith in Devlin," Sherwin said.

Wyn half chuckled, but seriousness instantly swept over her. "What?"

"Wyn, the band of men that we met on the highway…that wasn't Devlin and his men on their way to help your father," Sherwin was beginning open up to his traveling companions

"What? What do you mean?" Wyn stared at him with interest.

"That band *was* the rebels. That was the men on their way to attack the inn."

"What are you saying?"

"There is no small band of rebels secretly raiding the towns and villages across the country, it is Devlin. It has all been Devlin."

"That's not true. Devlin is a rich man, he would not pillage like a common thief!" Wyn defended.

"Wyn, it is not gold that he searches for. He is an evil man. He is concerned about only one thing—Devlin. He is trying to take the kingdom and to overthrow the king! There is no band of rebels; it is the king's own men doing the evil deeds."

"What?" Royce and Wyn said almost simultaneously. Wyn continued, "How could you…"

"Devlin has cunningly deceived the highwaymen and the Elite into thinking they are doing the kings will."

"I know Devlin; he would not do such a thing! He and Father are friends!" Wyn defended, and then turned to Royce for help.

"I'm sorry, my la…Wyn." Sherwin was not sure whether to pursue it any further or not.

Wyn turned back to Sherwin. "Sherwin, you are mistaken! Devlin we have known as long as we can remember." Then she turned back to Royce again. "He would never…"

"He and Father worked together for many years, but they never did see eye to eye. They have now gone their separate ways." Though he did not want to believe it, a feeling deep within told Royce, Sherwin was right.

"Devlin is not even in the linage. He has no right to the thr…!" Wyn cried.

"Who is to be the king anyway?" Keli asked. "I mean, when he passes on."

"The king is getting old and has no children. There are no heirs to succeed him," Royce threw in.

"But there is an heir," Sherwin spoke so softly the rest were not sure they heard what they heard.

"What?"

Royce, Wyn, and Keli were all staring at Sherwin. "Very few know this, but there is an heir."

"Who is it? Where is he?" Wyn asked.

"Who it is, I cannot say. And as for where…" Sherwin paused while he looked around at the three wondering faces, "no one knows.

"Well, if he really cared for the kingdom, he should come forward; maybe he could put an end to the unrest."

"Yes…I am sure he would." Sherwin looked away from the others and stared at the fire.

"If that is true, then the king will appoint the next true heir to the throne before he dies," Wyn said.

"He will if he is able, and if he is found," Sherwin added. "If he doesn't, the trials will start all over again. This is what Devlin wants. The king *is* getting old; he is not the ruler he once was. Devlin knows this. He is not going to wait around until the heir is found. He is too power hungry. Devlin is madly searching for the heir. He is searching, not to bring him back, but to destroy him. He will stop at nothing, trickery, deception, or force, whatever it takes. I know him well."

"What?" Wyn looked seriously at him as she considered the thought. "I don't believe it!" Wyn had always liked her uncle or acting uncle. "This is Devlin we are talking about!"

Sherwin continued, "If it were just a small band of rebels causing all the trouble, the Elite would have put an end to it, and you would have been safe at home, but that is not so. Devlin is a powerful man, and he has free run of the kingdom. He is deceiving the king.

Your father knows this. Unfortunately, the king trusts Devlin! He is the king's first consultant. Your father is trying to stop him and that is good, he needs to be stopped. If your father fights Devlin, he is fighting against the king."

"No! That's not true," Wyn defended.

"The only way your father had to keep you safe was to have you disappear. Your father knew this. That's why he sent us the way he did, instead of the highway. Devlin has command over the highwaymen, the 'Elite', the whole army. Very few know about the chalet in the mountains. Let's hope Devlin does not. If not, we will be safe there. The chalet in years past was used for the king's refuge in times of emergencies, war times—times as these. It has been long since abandoned, not needed for ages. …The king needs to know about Devlin and his treachery!" Sherwin affirmed. "We should be headed to Ary Brysta, not Hestia!"

"Ary Brysta?" Keli asked. "What is that?"

"Oh, I mean the king's castle."

"I never heard it called that before," Keli said.

Royce stared hard at Sherwin. Did he really know what he was talking about? He knew way too much to be a staff boy. Who was this boy, and how could he know so much about the king, the kingdom and Devlin?

The third evening in the woods passed with a somber mood hanging over all. Fear for their father, fear for the kingdom, and a fear for themselves, had caused a feeling of helplessness to descend. They felt completely separated from the rest of the world. That night, in Royce's prayers, again he asked God to watch over their father, watch over them, and he thanked Him for his two sisters. He prayed that Sherwin was wrong about his views of Devlin, but somehow he knew he was not.

***

The morning came once again. Once again, the clouds hid the sun. With luck, two more days of travel should bring them to the chalet. Fortunately, the rain had moved on up higher into the foothills of the mountain country. Unfortunately, as a result, the runoff from the high grounds had swollen the river. The peaceful river that had seemed so beautiful at first sight had now become a wild, raging torrent, attempting to handle the extra water. It was as if overnight it had become angry with the travelers and was not going to let them pass. This was not a problem until they found it necessary to cross in order to stay on their route. The river split into two waterways, just as their father had described. The ridge rose up between the two waterways, also as he had described. In order to keep following the ridge that led to the chalet, they would have to cross, for the ridge pared away at an angle from the river. They began looking for a suitable place to cross.

They stopped at a place where the river was wider than they had ever seen since the fork. If the river ever did recede enough to cross, this would be the place. Though the current was slower here, with the river at flood stage, a crossing would now be impossible. The opposite bank rose from the water and continued up to a steep rocky slope to the ridge. The climb up to the ridge would be treacherous, but it could be done.

Wyn dismounted her horse, and then Royce and Keli did the same. They walked out onto a gravel bar at the edge of the river to size up their adversary. Should they wait it out until the river went back to normal, or keep searching upstream hoping to find a place that would more suitable? The latter would take them farther off their course, because the river began to veer to the south. It was decided that Wyn and Keli would wait while Royce and Sherwin scouted a league or so up the river to look for a better crossing. Upstream they found nothing but more rapids and faster moving water. The farther the river went the more it veered to the south, winding more and more away from the ridge. Presently, they returned. They had found no better place.

"Lunch is served."

The girls had spread a blanket over a large flat rock and prepared the last of the dried fruit. They gave thanks and then prepared to eat their lunch picnic style. The sun broke through a gap in the clouds. It warmed their backs and their hearts. They began to cheer up from the gloom they had been feeling.

"How long do you think it will take for the water to go back down?" Keli asked.

"It all depends on how much it has rained in the mountains," Royce explained. "It could take a few hours, it could take days. … I don't really know."

"Well, I think…EEK!" Wyn suddenly let out an earsplitting scream and jumped up.

Royce whirled. He first looked at Wyn, then to what she was looking at. In a split second, he too was up hollering.

A big black bear had come through the brush a short distance from the children. Possibly, it had smelled the food. It jumped back a foot or so, reared up on its hind feet and raised its front paws into the air. It gave a roar to try to intimidate the children. It worked. The sound filled the small clearing.

"Run!" hollered Wyn.

All began to run, but something Royce's father had taught him popped into his head.

"No!" Royce shouted. "We can't out run a bear. Everyone up on this rock! Quick!"

The bear watched as the four children scrambled up on a boulder and huddled as close as they could. It wasn't a large rock, but it was big enough to make them a bit taller than the bear.

"Make as much noise as you can!" Royce yelled, pulling his sword from the scabbard.

All the children began screaming at the top of their lungs, howling, hollering, and flapping their arms. The hope was that the fierce animal might decide against any attack by the mere fact that he had never come across the likes of such shrieking humans. Did it work? The bear stared for a moment, looked to the side, then back at the children. Indecision caused the bear to hesitate. Then they started waving their arms and kicking their feet more than ever. It was apparent that the bear did not know what it was he had stumbled upon. It soon paid them no more attention, for it found something else much more appealing. The scent of the fruit spread on the blanket pulled his attention away from the shrieking children. It ambled over, nosed up to the rock and checked out the banquet left by the hungry children. It began to feast upon their picnic. Their screams of fear turned to yells of anger. The bear continued eating despite the protests that were made. Soon, and it did not take long, all was devoured, down to the very last crumb. The bear then looked at the children, whom by now had quit hollering and stood sadly watching. It dipped its huge head as if to say thank you, dropped its front paw down from the rock and waddled back into the brush. They were relieved for a moment, for a brief happy moment. The intruder had arrived quickly and it left equally so! The bear was gone, but so was their lunch. Something else was also gone, their horses!

The Crossing

The thought occurred to Royce that everything they had was still attached to those three horses, their food, their bedding, and all their supplies. Without them, all they had were the clothes on their backs, and of course, the sword that Royce went nowhere without. Unfortunately, the bow and arrows that had almost never left Wyn's shoulder since the panther attack was at this time still attached to Whirlwind's saddle! She had temporarily relinquished it to prepare the lunch. They would not survive long if they did not get those horses back. This was the second time they had lost their horses on this journey. Both times were because of wild animals. It seemed to be a lesson not easily learned. Royce decided that this was a mistake he would not make again.

All the horses had left in a direction perpendicular to the river, that fact was unmistakable. The tracks in the mud made the search easy.

"As long as the horses did not keep running, catching them should not be much of a problem," Royce told the other three.

The not much of a problem became quite a problem. It took much longer to correct than anyone would have ever thought, but they recovered all, eventually. It was nearly five hours later before they found themselves standing at the same sandbar pondering the same river crossing. Fortunately, in that time the river had receded a great deal.

"I think we should go ahead and cross. I do believe the river has gone down well enough," Royce spoke, hoping to encourage the girls before the crossing.

"How can you tell?" Wyn walked up and stood beside him, eyeing the swift moving water.

"Look at our tracks in the gravel. When we first arrived here, we stood right at the waters edge," he told her. "Our tracks, now, are a good distance back from where the edge of the water is now."

"It still looks rough to me. If it is still going down, why don't we just wait until the water goes back to normal? Then it would be an easy crossing."

"We should cross, the clouds are moving back in. If the rains set in, it may take days for it to get this low again," he urged.

Royce was of the mind to move on, not wanting to spend another night as the one before. By now, the sun had disappeared completely behind a bank of dark clouds. No doubt, it was an approaching storm system. Royce thought if they were going to cross, this was the time and place that would be most suited. Maybe they could find a shelter among the cliffs on the other side of the river before the rain sat in again.

Wyn glanced over her shoulder; the sky did look pretty dark toward the west.

Royce mounted Ole Murdoch and urged him forward. "You three stay put for a minute; I'll find a good path to cross over."

"I hope you can swim!" Wyn hollered to him sourly.

He turned and looked at her displeasingly. The horse was not too happy about entering the cold water of the river, but it reluctantly obeyed. The first half of the crossing, water only touched the stirrups, which caused no problems. But the riverbed dropped deeper in the second half. So much so, that his knees were now in the water. The water filled his boots. It was cold, coming from higher in the mountains. The flow began to push hard on the horse and rider. Royce found that by facing the horse up stream, it could withstand the force of the current. He had to side step to keep from being forced down stream. Ole Murdoch was much steadier this way. It worked quite well until Murdoch's left front hoof hit against an uneven rock on the bottom. He stumbled slightly, lowering Royce into the water, soaking him to his belt line. When the icy cold water soaked in, Royce gasped for a breath.

Wyn watched nervously from the gravel bar. "Come back! If it is too rough, we'll wait it out. Come back!" she hollered.

"It's fine! I'm okay!" Royce hollered, not willing to give up that easily.

He was okay. Murdoch recovered quickly. Unfortunately, their bedding was soaked again. The horse rose up out of the water and onto the opposite bank. He had made it safely across. He proceeded to unload the supply pack and the blankets. He then headed back across the river, avoiding the spot with the uneven rocks where Ole Murdoch had missed his step before.

Royce decided riding double would not be a wise act crossing the river. Keli and Sherwin would wait on one side, while Wyn crossed over on Whirlwind, following close behind Royce. He would then return for Keli who would ride Whirlwind. Last, Sherwin would cross over on Victor.

Wyn mounted her horse.

"If anything happens, just stay on Whirlwind, he'll get you across. Just don't let go!" Royce instructed.

"Oh, don't worry," Wyn answered.

Royce suggested she pull her dress up and hold it around her waist so it would not soak up water and cause more resistance. She understood his reasoning, but she did not like the idea at all. She only agreed to it if Royce and Sherwin kept their back to her the whole time. They promised. Even then she would not pull it up higher than her knees.

The crossing went without a hitch. When they climbed up on the other side, he unloaded the supplies off of Whirlwind. He left Wyn alone with the supplies and returned for Keli.

"Are you ready?" he asked.

"For sure!" Keli was smiling brightly, obviously enjoying herself. Her spirit seemed to know no fear!

"As I told Wyn, hold your dress up out of the water as best as you can and just hold on tight to the horse. Got it?"

"I got it." She smiled trustingly at her older brother.

Royce mounted his own horse and they started into the river. He kept a hold on the reigns of Keli's horse for fear that her lack of riding experience just might get her into difficulty. They rode side by side, he keeping her close by in case there was trouble. There *was* trouble. As soon as they entered the deeper section, the resistance increased. What Royce did not realize was that the two horses close together caused more turbulence, thus creating more drag. The increased pressure was pushing both horses down stream.

"Whoa, Murdoch, take it easy! Easy now!" Royce tried to calm Ole Murdoch, but it did no good. He fought to keep the horse facing up stream, but he was having trouble keeping a sure footing on the gravel bottom. He soon found it impossible to hold both horses together. Murdoch reared up and he had to let go of Whirlwind's reigns or be pulled off his own horse. Then he struggled to prevent his horse from panicking.

"Keli!" he hollered. "Just hold on to the horse! Stay on the horse! … Stay on Whirlwind! He'll get you to the bank… Just hold on, Keli!"

Royce's horse found his footing again and began to move up and out toward the bank. It was then that he heard Wyn scream!

"KEELLLII!"

Royce glanced up at Wyn for only a split second to see the horror on her face. She was looking past him. Royce whirled around; immediately he understood, his stomach leaped up into his throat.

"ROYCE! Royce HEEELLLLP!" Keli began hollering at the top of her lungs.

Keli's horse had dropped off into an even deeper section of the river and was being overtaken completely by the current! All that was visible was Keli's head and the horse's nose, eyes and ears! The current would only get swifter the farther they drifted! They were moving down the river fast! They were in real trouble!

"OH-NOOO!" Royce felt his heart nearly jump out of his chest. He had to do something, and it had to be quick. He knew there was no way Keli could swim in her water soaked dress. He could jump in, but he would never be able to get to her fighting this current. That might just drown him. *What to do?* The rope! It was attached to the saddle right in front of him. By now, Ole Murdoch had climbed out of the water up onto the riverbank. He prodded him into a run and passed Wyn at a full gallop.

"What are you doing?" she screamed! "Where are you going?"

He did not have time to answer her. He headed Ole Murdoch down stream. The old friend seemed to understand the emergency, he ran as fast as Royce could ever remember. Dodging rocks, ducking under limbs and hurdling over the small bushes, the horse darted. Sprinkles of rain began stinging against his face, but he hardly noticed this, for all of his concentration was on Keli. Apparently she was doing just as she had been told, for she was still on the horse's back. Keeping an eye on her, he rode well ahead to buy himself just a little time to get setup. He had to ride a good distance because of the speed Keli and Whirlwind were drifting. Choosing a large boulder that jutted out well into the river, he pulled the horse to a stop. He dismounted, grabbed the rope, and scrambled out to the edge of the boulder.

"Keli! Grab the rope!" he hollered to her upstream.

He heard her say something in reply, he wasn't sure what. He readied the rope, making sure it was not going to tangle when it was released. Accounting for the speed she was moving, he figured there would not be a chance for a second throw. He would have one opportunity and one only. The rope would have to land close enough to Keli for her to be able to reach it.

"Royce! Help me!" she screamed between coughs.

"You'll have to grab the rope!"

Royce was sure she understood this time by the nod she made. He slung the rope in a big arc out over the water. It landed just beyond her and a little down stream. The current pushed her right into the rope floating on the surface. In a second, she had it in her hand. Perfect!

"I got it!" she screamed, between coughs.

"Good! Now hold tight and I will pull you in!" As she and the horse came nearer, he took up the slack. They passed about twenty feet in front of him, Whirlwind still frantically fighting the current, doing a good job of keeping his nose out of the water. He braced himself. As the rope tightened, he began to pull. The force on the rope caught him unprepared, for it was way more than he had expected.

"Keli! Let go of the horse!"

The rope burned as it slipped in his hands.

"My boot! It's caught! Caught in the stirrup!" Keli screamed!

"Keli, you've got to get it loose!"

There was no way Royce was about to let go of that rope; no way he was going to lose his little sister. Letting out some slack, he took a second to brace himself better. He wrapped the rope around his arm and over his shoulder, and then dug in with all his might. The river took up the slack in the rope once again. Despite his greatest effort, he was no match for Keli, the horse, and the resistance the river created. His footing slipped out from under him, he slid over the edge of the boulder and plunged into the river.

The plunge put him well beneath the surface. Forcing his head above the icy cold water, he gasped for air. The force of the water quickly took him down the river. The steeper the incline of the riverbed, the faster the water flowed. He struggled to get his head above the water to take another breath. His head surfaced again, and he gulped in more air. The water soaked clothes made it nearly impossible to swim. Working his way around, he attempted to keep his feet downstream. He managed to touch the bottom once. It was then he realized he still held the rope in his hand; all he had to do was pull himself to Keli by the rope! The water became shallow enough that his feet began catching on some rocks on the bottom. This allowed him to work his way closer to the edge. He scampered up to safety on the bank. Bracing himself behind another rock, he waited for the hard pull once again. The rope went tight, but this time the drag was not nearly as strong. Keli had freed her boot from the stirrup. The horse was still being carried down the river, but Keli was not. Royce began to pull her to shore. With Whirlwind no longer supporting Keli's weight, she now found it hard to keep her head above the water. The more she held on to the rope, the more the current pulled down on her. She was being pulled under by the drag on the rope! At this rate, she would drown before he ever got her to the shore! Coughing and gasping, she had no choice but to let go of the rope. Royce felt the resistance ease up on the rope.

"Keli! NOOO!"

"Royce! … *Cough*! ... I couldn't...hold on! … *Cough*!"

What was he to do? Should he try the rope again? He quickly pulled it in and rolled it up as he ran to catch up with her. Maybe if he could throw her something to help her float, a log or something! He searched for a piece of driftwood as he went. He did not know where Ole Murdoch was, nor did he have time to look for him, so he ran on foot.

"Hurry, Royce, help!"   He heard Keli still coughing and hollering for him.

"Just hang on Keli!" he hollered again.   "Oh, please God, don't let this happen! Don't let her drown! Please!" he whispered a prayer as he climbed over the huge boulders lining the bank.   The water was moving more swiftly than he was able to. He could see her head still bobbing up and down.   The river was taking her away. Whirlwind was well beyond her now, way down stream. He watched in dismay as the horse caught its footing and pulled itself up onto the other edge of the river bank.   It disappeared into the trees a good distance down the river. A sick thought occurred to him; if he had not tried to save her with the rope, she could have stayed on Whirlwind. She would have been okay! "She's drowning, and it will be because I tried to save her! God in Heaven, HELP! Please help!"

Royce was near panic. So much so, he wasn't sure if what he began to see was really what was happening, or he was seeing things. A bird (what he thought was a bird) was flying upstream, several feet above the water's surface. It was headed straight for Keli! The sight disturbed Royce so; he stopped running, dropped the rope, and just watched in horror! As it closed in, he could see the bird or whatever-it-was drop closer to the surface. It had a wingspan of about thirty feet. This thing was huge! It had a pointed tail, four legs, and horns on its head and back. This was no bird! It slowed some when it reached Keli. With clawed feet, it plucked her from the water, much like he had seen an eagle do to a fish once back on Lake Lymere, near the inn. Once it had her, one claw under each arm, it took to the sky, flying right over where Royce stood frozen to the spot!

"ROYCE!" Keli screamed again as they passed above him. "HELP!"

This broke the spell of shock! "Don't worry! I'm coming! Just hang on!" *Don't worry? Just hang on? What was he saying? What could he do?* He stood watching in total helplessness as the enormous animal flew off to the rocky ridge with his little sister dangling in its clutches. What *could* he do?

A deafening crack of thunder echoed across the canyon. Even with the sound of the thunder ringing as loud as it was, ringing even louder in his head was the echo of his little sister screaming out his name over and over. The rain began falling in sheets. With no other option, he began climbing the stony bluff in the direction that the creature had taken his little sister.

***

Wyn stood in shock as she watched her little sister being carried away by the swift current. She watched until she could see her no more. In horror, not believing that this was really happening, she snapped into motion. Climbing up the riverbank, she started to run upstream to where the supplies lay. She hesitated for only a second, then began running on foot in the direction that Royce had taken. She was alone on the opposite side of the river from Sherwin, without a horse, but that did not dampen her determination. Moving as quickly as she could, though the rough rocks and the brush tried its best to prevent her, she followed the rivers edge, searching for her older brother and her little sister. Presently, she was encouraged to hear the sound of a horse headed in her direction, but when it came into view, it had no rider.

"Murdoch!" she cried. The horse stopped near her. "Murdoch, where is Royce? Where's Keli?" She caught the bridle with one hand as she wiped the tears from her eyes with the other, for they were clouding her vision. In an instant, she was mounted on Ole Murdoch and racing down the river's edge. It was then that the rain set in, just as it had the day before, coming down in torrents. She searched frantically. She rode a long way down stream watching the river and the bank for any sign of her siblings. She went all the way back to the place in which the river had forked. She found no one! Here the river was slow and gentle. They would not have come this far unless… unless they have drowned! No! She would not believe it. She would not let that thought dwell in her for long, not at this point. She turned Ole Murdoch around and started back. Slowly she went back up the river, this time looking for answers. She continued looking for clues as to what had happened to the others. She could not bring herself to believe they were gone. They were alive; they just had to be! It would soon be dark. The storm did not show any signs of letting up. As she headed back to where she had left Sherwin, the thunder rumbled, it was the loneliest sound she had ever heard.

Gone

Climbing the rocky cliff proved to be difficult, but Royce forced himself to continue. The lightning's flash kept blinding him. Several times it struck so close it jarred his entire body. Once, he felt his hair stand on end right before it struck a tree, not more than twenty feet from him! That was way too close, but he still kept climbing! As he scaled higher up the cliff the skies continued to darken. Night would not be far away. Because of the higher altitude, the wind gusts pushed on him hard. It caused the raindrops to hammer on him with a vengeance. None of this mattered.

The only thought in his head was to find Keli and save her from that…that beast. How he was to go about that, he had no idea. He prayed it would not be too late. Either way, he had to find her! He would not give up until he knew for sure, one way or another! He could not return to Wyn without knowing. These thoughts forced him to climb faster, but ever fearing what he might find whenever he caught up with that monster. Royce hoisted himself up onto one ledge after another. Climbing almost blindly, knowing only that this was the way he had last seen Keli and the creature.

He pulled himself up onto a particularly high rock ledge and started to get to his feet. When he did, he caught a glimpse of something moving on his right. He turned to realize he was being watched. Two snake-like eyes almost glowed in the dim evening light. Terror struck. Those two eyes were attached to a huge creature, twice as tall as he. Royce froze. It slowly eased closer. Its head was level with his own only because it was bending down to investigate him, his eyes intent with interest. The huge scaly beast just stared, not sure of the boy, the boy deathly afraid of the creature. Several unwary seconds passed. Moving its head closer still, it sniffed, trying to get a smell of the boy. Royce reached for his sword and pulled it from the sheath.

The creature raised its massive head and let out a deafening roar up into the air. This was the sound he had heard the morning when they did not know where Keli was! That was the same sound; it had come from this creature!

His heart pounded in his chest. Fully by instinct he raised his sword. His thoughts raced. He remembered his failure with the panther. If he could not handle the panther, there was no way under the sun he would survive this. The huge beast started forward. Royce backed away.

From out of nowhere, Keli appeared; she was alive! For a brief second his heart rejoiced, but only for a second! The creature had not devoured her, not yet anyway. His attention snapped back to the creature! She ran and stood between him and the beast. With her back to it! She was facing Royce! The beast stopped its advance!

"Run, Keli! Get back!"

"No! Royce!"

No? Why was she acting so? What was the matter with her? What was she thinking? She was going to be killed!

"Keli, run!" he yelled louder. "Get out of here!"

"No, Royce! Put down the sword! It will not hurt you!" She seemed to have no fear of the fierce beast.

Royce stared in disbelief. Amazingly, the huge creature had stopped its advance and now stood unmoving behind Keli.

"Are you mad? Run!"

"No Royce, back away and put the sword back in the scabbard."

"Why are you protecting that thing?"

"I'm not protecting it, I'm protecting you! It won't hurt you! … And it's not a thing! It's one of God's creatures! Same as you!"

One of God's creatures? Had she gone mad? She was speaking of it as if it were a pet! Royce stared in disbelief! The creature's massive head was well in reach of Keli, yet it did not move. It tensely eyed Royce with his sword raised.

"Trust me, Royce. Put the sword away." Keli's voice was most insistent!

The fear in him would not let him lower the sword. He stood frozen, his eyes locked on the creature, its pointed horns, its scaly head that towered several feet above him, and its razor-sharp teeth!

Keli stepped forward and spoke softly, "Royce, she only wants to live, same as we do. She will do you no harm if you do not hurt her."

"S-she?" Royce asked.

"She wants to be your friend." She waited for Royce's reply, when it did not come she spoke again, this time more urgent, "Royce, put the sword away!"

Royce could not believe he was doing it, but he found himself lowering his defenses. To his amazement, the creature began to relax its intense stare and back away, but it still did not take its eyes off of Royce's sword.

"Royce, she saved me from the river." She took another step forward and reached out to his arm. "I was about to drown, I would have, if she had not pulled me out…"

He tried to speak but was still too shaken. He could not believe what he was hearing. All he could do was shake his head with his jaw dropped open.

"…and the other morning, when you found me on the rock, she had just saved me from the wolves. They had attacked me."

Royce looked at his little sister trying to comprehend what he was hearing.

"She just wants to be our friend."

He slowly put the sword back into its place. The beast then began to relax more and move back towards an opening near the back of the ledge. The huge beast moved with surprising agility. In no time, the beast had disappeared into the cave. Only then did Royce recover enough to speak again.

"Keli, are you alright?" He hugged his sister like he had never hugged her before. Both were still soaking wet, though the rain had stopped. Even with her wet dark hair sticking to her checks, she seemed so beautiful and so grown up. Up until now, Royce had viewed her as his little sister, annoying and pesky at times as little sisters so often are. Nevertheless, now he saw a stunning beauty of a young lady having the same will to survive as Wyn. She was determined to survive, but still had the ability to love a creature that was as hideous as this thing. Where had she learned to be so brave?

"I'm okay." Then a sparkle came into her eye, and she began to speak with the excitement of the little sister Royce was used to. "Oh, Royce, it was so thrilling. One second I thought I was going to drown, and the next, I felt myself rising out of the water! I didn't even see her coming! Suddenly, I felt something wrap around my arms, and then I was flying above the trees! For a minute, I thought I *had* drowned and the Lord was taking me into Heaven! Then I realized I was still alive! I was so scared! I felt like an eagle soaring through the sky! If I hadn't been so scared, it would have been breathtaking!"

"You scared the wits out of me! Are you sure that … that … it didn't hurt you?" He leaned against a rock for support.

"I'm fine, Royce, really!"

"What is that thing?"

"I'm not really sure." She looked in the direction it had disappeared. "I think it is Sherwin's leviathan he spoke of the other day!"

Royce remembered Sherwin's description of leviathan, but he had been sure that that had been an idle tale. He had thought he had made the whole thing up. Maybe Sherwin did know what he was talking about. From now on, maybe he would start paying more attention to what Sherwin said.

"But she is friendly!" Keli looked back at the huge beast. "When she started to put me down, she did ever so gently."

"It didn't look friendly to me." He was still shaking from the encounter.

"Royce, it was the sword she didn't like. She was sure you meant to do her harm."

"How do you know it is a she?"

"I don't know. I just know."

"It is so hard to tell with reptiles." Then Royce remembered something Keli had said. "What did you mean when you said it saved you from the wolves yesterday morning?"

"When I was looking for berries, some wolves chased me. I climbed on the rock to get away from them. She chased the wolves away. When she heard you and Wyn coming, she flew up over the trees."

"That's why you were staring into the clouds when we found you."

"A-huh. You just missed her."

"Why did you not tell us?"

"I didn't think you would have believed me. I wasn't sure I believed it."

"I probably would have not. I'm so glad you're okay. I

thought you were going to drown for sure."

"Me too. Why, if it hadn't been for Shira, I would…"

"Shira?" Royce interrupted.

Keli grinned and nodded her head in a quick positive way. "Yeah, that's her name, Shira."

"You've already named her?" Royce could see he was going to have a big problem.

"No! I did not! … It's written on the inside of the cave!"

Royce could not digest that bit of information.

Keli just grinned again. "If she is to be our friend, she has to have a name!" She turned toward the cave. "Shira!" Presently, the huge creature emerged its head again from the hole in the rocks and looked at the two. Royce felt himself stiffen again, but Keli walked over to meet her.

"Shira."

"Keli… be careful." Royce's words sounded extremely nervous.

"Royce, it's alright. Watch." Shira approached Keli and lowered her head. She then proceeded to scratch her scaly nose above the nostrils, all the while Royce was cringing. She moved her head back and forth, obviously enjoying the attention. "Wait 'til Wyn sees her!"

"Wyn!" Royce jumped to his feet. "Oh, no! She'll think we've both drowned!" Royce took a hold of Keli's hand and started toward the edge of the rocky cliff. Looking over the edge, he could not believe he had climbed up the cliff just minutes before, for the edge was sheer and nearly straight down. With his adrenaline flowing, he had not noticed how steep a climb it had been. It would not be wise to start down with darkness nearly upon them. There would be no way he could get Keli down safely until morning light.

Keli and Royce were forced to spend the night on the stone ledge with a live, thirty-foot creature of the like he had never seen nor heard of before. The moonless night would again be as black as pitch. Not a star shown in the cloudy night sky. They worked quickly to find a suitable spot to spend the night before it got completely dark. They huddled together against the rock wall, well away from the edge, and hopefully, in Royce's mind, far enough away from that creature. Needless to say, he did not get much sleep.

This night in his prayers, Royce realized he had a lot to be thankful for! Particularly, the saving of his little sister, which was because of the intervention of a formidable looking monster! He was thankful for her and even mentioned her in his prayer.

***

Drown is exactly what Wyn thought *had* happened to the both of them. By now, she had made two full trips to the fork in the river and back. Finding only the rope neatly rolled into a coil where Royce had dropped it when the creature had flown over him. Retreating back to the place of the river crossing, she found Sherwin coming from down stream. He had been searching from his side of the river. She dismounted and looked at him. He shook his head. She knew what he meant.

"I'm coming over," Sherwin told her as he went for Victor.

"No!" she hollered. "No! Not until the water goes down more."

"It will soon be dark."

"No matter! It's too dark already! It's too dangerous!" she was adamant. "Find a safe place to spend the night. I'll do the same. We'll meet back here in the morning."

Sherwin reluctantly agreed. He said nothing for a great while. He gave her a very awkward shrug and mounted up. "Take great care, my lady."

She watched him disappear into the woods on the other side of the river. Only then did she begin to cry. He was the only other person for leagues. Had she been able to touch him, she would have given him a hug for no reason. Instead she had sent him away. Royce was gone. Keli was gone. She was all alone.

She stood there in total doubt. As the darkness enveloped her, sorrow did so as well. Not sure of what to do next, she just stared at the river in silence. The river—how deep and beautiful—now seemed deadly. She now wished they had never found it.

That is when she heard that frightening, horrible, evil sound, just as she had heard the morning of the wolves. It echoed once again, through the canyon. A cold chill ran right through Wyn as she waited for the sound to die away. Sorrow was compounded with fear, fear with terror. Realizing she could still be in great danger, shelter would be a must. She gathered the supplies that had been dropped by Royce and found a refuge several spans above the ground in a cleft of a rock. There she waited out the storm in what little protection she

could find. Eventually, the rain passed. Once the drops stopped
falling from the trees, all was quiet.

For Wyn, sleep would not come easily, though she was
completely exhausted. She sat sobbing in the darkness for hours. She
was cold, she was wet, she was wretched, and she was scared. She
had no idea what to do, where she was, where to go, or how to get
there. A wolf howled in the distance. Remembering what Royce had
said about the wolves, she pulled a soaking wet blanket up to her chin
for a little more protection. She began to pray for the morning.

A distant noise made Wyn sit up and listen. She rose up
trying to see in the darkness, but this night, even cat eyes would be of
little use. The night had long since fallen and the fog had rolled in. It
was impossible to see anything. She strained her ears to identify the
sound. Ole Murdoch whinnied out so big and loud that Wyn's heart
nearly leaped out of her chest. An answer came from her beloved
Whirlwind from somewhere far away across the river. Wyn wanted
desperately to go and find him, but the blackness prevented it, and so
did the river. It was obvious the two horses were longing for each
other, but the river was now a barrier between them.

It was also a barrier between her and Sherwin. The river that
they had once called beautiful, the river that had sustained them the
night before, the river that they had so longed to find, had now
become an adversary. She hated that river. Now the rain would cause
it to swell again and rise up even stronger against her.

Hearing Whirlwind across the river gave Wyn a glimmer of
hope. She hollered out several times, hoping, just hoping that Keli
and Royce might be with Whirlwind, but she received no answer. It
was just further evidence that they had, no doubt, met a dreadful end!
She spent the most miserable night, sure that they were forever, gone!

Flight

T he next morning, Royce was aroused at first light by the sound of heavy breathing. Without opening his eyes he grunted, "Wyn, you're snoring."

Hearing a loud snort, his eyes popped open. There in front of him, little more than an arm span away, laid the beast. Its head was way too close, and its large eyes stared right in his direction. Instantly, he returned to reality. It did not matter that he had never slept on a harder surface in his life and every part of his body was crying out in aches and pains. He was on his feet in an instant, scrambling away from Shira. It was the first sight of her in full daylight; she was enormous. His next thought was on Keli.

"Keli!" he said in a half whisper and a half scream.

"Oh, Royce, good, you're awake!" She skipped over to him, still glowing with excitement just as she had been the night before. "Look, Royce. I want to show you something."

She stepped in front of Shira. The beast raised her head and gave Keli her full attention. Keli bowed to Shira; Shira bowed low to Keli as if each to acknowledge the other. Keli gleamed at Royce to see his reaction.

"Wow... Keli... I..."

"That's not all!"

Keli raised her arms over her head; Shira sat on her back legs and raised her front claws up in the same fashion. Keli spread her arms apart as wide as she could; Shira unfolded her wings and raised them high above their heads. Keli looked at Royce again, this time with almost a twinkle in her eye. Keli then began to flap her arms up and down, as imitating a bird. Upon seeing that, Shira began to flap her wings. The wind stirred so violently that Royce shielded his face.

"Okay, Keli! Okay! I see what you mean. OKAY! Keli ... Hold up!"

Keli stopped; Shira also stopped. Keli was now smiling from ear to ear and had more than a sparkle in her eye.

"That's… that's amazing!" Royce stared.

"She is smart—really smart!"

"I think so!" Royce agreed. "But Keli, we have to start thinking about getting back to Wyn and Sherwin."

"Yeah, I know, and I'm so hungry I could…"

It was then that Shira took flight. Her wings stirred such a sudden rush of air, that the children took cover. She rose straight up into the sky. Both stood and watched in total amazement, keeping their eyes on her until she was out over the trees and completely out of sight.

"Now where do you suppose she is off to?" Keli asked, disappointment showing in her voice.

"I don't know, but we must get down and find Wyn and Sherwin." Royce started for the edge. "They must be worried…SICK!"

Royce took another good look at the sheer cliff in full daylight. He began to concentrate how to get Keli off the cliff. The rocks were so steep that getting himself down would be an undertaking, not to mention safely getting Keli down. Royce decided to look for another option. He searched every direction down, he checked the small cave for another entrance, he even considered climbing on up higher to find another way down from elsewhere, but no better proposal offered itself. The protrusion seemed practically inaccessible but by flight only. Their only option would be to go back the same way *he* had come, down the sheer rock wall!

With little warning, Shira was back. She hesitated in the air to allow the children to retreat to the safety of the cave, and then she settled softly on the stone surface. She had brought back something clinched in her teeth. She stepped forward and laid it down in front of Keli. It was a whole branch of a tree, a branch of an apple tree that still held its fruit. Again the children were amazed.

"Apples! Do you suppose she understood me when I said I was hungry?" Keli reached out and picked one of the apples from the branch.

"I don't see how…" Royce doubted.

"How else would you explain it?" Keli interrupted. "They're almost ripe."

Royce could not argue with that, they were delicious, sweet with the morning dew!

"I should take some of these to Wyn, she loves apples."

Royce pushed several into his pockets.

"I will put some in my pouch," Keli agreed.

"We should thank her some how." Royce was feeling a little ashamed of his gluttonous appetite.

"Just tell her!" Keli piped, as she picked the rest of the apples.

"What?"

"Just tell her!"

"Like I'm supposed to step up to her and say, 'Thank you, my lady!' And she is going to…"

After Royce said thank you, Shira looked him right in the eye and bowed, just as if she understood.

"Did you see that?"

Keli just nodded and giggled.

"You know, if I didn't know any better, I would have thought she knew what I meant."

"She did!"

He could not argue with that either, but what they needed now was to get to the others.

"Come on, Keli, we should go," Royce said.

Keli agreed, for Wyn's sake, although she could have stayed on the ledge with Shira all day!

"If I only still had the rope, this would be a lot easier," Royce said, as he checked the cliff's edge again.

As Royce instructed Keli on the arts of rock climbing, her eyes stayed on Shira. The huge beast seemed to be listening to Royce's plan for getting off the ledge, and if she did indeed understand what he was saying, it would explain her behavior. She was beginning to get very uneasy. As Royce started for the edge, Shira quickly positioned herself between him and the sheer drop. Then she began to act very strange. Flapping her wings and lifting off the rock a time or two, she then settled down, folded her wings and put her head flat on the ground.

"What is she doing?" Royce asked.

"I …I think…she wants to carry us down."

"What do you mean ca…? Keli, NO!"

Suddenly, Royce knew exactly what she meant, and he was not too happy about it. Keli had already run around Shira's head and began to climb up onto her back. He started forward, then, realizing he was too close to the huge creature that lay before him, he backed away.

"Keli, are you mad?" Royce cried, wondering how she could be so fearless. "Come down here, now!"

Keli did not; instead she crawled up to a spot on the huge animals back and settled down, sticking her leg right between the two rows of fins at the back of the neck.

"Come down here right now!"

"No Royce, you climb up!"

"Come down or I will get you down!"

All this hollering did not seem to bother Shira in the least; she kept perfectly still. Royce thought he would be able to reach Keli and get her off the creature. For that reason, and the fact that he was quite aggravated with Keli, he cautiously moved around the head of the beast and pulled himself up to get a hold of Keli. He was determined to remove her from this creature. This was just what Shira was waiting for, because as soon as he had reached Keli, she raised her head and unfolded her wings.

"Get a hold, Royce," Keli screamed.

This was excellent advice! For a second, he was dangling from one of the fins. The powerful wings began to raise the massive animal off of the ground. Royce pulled himself up and in behind Keli, placing himself between the fins as she had done! What else could he do?

"Oh… Oh! Keli, what have you done?"

"HANG ON, ROYCE!" Keli hollered at the top of her lungs.

Into the air they flew. Leaving the safety of the solid rock ledge, Shira flew out over the treetops. In seconds, they were a couple hundred feet above the ground. The wind was roaring in Royce's ears. His brain was going into a spin and his stomach was rising into his throat. All the while, Keli was laughing aloud, thoroughly enjoying the ride. Once Shira reached her flight speed, she soared like an eagle, only occasionally flapping her wings. It was then a smooth, comfortable ride. It was also then that Royce opened his eyes. What he saw was just as Keli had said it was, breathtaking! The view was spectacular! The rock cliffs were to their right, the trees gliding beneath them, and the majestic River Terranera winding its way through it all. Though his heart was beating madly, his hands clutching to maintain a hold, eventually, he found himself enjoying the ride. Once he relaxed, he found it relatively easy to hang on by putting his leg between Shira's fins just as Keli had done. He could not fall off unless she flew completely upside down. Though the thought had crossed his mind, he prayed she would not.

Shira followed the ridge for approximately a league or so, then turned around and followed the river upstream. Royce could see all the landscape they had trekked, from the cliff where they had first seen the gorge, to the river where they had tried to cross. To his surprise, she drifted down and landed ever so gently (just as Keli had said she would). She landed in the clearing right at the edge of the riverbank where the bear had stolen their lunch. He recognized it at once! It was the same bank, the same sand bar that they had attempted to picnic on. It was the same spot they had attempted the crossing! It just also happened to be the only place in the area big enough for an animal of such a nature to land. Royce lowered himself onto the sand. His knees were so weak they almost buckled under his weight. After steadying himself, he helped Keli down. Walking around to face the huge creature, he bowed. She bowed.

"Thanks. We are in your debt."

When he had said this, Shira bowed again, then turned to Keli, bowed and winked. After a couple seconds of silence, she took to the sky and disappeared over the trees once again. Both of them on the ground, stared until she was out of sight.

You're Alive

Just after sun up, they were once again standing on the bank of the River Terranera. The river had gone down more overnight, even despite the rain. So much so, that a crossing would now be completely safe on horseback.

That's when they heard a welcome sound. Whirlwind whined. Royce spun around to see Wyn's horse coming from the trees behind them at the edge of the clearing, still saddled and bridled. What a welcome sight. He caught the horse and checked him over thoroughly. He seemed to be in relatively good shape. He made a promise to Whirlwind there on the spot. The right for a good long rest would be his, if he would just carry them safely across the river again. The horse was not fearful of the water after what he had been through, as one would think, but stepped right up to the challenge. Once again, they found themselves on horseback in the middle of the river. Once again, the water filled his boots, but it only came a little higher than his ankles. It was just as cold as ever. Once again, the horse made a misstep.

"Oh, no! Not again!" Keli cried. She grabbed on to Royce tightly.

"No, not again," Royce reassured her.

Whirlwind immediately recovered, continued and climbed out on the other side. Climbing down from the horse, Royce removed the saddle. It was too cruel to make him wear it any longer, having had it on now for well over twenty-four hours. From there on, Keli led Whirlwind while he carried the saddle. He watched the ground for signs that would tell him of Wyn's direction. Though it was difficult, he did manage to find horse tracks still visible in the rain beaten mud.

They found the supplies. Wyn had left them in the cleft of a huge boulder. After a quick search, they found her right above their heads. She had heard the wolves howling in the night. For fear, she had climbed up into a tall fur tree and secured herself with the rope. She was asleep. Because of her sheer exhaustion and being up most of the night grieving, she did not hear them arrive.

"Wyn!" Royce hailed up to her.

She was awake instantaneously, her eyes popped open, wild with fear. She sat straight up with a jerk. Forgetting she had tethered herself to the tree, she began struggling against the ropes.

"Wyn!" Royce hailed again.

This time she came to and remembered where she was. She quickly freed herself and dropped to the ground. "Royce! Keli!" She was tightly hugging her little sister in an instant. Royce could not ever remember having seen her do that before! She was truly overjoyed to see them.

"Keli!" she shouted. "You're alive!"

"I'm alive!" Keli repeated.

"Thank the Maker of heaven and earth. I thought you were drowned!" She had dropped to her knees and hugged her for a long while. Now the tears on her cheeks were not tears of sorrow as they had been most of the night, they were tears of joy! Suddenly her expression changed to anger when she looked up at Royce. "Don't you ever do that to me again! I thought you were dead!"

Royce just smiled at her and shrugged his shoulders. "For a moment there, I thought so too."

Then she smiled back. She rose and started to give him a hug. "Come here you big..." Suddenly something else caught her attention. "... DRAGON!" she screamed and jerked back!

"A what?" Royce jumped, for she had screamed right in his ear.

Wyn was in near panic state by the sight of the huge creature. She was grabbing for Keli and her bow at the same time, ready to retreat or fight, whatever the need be.

Whirlwind reared and would have bolted had Royce not still held tightly to the reigns.

"A dragon!" She pointed past them.

Royce had to move quickly to prevent her from raising her bow.

"Shira! Royce, she followed us!" Then she noticed the fearful look on Wyn's face. "Wyn! It's all right! She's a friend!"

"What?" Wyn's eyes were wild, not registering what her little sister was saying.

Shira eased out from under the trees slowly, she seemed to be trying not to frighten the horse more than necessary. She carefully approached Keli who went to meet her.

"Keli, get back!" Wyn was almost hysterical.

Keli ignored the warning. The dragon extended her claw as if to give her something. Keli extended her own hand to receive what Shira was offering. Shira's claw contained nearly a dozen red, ripe apples. Keli caught some, but most fell to the ground around her.

"Where did you find these? Look, Royce! She's brought us more apples! Thank you, dear friend!" She rubbed her snout. "See, she *is* a friend."

"It is true—a good friend, indeed!" Royce agreed. He sampled one of the apples. "Here, catch," he hollered, as he pitched one of the apples to Wyn. The apple bounced off her shoulder and hit the ground. Wyn took no notice, for she was staring at the dragon with a look of pure exasperation.

"Wyn, Keli would not be with us now except for this …ah…what you called a dragon."

"What…what do you mean?" Wyn spoke, not taking her eyes off of Shira.

"Yeah! I was about to drown, but Shira plucked me out of the river and flew off with me! Oh, it was a thrilling ride! She took me nearly to the top of the ridge. I was soaring above the canyon like a bird."

"I don't believe it!" Wyn listened in amazement.

"Yes, she has a cave high in the canyon wall," Royce explained.

The great lizard stood listening to the conversation as they conveyed the whole story, from the point of falling into the river to the landing right back where they started on the gravel bar. With a gleam in her eye, she looked back and forth between the three as if she understood every word.

"That's not all. Two days ago, she chased some wolves away that tried to attack Keli," Royce explained.

"What? Why did you not tell us?" Wyn glared at Keli.

"I didn't think you would believe me. I did not believe me. I thought I was going mad."

"Wyn, what is a dragon?" Royce asked.

"A dragon!" she repeated. "I can't believe it's a real living dragon!"

"So this is a dragon?" Keli asked.

"I thought they were only a myth. I have only read about

them, and I've seen sketches, but I never believed there were really such things. I thought they were just stories. The stories describe them as mean and ferociously evil creatures, creatures that seek destruction, creatures to be feared!"

"People just don't understand them," Keli defended. "Who ever wrote that, well, they could never have known one."

"You might be right, Keli," Royce said. "But remember what she did when I held the sword?"

"She was only defending herself. That is understandable."

"I think she has been around people before, most wild animals fear man. She has no fear of us whatsoever, she only fears the sword. Maybe someone tried to use one against her." Royce extended his hand and touched Shira.

"Why would she need to fear anything?" Wyn thought aloud. "She is as big as a…"

The dragon extended its claw and touched Keli's hand. She nudged her with her nose, then unfolded her extensive wings and flew into the air. Again, the wind generated by her lift off caused them to take a step back. The three children watched until they could see her no more.

Keli turned to her sister. "Wyn, where's Sherwin?"

"Oh, no! Sherwin!" she screamed in answer. "We have to find him!"

* * *

Wyn told the story of how the river separated them and what she had told Sherwin the night before. They crossed back over the River Terranera. While they searched for Sherwin, Royce told Wyn the story of the river rescue in detail. While he spoke, he followed Victor's tracks in the mud. Luckily for them, it had not rained much more after Sherwin had left the river.

Royce was true to his promise to Whirlwind; he let the horse have a much deserved rest. He was not ridden, but Royce led him, and Wyn rode Ole Murdoch. Wyn was quite tired after the sleepless night in the tree. The events of the night had taken a toll on them all. Royce agreed to lighten up and not push so hard from then on. Whirlwind's saddle and bridle were left at the cleft of the rock along with all of the supplies, except the food. It was assumed that they would get Sherwin and return in a few minutes. It was decided that once they found Sherwin, they all would rest for a bit. However, finding Sherwin proved to be more difficult than they expected.

"How far would he go?" Wyn questioned after they had traveled a great distance from the river.

"Not this far! Something is not right." Royce stopped.

"Where could he have been going? I can't believe he would go this far," Wyn said. Suddenly, she remembered something. "Remember how he was babbling about telling the king about Devlin? You don't think he would try to go warn the king do you?"

"No, he would not, not on his own!" Royce hoped not anyway. "Look, he is not on his own any longer. Look at the tracks!" He pointed to the tracks on the ground. "Foot prints of a man!"

"Where?" Wyn searched the ground where he was pointing. She just could not believe that someone else would be this far out into the Black Forest.

The imprints of a boot among the markings of the horse's hoofs were definitely not Sherwin's.

"Notice here." Royce was down near the ground trying to decipher the markings. "There are a lot of Victor's tracks here. It looks as if there was a struggle. Something was dragged across to here. Then the man's prints and the horses lead off in that direction." He pointed. "The horse must have been led away, because the horse's tracks are on top of the man's." Royce was somewhat proud for what he was able to figure, but the meaning hit him like a stone from a castle wall. He looked up at Wyn horrified.

"Do you know what that means?" Royce asked.

She was perplexed at his horrified look.

"Yes, we have to go that way," she said calmly

"It means something has happened to Sherwin! He's been attacked or something!"

"Are you sure?" Keli looked worried.

"I can't be sure of anything, but…"

"Right! We don't know anything for sure." Wyn was trying to keep calm. "Let's not panic."

"One set of tracks made by a horse. Signs of a struggle! Something is dragged across the ground! Two sets of tracks out, one of a horse and one of a man. These are not Sherwin's! It doesn't take a sorcerer to figure what happened!" Royce was getting more upset with every word.

"I don't believe in sorcery!" Wyn snapped.

"Oh, Royce, something bad has happened to Sherwin!" Keli was getting worried too.

"Calm down both of you. Let's just go find out what really happened. Just be careful and alert."

"Right," he agreed. He began to follow the tracks that led off to the south, farther from the river.

"Oh, Wyn," Keli said. "Poor Sherwin."

No one could argue with Royce's deductions. He seemed to be right, for it did seem as if some evil had befallen Sherwin. He was supposed to meet back at the river that morning. This *would* explain why he hadn't been there.

"So, you think someone has taken Sherwin?" Wyn was quite disturbed. "What are we to do?"

"All that we *can* do is follow the tracks, and hope we find Sherwin unharmed."

"I refuse to believe someone would harm Sherwin!" Wyn retorted. She did not even want to consider the possibility that Sherwin may have been taken against his will. "You think he was taken by force?"

"We don't know who we are dealing with!" Royce cautioned.

"Or how many!" Keli added.

"By the tracks, there seems to be just one," Royce assured.

"Right, Royce," Keli praised.

"But there's one thing that does not make sense. Where did Sherwin spend the night?" Royce shook his head in thought.

"Maybe he was taken last night," Keli interjected.

"Sherwin had no weapon," Wyn cried. "I sent him away last night with no protection!"

"Strange indeed. We had better be on our guard." He instinctively pulled his sword from its place. Wyn gave him a disapproving look.

The Hermit

They followed the tracks deeper into the woods. Royce tracked Sherwin while Wyn now led Whirlwind. Keli rode Murdoch. They had not gone far when Royce whispered loudly. "Get down!"

Keli jumped from the horse. All ducked behind a thorn bush. A distance in front of them was Sherwin's horse, Victor. Sherwin was nowhere to be seen, but a man was kneeling upon the ground with his back to them. He was very short. A hooded cloak covered much of his head and most of his body. It looked as if it was much too long for him. The years of use had worn it nearly threadbare. He used a belt to gather the cloak at the waist and also to hold a few weapons close by. His brown trousers showed only from the knees and below. He had taken one of the supply packs from Victor's back and was rummaging through it, spreading the contents across the ground.

Royce was not having this. Their survival depended on what was in those packs! He started to move. Wyn grabbed his sleeve.

"Be careful. He could be dangerous!" she whispered, as she made a motion of the sheath that was visible at the man's side. Royce nodded in reply.

He stepped out into the small clearing cautiously, quietly approaching him. Before Royce could speak, the man spun around. In a split second, the old man had pulled his sword and was facing him. Instantly, he swung it at Royce. Royce, not expecting a fight, jumped back, but instinctively brought his own sword up in defense. The blades clashed together. The man brought his sword around again. Royce blocked it. All that his father had taught him came back to him in an instant. The art of self-defense and elements of swordplay took over, only this was not play, it was the real thing. The man attacked again and again. Each time Royce retreated back a step, the man advanced. All his concentration was on preventing the man's sword from reaching his body. Every time the attacker swung,

Royce's sword deflected it away. He defended himself rather well, never having tested his father's training in real combat. Nevertheless, he could not stand his ground but continued to fall back.

This man was a foot shorter than Royce, and he had much less reach in his arms. His sword was only the length of three spans, which also greatly prevented his reach. This accounted as much as anything to Royce's successful defense. Even with this great disadvantage, he kept advancing. Still, if the man lacked anything, it was not resolve. He kept advancing. Royce kept retreating.

Presently, Royce's ankles caught on something, and he could not back any farther. When he could not free his feet, he fell to his back on the ground. Instantly, he was enveloped in a mesh of vines and rope. Seconds later, he was dangling above the ground in a trap that most likely was meant for a large animal. The man broke off the attack, backed away a little and stood chuckling.

After that, Wyn and Keli ran from their place of hiding. "Royce!" they hollered in unison.

"Oh-oh, a lass! Two!" His high-pitched raspy voice just did not sound natural. The man seemed perplexed at the sight of the two girls, particularly Keli. He stared at her, unmoving.

Royce did not care for this situation at all. They had no defenses, for Wyn's bow was still hanging on Ole Murdoch's saddle. His own sword was still in his hand. Of course, his sword! He began violently chopping his way through the web of vines. In no time, he cut through his prison of foliage. He broke through and landed on the ground. Within seconds, he was between the man and his sisters. He did not know what the man's intentions were, but he was not going to take a chance. This man was not about to get near them if he could help it! This time, *he* was on the attack! He swung so hard and so quickly that the old man could only block Royce's blows.

"Royce!" Wyn screamed out.

Now Royce struck again and again. This time it was the old man who retreated quickly. A particularly hard swing hit the old man's sword with so much force that it shattered in two. The blade flew by Royce's head, missing him by inches.

"My sword!" the little old man hollered, as he now fell back onto the ground.

In terror, the man looked first at the hilt left in his hand and then up at Royce. His defense was now gone. Royce stayed his attack, but kept his sword ready. He stared back in astonishment, for the hood had fallen away to afford him a clear look at the old man. It was not a man at all; Royce's attacker was a woman!

The woman looked up in frustration. "If it is valuables you seek, I have no such things!" her voice now seemed much more natural, knowing that she was a woman. She spoke rather fast and quite intelligently for an old forest hermit. She stared at the sword Royce held over her. Her expression changed. "Who are you?"

"We will ask the questions." Royce was not about to let her control the conversation. "Who are *you*?"

"Where is Sherwin?" Keli hollered.

"And why have you stolen his horse?" Wyn cried.

"Stolen!" she said defensively. "I am no thief, my dear child! This horse be not stolen. Its owner is a young man named Edwin, best I can gather."

"Edwin? Royce asked in confusion. "His name is Sherwin. Where is he?" Royce was ready for some answers and not this double talk.

"Oh, well now." The woman began to relax a bit. "Friends of his are you?"

"We be! ... I mean, yes." Royce was growing impatient. "Where is Sherwin?"

"Safe he is, but not well. Resting inside. Still asleep, I think," she answered. "Come and see ... see for yourself. Found him late in the night, soaked to the bone and burning up with fever. Speaking quite out of his mind! Said he had to get to the palace! Fever broke this morning. He will recover. Come and see for yourself! He is safe!" She moved to go, but Royce prevented her. "Many travelers enter the Black Woods, not so many leave. For man, forest is not safe, much less children! What is your purpose here?"

"You were going through our supplies! Why?" Wyn demanded.

"Clues I search for. Who is this child I find in such a state? A clue I did find. This traveler's not prepared for a long journey in the Black Woods."

"Why did you attack me?" Royce was still breathing hard.

"Why? ... I see a man with sword drawn! Who attacked whom?"

"We are sorry. We are just worried about Sherwin," Wyn said.

"Don't apologize, Wyn, we still haven't seen him," Royce

said.

"Defending myself I was. One still has that right, does she not, even in your world?"

"Yes," Wyn answered. "In everyone's world!"

Royce considered that fact. Maybe he did look to be on the offensive when he confronted the woman. He backed up, lowering his sword. The woman got up from the ground.

"Forgive me, but robbed, I have been more than enough." the old woman defended.

"I am sorry to hear that. We would never rob you," Keli said boldly, as she stepped out from behind Wyn. Keli never met a stranger and could strike up a conversation with almost anyone. She had an ability to get people to open to her even if they had a mind not to. "What world are you from?" she asked.

The old woman half chuckled. "My child, there is only one, no more. I am a part of it no long...er" Her eyes fell upon Keli, and a strange look came over the old woman. "Anni?"

"Sorry, my name is Kelina. Everyone calls me Keli."

"Why sorry? Kelina a good name." Anoka looked at her slightly puzzled. Keli returned her gaze. "Still, Anni, you do look like to me."

"Are you a dwarf?" Keli asked timidly.

"Keli!" Wyn reprimanded.

"You mean those little people that live in the wild, with mysterious ways and magical powers?"

Keli nodded meekly.

"They do not exist! No! A human I am just as you!" she answered slightly annoyed, and then she softened a little. "Just very short, unfortunate though it may be."

"Sorry," Keli said.

"Not anymore, bother me it once did. Not anymore. I am...I am... well bless me. Forgot nearly I did. Anni called me Anoka! You can call me Anoka. A long time it has been."

"Your name has been Anoka for a long time?" Keli asked.

"No, I mean, yes. A long time it has been since I have spoken of it," she restated. "I have not seen another soul, not in years, aside from your sick friend."

"Oh. Pleased to meet you, Anoka." Keli stepped forward. "This is Gwendolyn. We call her Wyn for short. And this is Royce. We just call him...Royce.

"Pleased, to make your acquaintance, Anoka!" Wyn greeted.

"Gwendolyn?" She half grinned. "Pleased aye? Get to know me and we shall see."

Wyn offered her a hand, which made Royce very uneasy.

"It's alright big brother. I pose no harm. Insured that, you did, quite well." She held up the hilt that was still in her hand. She spoke to Royce at the same time she shook with Wyn.

"How did you know he was our brother?" Keli inquired.

"All share same image," she replied. "Also, only for one so close does one fight so fierce. Loves you greatly, he does."

Royce began to blush a bit. "Anoka, I am sorry about your sword."

"Better fail it now, than with a real opponent."

Royce frowned at this. He was not sure how to take that comment. Did she not consider him a real opponent?

"Well, Anoka, it is nice to meet you, but we want to see about Sherwin." Royce sheathed his sword. "If you do not mind, will you take us to him now?"

"Did I not say I would?" She started off in the direction of her dwelling. "Impatience!" She shook her head as she walked. "Four siblings. Strange traveling band you are. Where are your mother and father?"

"Father is away right now and our mother is… gone." Keli said sadly.

"You mother? Gone?" Anoka paused.

Keli nodded and continued, "Oh, Sherwin is not our brother, he is a good friend."

"I see."

"He doesn't talk," Keli explained.

"Not talk? Born that way or did some misfortune befall him?"

"No, I mean he is just quiet." Keli giggled.

"I see. You must not rush off, please. A visitor I haven't had in ages."

"Thanks, but we have a long way to go," Royce replied. "We will just be getting Sherwin and then…"

"Much time for that later, hot stew is now waiting," the woman cut him short.

"That is very kind of you, but…" Royce's answer was indefinite. He glanced at his sisters.

The three children looked at one another as they followed the old woman. They *were* hungry. A hot cooked meal sounded very tempting, but they knew nothing of this Anoka.

"Much to speak of. Much to discuss." The woman continued to walk briskly. "Edwin must rest a while before he travels again." She glanced behind her. "Keep close."

"His name is Sherwin," Keli corrected.

"I suppose we could stay for a while," Wyn said carefully.

"Wyn?" Royce looked at her in doubt.

"She seems harmless to me," Wyn defended quietly.

"I hope so." Royce pulled the horses together, and they reluctantly continued after the strange little woman.

They were walking among a grove of the largest trees that any of them had ever seen. Towering higher than any castle in the land, their branches seemed to stretch nearly to the clouds. These trees had a base of which would take a man twenty paces to encircle.

"I perceive someone searches for you," Anoka said abruptly.

"How did you know that?" Keli asked.

"Keli." Royce shook his head in a way that told Keli to watch what she said.

Anoka recited:

> *"The one pursued, move on he must,"*
> *"Lest he is caught for lack of dust!"*

"Who said that?" Keli asked, catching up with her.

"It was I, my dear Anni, just now." Anoka again looked puzzled at her.

"Keli!" she corrected, but Anoka paid her no attention.

"She knew that *you* said it," Royce replied in aggravation, "she meant…"

"For what reason did she ask?" Anoka said.

"What does it mean?" Keli wanted to know.

"What does what mean?" Anoka asked.

"What you said about *'lack of dust'*," Wyn said.

"Aye. When one begins to run, one will run until caught."

"What does *that* mean?" Royce was tired of waiting for answers.

"Running from a problem solves it not. Confronting it with careful consideration works better."

"What if the problem is a band of rebels?" Keli asked Anoka, to Royce's disapproval.

Anoka whirled around. "Rebels! In Rupert's kingdom?" She wrinkled her face at Keli. "Rebels you say? In that case, running might be a smart decision. Still, no solution! Safe you will be here tonight and you may be able to cross the river in the morning."

"Who said we were going to cross the river?" Royce asked, still trying to keep as much of their business to themselves as possible.

"Ah, my dear boy, four directions you may go from where you stand, three require a crossing of the great flowing River Terranera and one does not. I think that you came here not to retrace your steps, therefore if you continue forward, you must cross the river."

"How do you know that we haven't already crossed?"

"When the river becomes so angry, no one crosses."

Wyn gave Royce an 'I told you so' look.

The woman paused. "Ah, arrived we have."

Anoka had stopped at an unusually large tree, but it looked as so many others. The children saw nothing different here than any other place in the forest they had passed.

"Where?" Wyn said doubting.

"It is here that I dwell," she answered. "Your friend is here."

"You stay here?" Royce thought it strange too. "I see nothing of a dwelling."

"Not here, up there." Anoka looked up and began to climb a ladder of limbs that looked as if it were a perfectly natural part of the tree. She disappeared into the green boughs. The three hesitated. She soon reappeared.

"You live in a tree?" Keli hollered up, grinning. Her interest was peaked.

"Anni, you know the ground is too dangerous at night in the Black Woods. Safer if on the ground you are not. Many times I have told you this."

"Keli!" Keli shrugged her shoulders and made a face at the other two.

"We have slept on the ground for four nights now," Royce said, and then looked over at Wyn, remembering where he had found her that morning. "Well, almost."

"Then fortune has been on your side," she said. "If any food be in your packs, bring them up. Otherwise, remove the saddles from your horse and set them free."

"Set them free?" Royce questioned. He looked at Wyn and lowered his voice, "This woman is out of her mind. We lost the horses twice already."

"They will not leave, unless they need to. Safer they are if free, tethered they cannot run," she said firmly, as if hearing Royce's words.

"Run? From what?" Wyn wanted to know.

"The wolves, Wyn," Keli said.

Wyn answered only with a curious expression.

"Seen the wolves have you, Anni?" Anoka asked. This time Keli did not even try correcting her; she had given up. She only rolled her eyes and nodded her head.

"We have seen a panther and a bear, but only tracks of the wolf," Wyn explained. "We have heard them nearly every night."

"I have seen them," Keli said quietly.

"Then lucky you are! But have you yet to see...?"

"Seen what?" Royce asked.

"Mind you, we'll talk later. Work to do now," Anoka said softly to Keli and started up the ladder again. She hollered back down to Royce, "Tend your horses and come up. And the thought of tethering them put out of your head!"

"Wyn," Royce said.

"We need to check on Sherwin." She had started up the ladder, but Royce motioned to her. She backed down and came over to him.

"Something is not right about this Anoka," Royce whispered to Wyn, as he unsaddled Ole Murdoch. He laid the tack up under the cover of the tree house.

"She seems kind enough. Besides, what are our choices?" she defended. "She has Sherwin. If what she is saying is true, we owe her a debt."

"I don't trust her!"

"You don't trust anybody!"

"I am not supposed to trust anyone, am I? Father's orders!"

Wyn just shook her head in answer.

Who's Child Are You?

They followed Anoka up the little ladder into the tree house. Anoka was busy removing a small cauldron type pot from over the fire. She placed a few more sticks on the coals. Quickly they ignited. The flame lit the whole room.

With that light, they could now see they had climbed up through a trap door and found themselves in a house completely supported high above the forest floor by one single tree. The living area was one round room, but it was very spacious, it wrapped completely around the huge tree trunk. The floor was sturdy, consisting of ax-hewn logs covered by closely fitted board, also hand carved. Boughs of fur arched from the floor over their head to the trunk of the tree, forming both the walls and the ceiling. They were so tightly woven that it easily shed the rainwater and stopped the wind, even in the roughest of storms. Anoka had obviously constructed her house to fit herself, for Royce could barely stand up without hunkering over. A fire pit had been constructed of flat stones carefully mortared together. They were laid up and over to form an ingenious chimney. This amply served as Anoka's kitchen. Opposite the fire pit was a ladder that apparently led up to even higher levels.

"Over there is your friend." Anoka pointed to a pallet on the floor on the other side of the fire pit. She continued, as she tended to the pot over the fire, "Lucky for me, he walks in his sleep. Otherwise I would not have been able to get him up here. Sleeping on the ground I found him late last night, his mind quite out of him. Lucky it was that I found him." Then she looked up toward the ceiling. "Right Andre'?"

Royce glanced up in the direction Anoka had looked. When he saw nothing, he looked uncomfortably at Wyn.

Anoka continued, "Get him on his horse, I almost didn't. Arouse your friend you may. Eat, we will soon."

Royce and Wyn went over to where Sherwin was lying on a mat. Keli was already kneeling at his side. She touched him on the shoulder.

He aroused and looked directly at Keli. "Keli!" he said groggily. "You're not drowned! How did you get here? … How did I get here? … Where are we?" Every one laughed quietly. For a moment, Sherwin looked confused, but continued, "It is good to see you again. I feared the worst." He extended his hand.

Keli ignored his hand and gave him a big bear hug. "Sherwin, it is good to see you too! And I mean that!"

Sherwin did not quite know how to react, but awkwardly returned the hug, looking very embarrassed.

Royce chuckled at the sight. "It is good to see you Sherwin. How do you feel?"

"Head hurts a little, but fine otherwise."

"Nourishment is what you need," Anoka added firmly.

The pot, which steamed with an inviting aroma, had been warming above the bed of hot embers awaiting Anoka's return. She washed, and then offered the children that unforgotten luxury. She then proceeded to serve the supper. Dipping a large wooden ladle into the pot, she filled four hand-carved wooden bowls with stew. They thanked the Lord as Anoka listened quizzically. They then thanked Anoka and began to eat. The four children had not tasted of such food for several days, and they told her so. The quality of Anoka's cooking surprised them, and they gave her their greatest compliments. How she could cook something so delicious from things only from the wild was beyond them.

"So how long have you been living out here all alone?" Keli asked, making polite conversation.

"Oh, I don't live alone, child. I have Andre'."

"This is really good, what is it?" Wyn praised.

"Turtle!" Anoka replied.

"Oh." A repulsive look crossed Wyn's face. Suddenly, it did not taste nearly as good as she thought and was immediately sorry she had asked. She continued to eat in fear of insulting their hostess.

"Andre' just loves turtle. Don't you Andre'?" Again Anoka looked up as she spoke of Andre'.

The children looked up and saw nothing but the tree limbs supporting the roof. They glanced at one another nervously.

After supper, Anoka began to ask all sorts of questions, most of which concerned the kingdom and its welfare. Wyn told her of some of the unrest plaguing the land.

"Poor King Rupert, his hands be full no doubt," she said sadly.

Royce looked at her seriously. "King Rupert died thirty years ago!" he corrected.

"Oh dear! ... Then out goes my heart to the peasants. If that be true, then Galleed be king now. Oh, in a wretched state the kingdom must be now... I see why!" she moaned.

"Actually, he is dead too," Royce said. "William is the king now."

"Oh, my! That little whip? Why, when last I was in Ary Brysta... I knew him when he was no higher than a knee cap."

Royce took notice, remembering Sherwin had used the same words. "Where?"

"The palace, my boy."

Wyn had taken notice of something else. "King William must be all of sixty years old. How could you have known him back when he was little?"

"Take that as a compliment I will, for my appearance must deceive. I am well beyond sixty!"

"Why did you leave and come out here to live?" Keli asked

"Reasons I have," she said sadly. "Mostly long forgotten by all but I, to be sure. It is important no more." Then her expression hardened. "More important is, why are *you* here? What reason have you in the Black Woods?"

Royce looked at the other three. What could he say that would satisfy the old woman's curiosity? "We're on an errand for our father. When it is complete we shall return."

"Your father, knows you're here does he?" Anoka questioned. "Well, I will help you find what you seek, if you tell me of it."

"Thanks, you are very kind, but we know what we seek and where it is," Royce covered.

"You may find what you seek, careful lest you also find what you do not seek."

They spent the afternoon talking. Anoka did most all of it; the children mostly listened. She told of her life among the woods, the animals she had seen, and the troubles she had encountered. This old woman's words were harder to follow than Sherwin's. They were getting too peculiar for Royce's liking, but he still found himself strangely interested in all that she had to say. He finally rose from his place in front of the fire and announced; "I am going to check the horses. Wyn would you like to check on Whirlwind?"

"Ah ... Yes." She quickly caught his meaning and followed him down the ladder to the ground.

There was still enough light to make out the surrounding landscape. Soon the last of the day would give way to complete darkness, for the clouds were still heavy and would prevent the moon and stars from casting their shadows this night. The horses were fine. They were close to the tree house. Royce walked among them and petted each one. Wyn approached him.

"What is the matter?" Wyn questioned.

"Are you sure we should stay here tonight?" Royce asked.

"What do you think we should do, move on in the dark? We can't leave Sherwin, and he is in no shape to travel."

"I am not sure about Anoka. She is strange—very strange. She could be after something."

"Or she could be just an old woman who is very lonely. She is a little strange, yes, but surely we are safer with her than out on the forest floor."

Royce felt a little better. Wyn had always been able to read people far better than he could. Trust was something he had always had trouble with. It was the one instruction his father stressed upon him explicitly upon the beginning of this trip. It was one thing he had no problem complying with. As they talked, a single wolf howled far in the distance, and the tough decision of whether to stay with Anoka suddenly became a whole lot easier to make.

"Wyn, I hope you are right!"

They stayed. This night they rested on soft blankets under the shelter of a roof, a luxury they had not enjoyed since the inn. For that, Royce gave thanks to their Protector above. Still, it seemed strange, not to see the stars or hear the crickets and the frogs. They all three fell asleep wondering where their father was and what he was doing.

***

Staying turned out to be a good decision—it drizzled rain all that night. Sherwin was still so weak the next morning that Wyn made the decision to stay one more night, giving him a chance to gain a little more strength. Anoka did not seem to mind. She started to become very fond of the children being there.

After breakfast (which was turtle again), Royce went to check on the horses and found them gone. In thirty minutes, he had rounded them back up under the tree house once again. He was getting tired of chasing after them.

That afternoon Wyn decided to go fishing again. She just could not stomach another bowl of turtle, though she would not dare tell Anoka this. The river was a short distance down the slope from the south side of the tree house. She retrieved her bow and arrows and left with Keli following along behind her.

While they were gone, Anoka approached Royce.

"Royce, you children are in real trouble are you not?"

"Why would you say that?"

"Your sword, I know it well. Its owner knows you have it, does he?"

"This is my father's sword." He glanced at it. "It's not stolen. He sent it with me when we left."

"Your father's?" She looked at him seriously. "Be aware, such a sword can bring you much trouble, much trouble indeed if you do not learn how to use it."

"I know how to use it!" he replied defensively.

"Your father taught you?"

"Yes!"

"He was not finished with the lessons was he?"

"Why do you ask?"

"Defend you do well. Attack you do poorly."

"What?"

"Show you I can." She picked up two wooden sticks about arms length. She pitched one to Royce. "I will attack. Make ready."

As soon as Royce had the stick in his right hand, Anoka took a swing at him. Royce quickly deflected it away. She swung two more times and he did the same.

"Good," she said. "Very good defense. That is the first you need to know, you do. Now, attack me."

"Very well," Royce replied uneasily.

He swung lightly. Anoka easily evaded his movement.

"Harder!" she instructed.

He swung again. She dodged again.

"Swing like you were protecting little sister!" she said forcefully.

This time he swung hard. Anoka used the stick and deflected Royce's swing in another direction. Instantly, she brought her stick around and tapped him soundly on the side.

"Oh!" he yelped.

In the time it took for Royce to swing and recover, Anoka had defended and counter attacked.

"First lesson. Immediately after attack is one most vulnerable. Attack only when you must, but defend always. If you cannot defend, do not attack."

"I see," Royce said, rubbing his side, "let me try again."

This time the result was about the same, only this time her deflection caused Royce to come down on his right leg. She tapped him on the other.

"Oh!" he cried in pain. Royce began to realize what she had meant about a worthy opponent.

"Second lesson. You must never lose your balance. A powerful stroke can be a great advantage it can, but a deadly enemy just as well. Again try. This time do not swing down. Swing from the side. Much harder to deflect."

Royce's side and leg were still stinging, but he agreed to try again. He swung from the right. Instead of deflecting the blow, Anoka could only block it soundly. Nevertheless, as Royce followed through with his swing, she still had time enough to tap him lightly on the side before he could bring his stick around to defend.

"When swinging, you must be prepared to block."

"I see," Royce said rubbing his wounds.

For the next hour, Anoka showed him the fine art of defense and attack. By the end of the session, Royce was quite sore, but he *was* beginning to grasp some of what she was teaching. When he would swing, she would block and then swing. Royce would then block. The sticks tapped together over and over, almost creating a rhythm. When Wyn and Keli returned from fishing, it looked as if an epic battle was raging between Anoka and Royce.

"Royce!" screamed Wyn. "What are you doing?"

Royce immediately stopped. Anoka did not. She popped him once more on the side.

"Ouch!" he hollered.

"Lesson ten. Never let something break your concentration!" Anoka laughed when she saw Wyn's disturbed look. "Worry not, my dear. Fine he is. Teaching me, your brother was."

"No, Wyn, turn that around," he said. "Teaching *me* she was."

Wyn looked between the two in confusion.

Keli interrupted the awkward moment. "Look what we found in the river," she said, holding up several fish.

That put a smile on Royce's face.

***

That evening after supper, Royce and Wyn went out to check the horses. Keli collected the bowls from supper and meant to clean them in the washbasin.

"Anni, do that I will." The old woman rose from her seat near the fire, walked over, then she and Keli began the washing.

"Why do you call me Anni?"

"Oh, oh. Keli, mind me not. Nothing I mean by it. … Anni was a young girl about the size of you when she first came out here. Friends we were for many years. You remind me so much of her, you do. Doesn't she Andre'? Miss her I do."

"I suppose so." Keli sighed as she looked up.

"But left something with me she did. Keep it in good care, she told me. Watched over it all these years I have. She visited almost every year, except for these last few. Now, I'm afraid she's grown up and forgotten all about me and the promise we made."

"What was it that she left with you?" Keli asked curiously.

Anoka glanced at Sherwin, whose belly was now full of fish. He had dozed off lying on the floor in front of the fire pit. Satisfied that he was not listening, she continued.

"A dragon!" she whispered.

"What?" Keli whispered back with a gleam in her eye.

"An animal like none other found in creation! An animal with intelligence, with heart, it is as she would have... a heart!" Anoka said, with a glint in her eyes. "Your best friend or your worst enemy, she is. You choose."

"What do you mean?"

"If she doesn't take to you, live to be an old woman you will not. If you see her, do not approach her. Keep your distance, mind you. She never welcomes strangers. Reads you like a book she can, looks into your very heart. Knows your intention before you do your own, good or evil, she knows." She nodded as she talked. "If she takes to you, a friend you will have for life, you will. More than one time, she has saved mine, but years ago that was. But to gain her trust takes years, decades! I never gained her trust like Anni did."

"What does she look like?"

"The size of a hound she was when Anni first brought her here. Sharpened her claws on this very hearth she did. Alas, through my door her head would fit no longer!"

"Does she have the tail of a lizard?"

"Yes!" Anoka answered in a snap.

"With the claws of an eagle," Keli continued. She knew exactly of whom the old woman spoke. "The fangs of a tiger? The eyes of a serpent?"

"Seen her have you?" Anoka looked at her in amazement.

"Does she have wings greater than that of the condor and can soar through the heavens as a great bird in flight?

"Wings of a condor! Seen her, you have!"

"Yes."

"Magnificent isn't she?"

Keli nodded excitedly.

"My dear child, a good sighting of her you did get by the sound of it. But, as I said, I did...nothing to fear as long as you stay your distance. How far away from you was she?"

"Close."

"How close?" She peered at her intently.

"Very close."

"What do you mean, child?"

"She picked me up, and carried me."

Anoka dropped the last bowl she had just washed, it clang hard against the washbasin. She stared at her in disbelief. Keli stared back, realizing that what had transpired between she and the creature the last two days must have been something absolutely unheard of by Anoka. For even she, who had watched over the creature from the time it had been a baby, did not go near her now. She had grown so huge and so fearsome, that even she was now afraid of her. It was the first time Anoka was found with a loss of words. She acted as if she were about to say something but then stopped. She stared at Keli, then at the roof.

"Did you here that Andre'?" she said strong and loud, then looked down at Keli again. "Of course Andre' never did get along with her," Anoka said sadly. "Did you Andre'?" She looked to the roof again.

Keli glanced up and then at Anoka. "Why do you keep speaking to this Andre'?" she asked, not sure whether she should speak of it or not. "There is no one else here."

"Have you not seen Andre'?" she said in disbelief. "Andre', Keli has not seen you, show yourself."

Suddenly, Keli was very nervous. Was Anoka going mad?

She was speaking up to the ceiling again. Was Andre' an invisible friend? She wished she had not asked.

"He is harmless, he is," she said, as she pulled a three legged stool from the wall and set it in the middle of the room. She stepped up and reached for one of the branches supporting the roof. "He *is* sometimes very hard to see."

Suddenly, one of the branches came alive and began to slowly move. Keli gasped in horror. It wasn't a branch at all. Andre' was a snake! He was a python longer than Keli was tall.

"Oh, Oh!" Keli cried.

"Worry not. Andre' will not harm you," Anoka doted.

"Did we sleep here last night with him hanging over the top of us?"

"Oh, no!" she said. "He hunts at night. He was here yesterday afternoon when you arrived, he was. Came back in this morning, he did."

"We best not tell Wyn, she hates snakes."

"Then we will not tell her!" Anoka whispered, with a chuckle.

Keli watched in amazement as the huge snake slowly disappeared through a hole in the ceiling next to the tree trunk.

Bang! Keli nearly jumped out of her skin. The trap door had been opened back, and Wyn and Royce reentered the tree house.

Anoka was very quiet the rest of the evening, glancing at Keli quite often but not speaking. Keli wanted to talk with her more about Shira. She desperately wanted to know more about the creature she had befriended. Anoka kept herself so busy that Keli did not get another chance that night.

Royce had them all turn in early. He had plans to head back to the river at first light and cross if the water levels would permit. Then climb to the ridge and on to the chalet.

***

Royce was awakened just before dawn by an awful commotion. The horses seemed to be running around under the tree house. The sound of the hoof beats pounding hard against the ground was so loud it seemed to jar the whole tree. He lay there for a second, wondering what would make them carry on so. The answer came soon. First it was a howl of a single wolf, then another and another, then, it sounded as if it had to be thirty or forty. Royce was up instantly, pulling on his boots and reaching for his sword. By the time he reached the trap door Wyn was by his side, bow in hand. He unlatched the catch and pulled up. A foot slammed it back down.

"Mad are you?" Anoka hollered. "What reasons have you to risk your life?"

"The horses! They will be killed!" Royce yelled.

"Better them than you!" she yelled back. "They can run, get away they can! You go down now, and you would not have a chance!"

Royce looked at Anoka in a rage but said nothing.

"Left them free did you not?" Anoka asked, but Royce did not answer.

Somehow she knew, by the look on Royce's face, she knew that he had not done what he was told. The howling was louder now and more nerve piercing than ever. Keli was now beside Wyn and pulling on her arm.

"Well?" Wyn now turned on him.

"I did not," he answered guiltily.

"Did I not tell you to leave them free?" Anoka's anger was evident.

"We have lost them three times already!"

"Lose them for certain now you will!"

"We are going to lose them like we lost Dante'!" Keli screamed. "We need something to scare the wolves away! We just can't lose Murdoch, Whirlwind and Victor like we lost Dante'!"

"Keli! Please calm down! The horses will defend themselves as best they can!" Wyn held her tightly.

The howling stopped. Then the growling began. It started soft and low but soon got louder. Keli knew what would happen next. They would growl, they would surround, they would move in, they would attack, just as she had seen before. The horses would have little chance!

"SHIRA! HELP! SHIRA!" Keli screamed with everything that she had. She ran around to the little circle window! "SHIRA!"

Wyn thought she was going into shock! She grabbed her and tried to hold her down.

"Keli, it is alright! We will get through this. It will be alright!"

"NO! WE NEED SHIRA!" she screamed again!

Royce was so confused! He wanted to go down and try to protect the horses, but what could he do against thirty wolves! He could not think straight with the wolves growling and Keli still screaming. He tried to help Wyn hold her.

"SHIRA!" Keli screamed one last time.

Suddenly, there was a deafening sound that shook the whole tree. A deep sound was as of a lion's roar, coupled with a screech of an eagle amplified ten times over. The whole tree house vibrated as if a mighty wind had slammed against it. The horses were prancing and pulling against the ropes, snorting and whinnying. The sound of wolves running was heard from all sides. They were fleeing in every direction. There was a quick yelp of a wolf, as if in pain, then another. Then it was all over. The sound of the retreating canines died away, leaving only the heavy panting of the horses to break the silence. The only other sound was a gentle breeze whistling in the top of the trees, and then it too, faded.

"She has followed us." Keli spoke in a now relaxed voice, but her eyes still watery with tears.

Anoka looked at Keli, her eyes wild in fear. She stuttered, "My...my dear, who's child are you? The daughter of whom?"

"I told you, I am Keli." Anoka's stare was suddenly making her quite uncomfortable. "The youngest daughter of Spencer and Alaina Windmere."

"Well, youngest daughter of Spencer and Alaina Windmere, I think, she has chosen you! She has!"

She said those words without a smile, only with a wrinkled brow and an expression none of them could read. Royce and Wyn could not figure what would make her say that, but Keli knew.

Bitter Disappointment

Royce was still set on moving out at first light, in spite of the rough night they had spent. He tried to hold tight to that plan, but Anoka insisted on feeding them a hearty first meal. Wyn and Keli were in no hurry to continue their travels, they suggested visiting with Anoka a little longer. Even Sherwin warmed up to her. While Royce was readying the horses and repacking the supplies, Sherwin and Anoka spoke on the subject of the ancient kings and the long-past history of Arielana. Royce could have used Sherwin's help, but decided not to interrupt. The woman proved to be a storehouse of knowledge about almost any subject that they were willing to talk about. Nevertheless, they never did get her to tell why she had left the civilized world to live in the wild, but they did not tell her of their own plight either. Royce made a good attempt to glean any and all information from Anoka without revealing their destination, or the reason for their travels. Carefully wording his questions, he got her to speak of where they were. She spoke of the river and the Hestia Mountains. According to Anoka, the wide place on the river where they had encountered the bear was the best place to cross, if it was a crossing that was required.

After all was said and done, even Royce had to admit that, despite her strange behavior, Anoka turned out to be a valuable friend. The fact that she presented him with a large package of dried venison for the trail did not hurt her reputation any either. She also gave him something else. She handed him something wrapped in a leather pouch. Royce opened it. It was her shattered sword. Upon a closer look it was a weapon made by a very skilled craftsman.

"It is customary to return a failed sword to its maker. You will find one Lanski of Wittakker. Take it to him. He will make good on it."

"Thank you," Royce said. "If he is still alive, I will do that."

"Oh, he is still alive! He is too ornery to pass on!"

She gave Wyn five new arrows for her quiver. They were

straight and perfect and obviously had taken her some time to make.

"Thank you," Wyn said, "but don't you need these?"

"Not as much as you will my dear."

Sherwin received a bottle of some concoction that she insisted would cause his strength to return in full, even though he said it tasted absolutely horrid.

Keli's gift was a small amulet that hung on a chain. This was not something she had made. It had small stones set in a shiny metallic substance. They sparkled in the sunlight. Keli squealed in delight.

"Someone very special gave that to me, now I give it to you," Anoka explained. "If anyone ever takes note of it, you may tell them about me."

Keli beamed at her. "I do not need this to remind me to tell people about you!" She gave her a hug. "But I have nothing to give you in return!"

"Oh, yes you have child and you have already given it."

***

Needless to say, the morning was well spent before they actually mounted and pulled away from the tree house. As they traveled that morning the *whole* story of Shira was repeated for Sherwin's benefit. From Keli's first meeting of the great dragon the morning in the woods, to the wolf attack during the night, not a single thing was left out. Most of their words seemed as idle tales. When telling the part of Royce climbing the cliff to get to Keli and pulling the sword on the dragon, Sherwin interrupted.

"Are you mad? A beast of that nature could have killed you! Why would you do that?"

Surprised by the question, there was silence for a spell. Then Royce answered, "Because… she is my sister. We are family. That is what you do for family."

"Do you?" Sherwin said. "You would endanger your own life for the sake of Keli?"

Royce nodded. "Yes," he said firmly.

"Why?"

"She is my sister and… I love her." Royce had never ever said those words before and they sounded strange from his own lips, but he knew they were true! Sherwin was silent, deep in thought. Wyn and Keli just stared between Sherwin and Royce not knowing what to say.

Royce unbuckled the second dagger from his waist and handed it to Sherwin. "Here, you need to keep this on you, in case you get separated again. You might need it. I should have given it to you at the beginning. Sorry about that." Royce looked at Wyn. She nodded approvingly.

Sherwin received the dagger. "Thank you, my lord." He eyed the weapon respectfully.

"Sherwin, like Wyn said, call me Royce. You are family now."

He looked up from the dagger to Royce, but said nothing.

***

The sun did not shine that morning, the weather stayed about the same. It did not matter to the children, their spirits were high. They were reunited. The events of the last several days had caused them to realize how much they needed each other, how much they depended on the other, and how much they cared. The petty bickering from the first few days of the trip now seemed so immature and senseless. The near loss of each other had taught them what was most important—each other! It reinforced the bond between them that now would become invincible, the bond of deep caring devotion, and the bond of love. Now that they had found it, they would never let it go! Even their feelings toward Sherwin had changed. As for Anoka, they learned that there were still some in the world willing to lend a helping hand to four children that needed her.

For the forth time, they found themselves standing on the gravel bar at the rivers edge, staring at the fast flowing water. Almost three days had passed since the first time. Nevertheless, there they were, contemplating another river crossing.

"We could just go back to Anoka's tree house!" Keli said teasingly.

They did not, but crossed over without incident and began their long ascent to the top of the ridge.

That night they positioned camp on a rocky ledge that would be easily protected from any wild animals that might try to attack. They built a fire and sat down to eat. While eating, they enjoyed the view of the great canyon they had just crossed. That of itself was a great accomplishment. Just before dark, the clouds rolled back and revealed the most glorious sunset. The nighttime sky came alive with a million twinkling stars.

***

The next morning, Wyn reminded them that it was the day of assembly. Their father had taken them to the assembly for as long as they could remember. This would be the first time they would not be able to attend, so Royce decided that they would have an assembly of their own. He tried to recite a passage from 'The Book', and with a little help from Wyn he succeeded. "Yea, though I walk through the valley of the shadow of death, I will fear no evil for Thou art with me..." Royce now had a greater understanding of those words. Afterwards, he led them in prayer, careful not to forget to thank Him for the safety they had been afforded thus far.   Lunch was apples and dried venison. They used a stone for the table, and a blanket for the spread.   This time they were not interrupted by a bear.   All the urgency of getting to the chalet was temporarily forgotten. They ate and rested. They were happy to see blue sky all that day. It had been nothing but clouds for so many days. They finished eating, then for two hours they acted as if they had no more cares than any other children in the world. They pretended the huge boulders were castles, and they were rulers of the great country that lay before them. Sherwin sat and watched. Try as Keli may, she still could not coax him to join in. That did not stop the rest from enjoying themselves. They laughed, they played, and they sang.

***

The following day Royce aroused everyone early and had them on the move by first light. The fog was so thick that it was difficult to see one another if they strayed more than a stones cast apart. The huge boulders and the extreme slope made the first part of the days travel very treacherous, but by being careful and taking their time, they maneuvered it safely. Up they climbed, despite the poor visibility. By the time they reached the top of the rocky hillside they could see that the sun had risen well into the sky. At this height, the sky above was clear, but as they looked below, the fog still covered the lower areas of the canyon as a blanket on a bed.   It was a fascinating sight to look from the ridge, down on top of the foggy clouds. Only the tree-covered ridges felt the warm morning sun, the fog extended up into each ravine as giant fingers of a hand. It too, burned away a few hours later.

A great distance was covered that day.   The ridge was followed just as Father had instructed. Though it was rocky, the traveling was somewhat easy. The highest point of the crest almost formed a path meandering back and forth in a westerly direction, but ever slowly rising in altitude. In front of them were the foothills of Mount Hestia. In the distance, they could see an outline of the mountain becoming ever more visible as the morning mist dissipated. It was their first glimpse of the mighty peak. They seemed to be climbing to the top of the world.

All day, they sang, talked, laughed, and munched on apples, apples they had picked from a branch of an apple tree they found in their camp that morning. Keli, sitting in front of Royce on Ole Murdoch, kept looking back often. He knew what she was looking for.

"Royce, when do you think we will see her again?"

"I'm sure I don't know, Keli."

"I am sure we will."

"How do you know?"

"I don't know. I just know. Every time we have been in real trouble, she has been there for us."

Royce agreed, but also thought of another aspect, twice, when Keli had been in real trouble, the dragon appeared. It had come when she called for her at Anoka's. There was much more to her relationship with Shira. It was more than just an acquaintance. He pondered on this, but did not voice it to Keli.

"I like that dragon," she announced.

"I know you do. I do too."

Royce did not worry so much about finding the chalet. It

seemed that Father's instructions were now working precisely. The fact that they were several days behind did not matter. He was confident they were going to make it. Once there, they would be safe.

Since they covered so much ground that day, it was decided they would stop early and set up camp. When a suitable spot was found, they unpacked. Wyn then had an announcement. It seemed that the water ruined all the cornmeal. It now smelled extremely bad. There would be no more bread. The dried fruit was all gone and very little of the dried meat was left, but they had the venison Anoka had given them, and they had a few more apples.

***

The weather the next day was just as beautiful as they could have asked for. They gladly welcomed the brilliant sun with its warmth and beauty! But a more welcome sight than the sun was the view they saw as the morning fog burned away. The sky was clear enough to see Mount Hestia in detail! The peak, still white with a snowcap, was vivid and brilliant in the full sun.

They had to be close now! They had followed their father's instructions completely. This was their ninth day of travel, finding the chalet today would be a must. Everything their father had told them had been almost exactly the way he said it would be. Accounting for some minor delays on the road, the two major ones at Anoka's and the river, today they were sure they would reach the chalet.

With very little obstruction, the view became more spectacular the higher they went. As they climbed in altitude the landscape changed. There were no trees, just shrub, brush, and rock. They could see for leagues in every direction, a very sharp contrast from the scenery the many days before.

"The chalet!" It was Sherwin who saw it first.

These wonderful words caused Royce to pull his horse to a stop. All looked in the direction he pointed. They had done it! It was what they had been waiting to see for many long days. The chalet, nestled neatly in the shadows of the mountain was surprisingly easy to spot after they cleared the last ridge. It was among a small cluster of buildings lying partially hidden by some fur trees far down in the valley below. Flat fields enveloped it on all sides. It looked to be a farming operation of some type, at some time long past. Cutting through the middle of the valley, passing near the chalet, was a crystal mountain stream sparkling in the sunlight.

"That is it! We are here!" A great feeling of accomplishment settled on Royce. He had succeeded in bringing them here at last, and now they would be safe.

"Oh, we are here!" Wyn sighed. She pulled Whirlwind to a stop between Royce and Sherwin. "Finally! Thank the Father above!"

"Let's hurry!" Keli urged.

Royce coaxed his horse to pick up the pace; the rest did the same. Down the hill and across a wide grassy field they rode, lighthearted and happy. The horses nibbled the tops of the grassy heads as they went. They would be as happy as their riders to settle here for a while.

A place to rest! Royce thought. *A roof over their heads, out of the rain! The chance to sleep in a bed again and off of the hard ground! Not having to worry about wolves attacking in the night.*

A chance to clean up was what Wyn was thinking. By this time, all were starting to look pretty grimy and dirty. No doubt, their smell was none too pleasant. Royce and Keli were the only ones to have a good bath in the river.

There would be provision! Their father had said that he left provision enough for them. At least they would not go hungry.

As they neared the edge of the field, not far from the chalet's outer fence, something caused a feeling of doubt to rise in Royce's mind. Smoke. At first, he did not say anything, for it did seem that it would be a natural thing, smoke rising from a chimney. Smoke was definitely rising from the chalet, but it was supposed to be vacant. Should there be smoke? Royce pulled to a halt so quickly that the others had to turn to keep from running into the rear of his horse.

"Royce, what is it?" Wyn questioned.

"Smoke!" he answered. "There should be no smoke."

"No," Wyn agreed. "But maybe it's Father. He has beaten us here! It did take us four days longer than it was supposed to." She started to urge her horse forward, but Royce stopped her.

"Maybe. Maybe not." He dismounted. "We had better be careful. You keep the horses here for a minute. I will check it out. Give me the bow."

"No." Wyn also dismounted. "Sherwin and Keli can keep the horses quiet, I am coming."

Royce started to argue, but he knew it would be useless. "Okay, but be on the alert!" He turned to Sherwin and Keli. "And you two, keep out of sight."

"Yes, my lord."

Wyn rolled her eyes in Sherwin's direction. After all these days of correcting him, he still would not stop calling Royce 'my lord'.

Sherwin climbed down and took the reigns to all three horses and led them up behind some brush at the corner of the compound.

Royce and Wyn cautiously eased their way up to the gate and into the courtyard. All was quiet; no sign of anyone anywhere in the compound, but what they did see was quite disturbing. The smoke was not coming from a chimney, as was Royce's first thought, it was coming from several structures of the compound. All the wood members of the building now laid in ashes and charcoal. Nothing was left of most of the buildings, in most cases just four stonewalls. Gone completely were the servant's quarters, the stables, the cook's kitchen, and a couple other small sheds. The only reason the main dwelling remained was because it was built completely of stone. The only other structure left untouched was the guard's tower, but that was pretty much an empty shell. All buildings that could have been burned had been destroyed. By the small flames that still lingered about here and there, the fires could not have happened more than a day earlier.

"What went on here?" Confusion reflected in Wyn's eyes.

"The place has burned!" Royce spoke in almost a whisper.

"How… Lightning?"

"No! These fires have been deliberately set! There is no chard grass between the buildings. No. Someone has purposefully burned these buildings!"

"Why would someone do that?"

"Don't you see they are after us? They must have found out we were coming up here, and they came here looking for us! Somehow they knew we were coming."

"Oh, Royce, that means that they must have Father!" The fear showed on her face.

"Not true! Father would have never told them where we were going!" he corrected.

Wyn shook her head in agreement. "We are just children, why would they go to all this bother to get to us?"

"I don't know, maybe they are looking for something of real value, and they think we have it!"

"We took nothing with us." On Wyn's face was complete dismay. "Only what we needed to survive!"

"What if we did take something with us?" Royce looked seriously at his sister. What if we left with something of great value?"

"What?"

"The heir to the throne," Royce had hesitated to say it, but he had to. He could not keep what he was suspecting to himself any longer.

"Oh, Royce. You mean Sherwin?" Wyn glared at him. "You have gone mad."

"No, it makes sense," he insisted. "Listen. Out of nowhere, he comes to live with us. He is supposed to be a staff boy, but he doesn't know how to do anything. Right away, the inn is attacked. Father sent him with us and tells me to take care of him just as if he is one of the family. Remember Father saying he was trying to protect something more valuable than the inn?"

"Royce, I…"

"He doesn't talk like you and me. Every time he says something, it is something strange. He knows more about the king's Elite than anybody I know. He knows about the king's horses. He knows Devlin."

Wyn kept silent as she tried to comprehend what Royce was saying.

"Think about it. Sherwin tells us there is a living heir. If… there is an heir, I believe it is Sherwin."

"If that is true, I don't see how he could have ended up with us," Wyn said, still in doubt.

"Consider this…" Royce started, but he stopped when Wyn motioned with her eyes to the gate.

By this time, Sherwin and Keli had eased their way up to the front of the compound. They were peeking in from the outer wall, and Royce waved them forward.

"What happened?" Keli asked in a loud whisper.

"It has been burned, Keli," Royce answered.

"What a stroke of luck," Sherwin said from a kneeling position. He looked up and noticed the others look of dismay. "These tracks are only a day old. Had we been on schedule, we would have been here when the highwaymen attacked."

Royce glanced at Wyn nonchalantly, who slowly shook her

head 'no'.

"The highwaymen? You know, this could just have been done by common thieves and robbers." Wyn still could not see how someone would go to so much trouble to find *them*.

"Not thieves," Sherwin spoke, still down on one knee looking at the ground.

"How do you know?" Wyn questioned.

Sherwin looked up at her and hesitated as if he did not want to answer.

"Well?" Wyn's impatience was showing

"It's the tracks…the horses all have shoes. Look at the marks. All have been shod."

"So, what does that mean?"

"Only the highwaymen's horses have *shoes*."

"How do you know that?" Wyn questioned.

"No, he is right," Royce agreed. "Only the knights and the king's highwaymen have shoes on their horses…because iron is so hard to come by. But…how *would* you know that, Sherwin?"

"I…I have been…I have worked in the royal stables. I have seen their horses!" Then he proceeded to show them all the many horse tracks in the courtyard. "See, every horse, shod."

"So, the king's highwaymen are after *us*?" Royce questioned.

"Yes. I think it is the same band of men we met on the road the first night."

"That makes no sense, we are just children!" Wyn was sure the highwaymen would not go to this much bother on their account. She was still not convinced Sherwin was the heir to the throne of Arielana.

"The king would never have ordered the highwaymen to burn the place to the ground. But these men are no longer the king's men!" Sherwin said.

"Sherwin you're not making sense!" Wyn said, thoroughly confused. "You said it was the king's highwaymen!"

"No. The horses still belong to the king, but the men do not. The men riding these horses are no longer following the king's orders. They may think they are, but they are now serving Devlin."

There was silence as they tried to figure what that meant.

Carefully they explored the main structure. Anything of value had either been destroyed or taken. There were no provisions, no storage of food; nothing was left! They found nothing at all that they had been hoping for. With no food, they could not stay here. The rugged mountainous region offered little essentials on which to live. With so little supplies, a hard decision had to be made; they had to move on, or they would starve.

"What do we do now?" Wyn looked at Royce.

"I… I am not sure, but it's not safe here," he stopped when he saw the fear in Wyn's eyes. "We had better go. The fires were not set that long ago. Whoever did this cannot be far away, and they may come back."

"Where do we go?" For Wyn, a definite plan must be in order, or she would be very unnerved. Since leaving the inn, they had always had a destination. They knew where they were going, even when they did not know how to get there. It would not do for them to just wander the country aimlessly. They needed a place to go.

"I don't know, but let's get away from here!" Royce answered.

It was not the answer Wyn hoped for, but she could think of no better plan.

That's all that had to be said. Soon they were mounted and on their way again. Not sure of where to go or what to do, they just rode.

A Lesson of the Heart

O ne thing was for certain, they had to eat. Their food would not last long.   With the hopes of the chalet providing the necessities they needed now gone, it was a fact that they would have to fend for themselves. Water was not a problem with all the many mountain streams available, but food was a greater concern. With very few food producing trees growing in the higher altitudes, living on nuts and berries would not be an option.

Which way would they go?

To continue to go east would take them over the great Mount Hestia, which would be ludicrous and would end in certain disaster.

Going north would take them into the badlands.   Three different countries laid claims to that region over the years, including Arielana. Nevertheless, a war was never fought to settle the dispute, the territory was considered worthless. Nothing lived there, nothing ever grew there; it was just a vast, arid wasteland of rubble, rock, and sand. Going that way would have the same end as going over the mountain. Sure, they would have been safe from their pursuers had they gone there, but only to perish in a few days time. Few that had ever entered that barren desert had ever been known to return.

West would take them back the way they had come, and none of them cared for that, except to return to Anoka's.

Nevertheless, fear and wonder of their father's wellbeing forced them south.

They had no idea where they were going. They paralleled the road so that they could still follow along to keep some direction. They knew to not use the highway, because of the fear of crossing paths with the king's men, as they had discovered that first night. Roads were designed for traveling; hills, ridges, and ravines were not. Therefore, as in the Black Forest, they covered little ground. Fortunately, the area was not overly populated.   The rugged, mountainous landscape was not a very hospitable place to live. They could easily travel undetected. Eventually, they began to see a cabin here and again as they descended down from the Hestia foothills. They were hoping to find a village where they would be able to purchase food. Their father had not sent them out penniless. They would just buy the things they needed, if they could find a merchant. Nevertheless, two full days of travel brought them to no such place, but it did get them back into the cover and protection of the woods. Being out of the open made them feel somewhat safer and raised their spirits only a little.

All were desperately feeling the pangs of hunger by late the second evening. Anoka's venison was all gone and so were the apples. That is why, when Wyn spotted a deer in a small clearing, she quickly loaded the bow and pulled the string taught, almost out of instinct. Poised in that position, she froze. Suddenly, realizing what she was about to do, a battle began raging within. The will to survive had, for an instant, overpowered the usually sweet, life-loving, carefree person that Wyn used to be. It was a clash between the person she used to be and the one she had now become, between the child that had left the inn and the young woman that had emerged from the Black Forest. She was not the same person she had been and it had happened all too quickly. Her child like spirit fought against her will to survive. The adolescent Wyn saw the deer as a beautiful, wholesome thing, unlike the panther that attacked them with claws and teeth bared. The young adult Wyn saw the deer as an innocent object that must die for her to continue to live. She sat motionless, unable to let the arrow go as a tear rolled down her cheek.

Royce, seeing the deer and Wyn taking aim, urged her to shoot. "Do it," he whispered softly.

Keli, after she saw what was about to happen, urged her not too, "Wyn, don't, please don't."

Wyn did not reply to either.

"Do it," Royce urged her again as quietly as he could.

Wyn still sat frozen. The deer stood staring into the distance, sniffing the air. The breeze must have been in their favor, because it did not run, it just stood with its nose in the air checking for danger. It then turned its head slightly; nature was telling it something was not quite right. Wyn wanted to shoot, she needed to shoot, but her heart just would not let her. As the old Wyn began to win over, she slowly lowered her bow.

Royce, seeing that she was not going to be able to kill the animal, grabbed the bow from her and set the arrow back into its place. The deer, seeing the movement, realized the danger and bolted for the trees. Barely able to get the shot off before it disappeared into the brush, the arrow missed the deer.

He lowered the bow, but kept looking in the direction the deer had disappeared. "It would have fed us for several days," he said lowly.

"Royce, I...I'm sorry," Wyn's voice cracked. "I just couldn't."

Royce looked at Wyn. A tear in her eye moved him. "Let not your heart be troubled, Wyn, the Lord will provide." He smiled at her.

A few short days ago, he would have berated her for not being able to be *man* enough to shoot, but this is the girl who had killed an attacking panther. She had supplied them with fish. She showed him how to kindle a fire. This girl that had taught him a thing or two about survival was now teaching him a lesson of the heart. After all that they had come through, he was glad that she somehow was able to keep that sweet Wyn character. The caring for another living creature is a quality that Royce would not want to see her ever lose.

Wyn had always been careful to show her tough exterior, to be a solid rock, the anchor in a gale, but on the inside he knew her heart was still just as tender. Seeing her like this, he could not say another word, but almost wanted to cry himself.

That did not restrain Keli, "It's fine, Wyn. It can now live too."

"Yes, and so will we." Royce forced a lump back down in his throat. "Let's go."

Sherwin just looked back and forth between the three, but did not say a word. They rode on.

***

The following day the weather had changed again. Gloomy clouds blocked out the sun once again, bringing a stronger feeling of despair over the travelers. They were hungry. They rode the ridge overlooking a huge valley. Far below, the road followed the flat, easy contour of the land. They kept close by it (but they did not dare use it), carefully checking it often to insure they were still going the same direction, for it would inevitably lead to a settlement.

A sound of distant hollering caused Royce to pull his horse to a stop. He raised his hand to motion to the others to be quiet. He listened. A man's voice yelled, then a woman screamed. The sound was faint, but there was no mistake of what it was. Royce dismounted and ran to position himself on a boulder where he could see down to the road.

A horse cart had been stopped on the road by a group of highwaymen. A family of four: a man, his wife and two children, who had been the occupants of the cart, were now running around on the ground. Chasing them were five men on horseback. Dressed in black, except for their armed breastplates of polished steel, they wheeled their weapons as they circled the cart as if fighting some great enemy in battle. The family gathered together in the ditch off to the side of the road in sheer terror. Three of the men dismounted and began to ransack the horse cart. It looked as if they were looking for something of value, as would a common thief. The two others turned their attention to the family. In an attempt to put as much fear in them as possible, they began threats of torture.

The sound of the woman's screams opposing the laughter of the evil men put a sickening feeling in the pit of Royce's stomach as he watched the event. He had to turn away.

Wyn, Keli, and Sherwin had slid in beside Royce. They too

were horrified at the sight, staring in disbelief.

"That's despicable!" Sherwin spoke in anger. "The king will be made known of such atrocities!"

"Let's go!" Royce whispered roughly. He withdrew to return to his horse. "Let's get out of here!"

"What?" Wyn replied in surprise. "Where are you going?"

"Anywhere but here!"

"We have to help them," Wyn cried. She pulled back from the edge of the stone that they had been hiding behind.

"How?" Royce replied. "Just how can we do that?"

"We can't just turn our back on them!"

"What can we do? We are just four children, what can we do against five highwaymen trained to fight?" Royce stared. "What do you suggest?

With a look of anguish, Wyn stared back. She was definitely of a courageous heart. Her eyes were enraged as she tried to speak, but she could not. For several long seconds the two stared at each other while they listened to the sounds from the men still taunting the poor family.

"We report it to the king," Sherwin said quietly, but no one replied.

"How are we to do that Sherwin?" Royce asked. When Sherwin did not answer, Royce walked toward his horse. "Come on. Let's go."

"Come on, Keli," Wyn said in sorrow and anger. Without looking back she mounted Whirlwind.

Keli did not follow. She could not turn away. She had not stopped watching the scene as it unfolded in front of her, but stared intently. Even when Sherwin withdrew, she did not move.

Suddenly there was a roar, a roar that was very familiar to the children. They knew that roar. Instantly, Royce was back peering over the edge of the boulder, absolutely amazed at the sight that unfolded before his eyes.

Shira had dropped right in the middle of the five men. The three unmanned horses fled. Using her claws, she took the two men still on their horses out first, knocking them from their mounts. In sheer terror they fled on foot with their horses leaving them far behind. One man charged recklessly with his spear. Using her tail, Shira easily knocked him aside like a rag doll. He rolled to the side of the road in the ditch, then scrambled up and ran. Another man froze in horror as Shira swung around to face him. He fainted, passed out cold and fell to the ground. The remaining one fled as fast as his legs would carry him. Almost, as quickly as it had begun, it had ended. Shira's efforts were no more to her than it would be to a man swatting flies, not much more than an annoyance. She waited a moment for the last man to vacate the area, and then she lifted off. She was gone in an instant, sweeping out over the trees.

The family still huddled together in complete dismay at what they had just witnessed. They began to recover. Slowly the father arose, checked each of his family, and then went chasing their horse and cart in the direction it had fled.

Royce could not believe what his eyes had just witnessed. He looked over to Keli who had never stopped staring at the scene. She slowly turned to Royce; her face had an expression that he could not read.

"Is she with us again?" Royce asked.

"She has never left," was all that Keli said.

Royce wondered how she had known that. Did she have something to do with Shira attacking the highwaymen and saving the peasant family on the road? Had she called her, like she did at Anoka's place? If so, did she know that to attack a highwayman would be in direct violation of the king's authority? He wondered, but he didn't ask. He was afraid to. At the same time, he was glad that something had been done about those wretched soldiers!

When he pulled back from the rock the second time, one from their party was missing. "Where's Wyn?"

Sherwin made a gesture with his head in the direction of the family on the road.

Moved with compassion for the poor terrorized family, Wyn had turned Whirlwind down the slope. After scanning the area, Royce caught sight of her near the bottom of the hill. She rode boldly up to the woman and her sons.

"What is she doing?" he said aloud as he watched helplessly from the top of the ledge.

She got down from her horse and made her acquaintance with the woman. The mother wore a tattered dress, dark in color, and her hair was quite raveled. Royce guessed her to be thirty years of age, the two boys to be around six and eight. Wyn picked up some overturned baskets. As she did, she and the woman began to talk. They talked for what seemed to Royce, a long time. He was too far from them to hear anything that was being said. About the time they had gathered all their belongings, the father returned with the horse and cart. Wyn then proceeded to help them reload the articles. They talked a little longer, and then they parted company, the family in their original direction, Wyn in the opposite. Once she was well out of their sight, she left the road and climbed back up to the ridge. A few minutes later, she rode up to the waiting three.

"Wyn, you should have told me where you were going," Royce reprimanded.

Wyn did not reply to that statement. She just looked at Royce in such a most solemn way that Royce dropped it. He could tell she had learned of something important to tell him.

"What… what did you find out?"

"The highwaymen! They *are* searching for us!"

"What did they tell you?" Royce asked. He had known it to be true, but now to hear Wyn say so seemed to drop a millstone upon him. If Wyn now believed it were true, then it was confirmed.

"It was better that I went alone," she explained. The soldiers are looking for children. Four children! They described us exactly! They are checking any and all travelers, searching every farmhouse, every dwelling!"

"Did the soldiers harm them?" Sherwin asked.

"No," she answered.

"Did they take anything from them?"

"No," she said. "I don't suppose they had that chance."

Horrible News

The father of the family had given Wyn some valuable information. There was a market in a tiny village he had called Dalimoore. It seems that they had been delivering vegetables there today. A half days travel away, they could be there by early evening.

It was decided they would stop at the village of Dalimoore, despite the highwaymen. The apples had long since run out and so had all that Anoka sent. A visit to the market would be necessary to restock the supplies. Royce would go into the township alone, as to not draw attention to them as a group. The rest would hide with the horses in the thick part of the woods. Again, Wyn did not like this plan, but could not argue with it. Royce instructed them that if he did not return in two hours, they were not to wait for him. If things went wrong or if they became separated, they decided to rendezvous one hour after sundown at the overlook where they had watched Shira save the family on the road.

The skies had darkened and a drizzle began to fall. This was both good and bad. It would be an advantage by making it easier for him to slip in and out of the village unnoticed, for there would be less people out and about, but it would be much harder to cover his tracks. He worked his way down the road on foot, leaving the horses for those hiding, in case they had to move in an unexpected hurry.

Into the sleepy little village of Dalimoore he trotted, keeping his cloak over his face to shield it from the rain. The village consisted of little more than ten buildings, an inn, much like his beloved home, a stable, several cottages, and an open-air market. Perfect! This was just what he was looking for. He pulled his cloak up tighter around his head and entered.

The market consisted basically of a crudely built roof attached to the front of the owners dwelling. Three sides were open to the outside, not making it easy to keep hidden. The shop was not empty as he had hoped, two men were haggling with the keeper over the price of some goods, and a few others were browsing the very limited selection. As soon as he had entered, it seemed as if all looked up at him. He thought that if he sort of slumped over and spoke in a gruff voice, it might appear that he was older than he really was. He even limped a little. It seemed to work for the time being. The three went back to their dealings, although the proprietor's eyes lingered on him a little longer. Royce tried to stay as far away as possible, hoping not to be noticed. That was not easy, for the place was quite small.

There were a few freshly killed fowl hanging around the perimeter, and a couple of make-shift shelves in the center, which were nearly bare. Royce figured, being late in the afternoon, the stock had been picked over rather thoroughly. Royce eyed all the keeper had to offer, which did not take long. What he needed was dried goods that would keep during the travel. How could he request that without raising suspicion? The proprietor finished with his previous customers and offered his assistance to Royce, who just grunted, and continued to act as if he was checking out the dressed poultry.

"Fresh as it gets, killed this morning."

The owner still kept eyeing him. This made Royce uncomfortable.

Then he leaned close and spoke in a quiet voice, "Ye the inn keeper's son?"

Royce, not expecting to be recognized, glanced at him in surprise. He quickly recovered, but he knew it was too late; he had given himself away by the look on his face.

Then the keeper rose up straight and spoke louder than needed, "Got dat lard yer mother was in fer' yesterday."

"My mother?" *Maybe he has got me mixed up with someone else,* Royce thought. He looked at the keeper, who looked down at him without turning his head, he shifted his eyes over to some men who had come in the other side of the market, then looked quickly back to Royce.

"It's in de back if'n she still wants it, but ye'll have to come fetch it yerself," again he spoke louder than necessary. He then started to walk towards the back room. He looked back at Royce and motioned his head inconspicuously as if to say 'follow me'.

Royce glanced at the men who had just entered. They were definitely highwaymen. He realized the keeper was trying to get him away from the others in the market. The words of his father rang out in his head 'Trust no one!' Nevertheless, he did not want to make a scene. The keeper had spoken to him as if he had known him. It would look more suspicious to the men if he did not play along with this man. The keeper looked harmless enough, although looks can be deceiving. He wore thick leather boots and his apron was stretched tightly over his rather large midsection. Apparently this man had not gone hungry very often. A heavy woolen shirt hung loosely to his belt. His sleeves were rolled back to the elbows. Gray hairs speckled his head except for a small bald spot on top. His bearded face had a certain gentleness that Royce felt comfortable with. He motioned with his hand, careful not to be seen by his other customers. Royce followed him.

The back room was small, but well supplied. It was stacked high with odds and ends and products that a shopkeeper would have, but Royce saw no lard! The keeper pulled the door tight behind them. This made Royce very uneasy. The keeper quickly turned to Royce.

"What are ye doing here? Ye are in real danger!"

Royce stared as if he was a mad man.

"Are ye sisters with ye? Are they alright?"

Still he did not want to answer, being caught off guard by a stranger who knew much more about him than he should.

The man read the disturbed look on Royce's face and cocked his head to the side. "Spencer Windmere's, ye father?"

"Y-Yes." Royce was not sure how to reply. "Who are you, and how do you know who I am?"

"Me think it be a lot safer fer the both of us if ye not know who I be. When ye leave, ye must forget that ye wast ever here! And, me'll do likewise! Is that to yer understanding?"

Royce nodded reluctantly.

"Well, ye're going to have to trust me if me be helping ye. I can't tell ye much, but I can tell ye this; I be in with those that help yer father. Well, what is left of 'em anyways. Me be a friend of Spencer. Go way back, him and me. Me knew yer mother too, even before she... before she..."

"Died?"

A curious look came on this face. "Err...I mean before...Yes." The shopkeeper stopped in mid-sentence. "Yes, died!"

"Before what?" Royce felt that he knew something that he did not want to tell.

"Never mind. Not important now, boy! What ye have to do now is get ye away from here, fer away!" He checked the door. "Me don't know how ye got here without being caught, but ye go right back the same way, and wherever it is that ye have been hid'n go back there and stay.   Mind ye!   And stay low, the highwaymen are everywhere!"

"Everywhere?"

"Yeah, looking for ye and yer sisters! Fer a week now they been in and out, asking questions!"

"For us? What do they want with us?"

"Do ye not know?"

"No!" Royce did not trust him enough to tell what he really suspected.

"One thing me know fer sure, they have their orders, and that is to find ye at all costs.   Anyone who knows anything of yer whereabouts is to turn ye in, straight way!"

This man knew so much that Royce had to ask the question most pressing in his mind, "Do you know where my father is?"

The keeper lowered his head; he did not want to answer. Royce could tell he did not want to answer. Quietly he spoke, "Aye."

"Where is he? Is he well?"

"Err... me guess ye'll find out in time." He wrinkled up his face and scratched his beard. "Son, ye father has been locked up."

"What? ... What are the charges?"

"Treason."

"Treason!" Royce was shocked. "My father has been fighting the rebels from the start.   How could he be charged for treason?" Royce suddenly recalled what Sherwin had said about Devlin, if he was against Devlin, he was against the king.

"Keep your voice down!" the keeper warned. "I know yer father well, he's no rebel. But, me sources say they plan to petition the king fer execution."

"Execution!"

"Let us worry about that. Right now ye have to worry about ye and yer sisters! That is why ye have to take them and go! Don't even tell me where. Just go. Hide yerselves! Ye need to know that ye are dealing with some very dangerous men. If they catch ye and yer sisters, well, let's just say it weren't be good!"

The mention of his sisters struck a raw nerve. "If they do anything to Wyn and Keli I will..."

"Ye'll do nothing! Ye can't fight the king's Elite!"

The keeper was right. What could he do? His only option

was to do just what his father had instructed. Keep Wyn and Keli safely hidden away!

"These men are desperate! They won't give up till they get what they be after."

"And what is that?"

"Can you think of nothing?"

"Nothing! We left in the middle of the night with only the four horses and food enough for five days."

"Four horses?"

"Yes. One for each of us, that is until Butch got attacked by..."

"There are four of ye?" The keeper looked at him seriously. "Who's the fourth?"

"Just a staff boy from the inn."

"Hmm." The man was quiet for a moment, deep in thought. "How long have ye known this boy?"

"He has been with us for a little while. Why?"

"Nothing. Well, ye need to be away. The longer ye stay, the greater ye chance of being found. Here, take des pail. Here's dried meat and here's some meal. Go, but talk to no one! If anyone asks ye of yer business, ye are taking this lard to yer mother! Keep yer head covered and above all, hide that sword!"

Royce had thought he had concealed it well, but apparently not.

"A young man on an erring fer his mother would not tote such a sword. Fer sure, not one that looked as that." The shopkeeper eyed the sword as Royce tried to tuck it farther under his cloak. He had thought nothing of it before, but the sword had been his father's for as long as he could remember. Looking at it now, it did look unusual. He had seen nobody carry one like it, not any highwaymen, not the Elite, definitely not any commoner.

"Now go," the keeper's words brought him back from his thoughts, "protect yer sisters, and God be with ye!"

"Yes." Royce cracked the door and peeped out. The men were still there. "You could let me out the back way."

"Can't do that."

"Why not?"

"Me don't have a back door."

The keeper opened the door and started to go out, but Royce stopped him and held out some copper coins.

"I'll collect next time, boy. Run on now and give ye mother my regards!" he started talking loud once again.

"My moth…" Royce gave him a weak smile. "I will not forget this, sir."

"Nor me, boy, nor me," he said low.

The Chase

Royce moved quickly through the market and out into the street. He pulled the cloak completely back over his head, for the drizzle had become harder. He rounded the corner of a cottage and started up the road, keeping to the side of the street. His heart ached from the news of his father. Should he tell his sisters of what he had learned, or should he keep it to himself? Keeping it from them would be tough, and it would not be fair. He knew in his heart that if the roles were reversed, he would want to know. He decided he could keep no secrets from them. Nevertheless, what if the keeper was making all of it up? What if it were all just a story? But why would he do that? He did know his father; it was obvious by how much he knew about the family. He did give him some food, but it still could be a hoax, a trick, or a trap! Deep in his heart he felt the keeper to be telling the truth. Royce's thoughts were a blur as he backtracked his way to the place were he had left the others.

A time or two he thought he saw something out of the corner of his eye, a movement of someone as if they were following, but each time he looked, he saw no one. Surely, all the talk of being pursued by the highwaymen had made him paranoid.

For this reason, when he found the others, he told them to mount up quickly, for they were leaving. Royce quickly packed the fresh supplies onto the back of the horses and led them back in the direction they had come. Minutes after they had mounted, they heard the sound of horse's hooves beating hard against the ground. Royce had been followed! It was a group of riders, no doubt the highwaymen! There were six of them and they were riding hard. Whatever it was they wanted, Royce was determined not to stick around and find out.

He hollered for Wyn and Sherwin to put it to the horses with all they had. They did without question. The horses were truly the finest his father owned. They carried the children as swiftly as any horses in the kingdom could. They crossed a small ravine, up a slight hill and turned onto a well-traveled road. It was then they found that the horses could really move.   Unfortunately, so could the highwaymen's.   Even though they were traveling at amazing speed, the pursuers stayed with them.   It was soon discovered that to outrun them was not going to be possible.   For the highwaymen's horses were trained for this very purpose.

Keli, riding in front of Royce was hanging on tightly.   She kept looking over their shoulders to check the status of the pursuers. For a while her reports were favorable, they were actually pulling ahead, that is until the horses began to wear down.   Though they had a good lead to start, the highwaymen were closing in.

"Royce, they're gaining on us!" Keli hollered.   "Now there are more of them!"

The group of six had now grown to twenty.   Royce urged his horse to go faster, but the poor animal was already giving all it had. Sherwin was well out in front on Victor, followed closely by Whirlwind with Wyn.   Carrying two was taking its toll on Ole Murdoch.   He was beginning to fall back.   Royce knew he could not keep up this pace for long, but he was not willing to give up.

"Royce, hurry!" Wyn urged them to catch up.

"Just go! Don't wait!" he instructed.

If they could not out run them, he would have to do something else. *Could he fight? Impossible! Maybe they could outsmart them. But how?*

"If we were riding Shira, we could outrun them," Keli shouted in Royce's ear.   "We need Shira!"

The road sloped down to a narrow wooden bridge, a bridge so narrow that one ox cart could not pass over beside another.   It was about the length of a stone's throw.   It crossed a small, but deep gully. Though, in its day the bridge was well built for strength, the years of weather had taken its toll.   The surface of the boarding was not of the most favorable for a horse's hoof.   Whirlwind did remarkably well for the most part, but near the end of the wooden structure his hoof broke through an old weathered board.   Down went poor Whirlwind!   Over the horse's head went Wyn!

Royce could do nothing but watched in horror at what was happening in front of him.

Keli screamed, "Wyn!"

Wyn took the fall amazingly well.   She rolled into a ball and landed just beyond the wood of the bridge, tumbling several times.

"Wyn!" Royce rode up to where Wyn had landed and pulled back on the reigns. Murdoch skidded to a stop. He jumped off Ole Murdoch and was at her side in an instant.

"I'm okay!" she assured him, still lying on the ground. She started to get up.

"You're bleeding!"

"I think I just bit my lip! It's nothing!" Though she was bruised and scratched, she would be sore for a good while, but was not seriously hurt. She was tough—tougher than Royce would have ever thought possible.

He had to take her for her word now, for the highwaymen were bearing down on them hard. Down the hill they rode, coming on at full speed. What would he do? Flee? Fight? Or surrender? He unsheathed his sword and lifted it upright in front of him. He stood stiff in front of Wyn, as if preparing to defend his sister to the end. His heart pounded in his chest. He knees felt weak. Sweat was trickling down his brow. Both hands were locked around the hilt of his sword.

The advancing foe kept right on coming. The bridge rumbled as the horses started across. Suddenly, to Royce's amazement, the bridge burst into flames. Fire erupted about center ways of the crossing and totally engulfed the passage. The first of the horses skidded to a halt and unseated several of the riders. Moving at such a speed, the riders in the back slammed into those that had stopped so quickly. Several men tumbled over the rail into the ravine. Two of the men who had fallen off, jumped over the rail to evade the retreating horses. Few stayed in their saddles. Whether they were on foot or in the saddle, all scrambled back to protect themselves from the intense heat. The men at the end of the band were so taken by what they saw in front of them, that they pulled their horses to a stop and sat staring at the disorder.

Royce looked on in disbelief. He had never seen such an occurrence. Taking full advantage of the opportunity, he pulled Wyn to her feet.

"Wyn, we must move on!"

He helped her to her horse. Only then did Royce realize that their beloved Whirlwind, Wyn's faithful horse, would be able to carry her no farther. The horse favored its right front leg so strongly that it would be inhumane to climb on him again.

The highwaymen were relentless. They began to regroup.

Driven by the fear of full retribution if they failed to apprehend the children, they determined not to give up their pursuit. The ones who were still able to ride had begun to cross the river by climbing down the bank and wading through the water. It would not be long before the chase would be on again.

Royce hurriedly removed the supplies from Whirlwind. The four would have to double on the two remaining horses. Sherwin and Keli rode up to collect the two standing on the ground. Just as they mounted and spurred the horses into action, they pulled them to a halt, for something was blocking the road, a huge something. A dragon!

Keli was off the horse in an instant, running up to her new reptilian friend. "Shira!"

"Keli!" Wyn shouted.

"Whoa! She's ...as big as a cottage!" Sherwin recoiled! It was the first time he had seen the great creature!

"It's alright, Sherwin. She's a friend!" Royce reassured him.

Keli greeted Shira with a hug. Royce smiled. Wyn winched. And Sherwin's mouth dropped open.

"Royce, Shira will carry us faster than any horse ever could! She will get us away!" As soon as Keli had said that, Shira lowered her head flat to the ground, just as she had done before. "See, she's offering to help!"

Royce thought for a second. The two horses would not be able to carry the four of them swiftly enough to escape from the Elite. Maybe this was the answer. Out smart the highwaymen, they would! Royce agreed, "Sherwin, untie the supplies from the horses. We are riding Shira out of here!" Royce was on the ground pulling the pack from Ole Murdoch.

"What? You mean that... that... that..."

"Dragon!" Royce finished for him. "Hurry!"

Keli was already climbing on the back of the great creature.

"Not me!" Sherwin was shaking his head. "I am not getting anywhere near that... that..."

"Dragon!" this time Keli finished for him.

"Fine, you can stay here and tell it to the highwaymen!" Royce shouted.

A shout was heard from the men in the ravine that told them it would not be long before they would be back on the road.

Sherwin changed his mind. "What are we waiting for? Let's ride!"

Under normal circumstances it would have taken some persuasion to get Wyn aboard, but the shouts of the riders nearing the top of the gulley convinced her too. Shira waited patiently for them to mount up. As soon as all four were seated on her scaly back, she whirled around on her hind legs and lumbered down the road on all fours, a rough ride to say the least.

"Royce...do you think...she cannot...fly with the...four of us?" Keli managed to say. All four were being thrown to and fro quite roughly.

"Fly?" Sherwin questioned. His face held a look of terror.

Both concerns were answered when Shira unfolded her wings and began to lift them effortlessly off the ground. She flew just slightly above the surface of the road. Once in the air, the ride became much smoother. As gracefully as an eagle, she rose above the trees. Realizing they had left the ground, Royce grabbed Shira's fins. Wyn grabbed Keli, as a motherly instinct would demand. Sherwin grabbed anything he could hold on to, as sheer terror would demand.

Royce noticed this takeoff to be nothing like his first experience on Shira's back. It was not nearly as frightening as the first because of the long horizontal liftoff. Royce thought this was possibly for the benefit of Wyn and Sherwin. Somehow, maybe Shira could sense their fear. Also, she was carrying four people instead of two. The extra weight may have required the running start. What Royce hadn't considered was that she had stayed completely out of sight from the highwaymen.

When the men finally did climb up out of the gully, the dragon had disappeared through the trees and around the bend completely beyond their sight. They were mystified, to say the least, by what they found: three horses, one lame from the bridge incident, two others completely unharmed, saddled and bridled. Though they searched diligently, the children were not found, not even a trace. Few of the dragon's tracks showed in the road because of the hard packed, gravelly surface. Those that did, the men did not recognize as unusual, for them to suspect a creature of Shira's nature never entered their mind. A thorough search of the whole area found nothing, not a clue as to what became of the innkeeper's children!

For this reason, the highwaymen, superstitious as they were, assumed that Royce had to be a worker of dark magic. Only a mighty sorcerer could have caused the bridge to burst into flames in such a way. Only a sorcerer of incredible power could have whisked them all away without a trace.   In the soldier's gullible minds, the only explanation for not finding the children was that Royce had taken them all away! The last they had seen of him was when he was in the center of the road at the opposite end of the bridge, standing stone still, sword outstretched. Then there was a huge ball of fire and they were gone, not even a trace. It is in this way the rational mind explains the extraordinary. If it cannot be explained, it must be magic! This was the story they carried back to their superior. In the ears of Devlin they retold the story of how the oldest son of the innkeeper had raised his sword in the air, cast a spell that inflamed the whole bridge, and then whisked them away by some form of dark magic. Did he believe them? He did not want to, but they showed him their singed beards and charred clothing to prove it!

A Safe Place

S hira, take us someplace safe!" Keli thought out loud.

        Shira picked up speed. A good distance from the bridge she lifted up and out from among the path of trees edging the highway. Soaring out over the treetops once again, she headed in a northwesterly direction. Royce had a keen sense of direction and soon realized where they were heading—back over the Black Forest! Keli had requested a safe place, no doubt, that would be a safer place than where they were. For it now seemed that the forest was safer than anywhere people were. Although, to go back seemed to be the wrong way, at the moment, he did not know which way would be right. Where else could they go? Well he would not think about that now. For now, he was happy to be away. He sat back to enjoy the ride, since he knew now that a ride on the back of a dragon was something that one could live through.

        Keli was thoroughly enjoying the ride too. She was sitting closest to Shira's head. She kept rubbing her and talking to her the whole flight. She was absolutely in total delight.

        Though he and Keli were enjoying themselves, Wyn had not opened her eyes since they had left the ground. She sat directly behind her little sister, arms wrapping tightly around her. Royce was seated behind Wyn.

        He tapped her on the shoulder. "Wyn, open your eyes!"

        Wyn did so reluctantly, even though what she saw caused her to gasp. The sight was so overwhelming she could not close them again. Far below, the ever-changing landscape was passing beneath them. From this height, the whole world was visible. Off to their right, Mount Hestia majestically towered still above them. To their left, were the canyons, the sheer rock cliffs, the tree covered bluffs, and the winding river making its way through it all. To top it off, the magnificent sun fought its way through the retreating clouds to create the most beautiful of sunsets. No, she could not close her eyes again.

        Sherwin was not enjoying the ride. He had not closed his

eyes, as Wyn had, but sat looking from side to side, taking it all in. When Royce looked back to check on him, all the color had left his face.

"What do you think of this, Sherwin?" Royce was sure he had to be impressed.

"Extraordinary," he answered weakly in his usual unemotional tone. *Did nothing impress this boy? He was sure of the unusual sort,* Royce thought. Actually, Sherwin was greatly affected by the ride; had there been anything in his stomach, he would have lost it there on the spot.

As they soared through the sky, something pressed hard into Royce's thoughts. It was what the shopkeeper had told him about his father. Was it true? He seemed to know what he was talking about. He had recognized him as his father's son and knew the whole family, including his mother. He was right about the highwaymen being after them, and he had not sent him away empty-handed. Though he did not want to believe what he said, his gut-instinct told him, the man was telling the truth. If his father had been arrested, where was he being kept? That is one piece of information that he failed to get from the keeper. Where would they have put him?

Something else also pressed hard on his mind as he pondered the events of the day; the family on the road, meeting the shop keeper, the highwaymen, the bridge bursting into flames, and Shira showing up right at their most desperate time of need. A thought suddenly popped into Royce's head. *'We need Shira.'* were Keli's words right before she showed up at the bridge! When she said *'Shira will carry us away!'* Shira had instantly dropped her head for them to climb aboard. He remembered the strange way Keli had acted on the ridge when watching Shira save the family on the road! When she had said *'I am hungry'* and Shira brought her apples! At Anoka's tree house, Royce was sure it had been Shira that drove away the wolves, but only after Keli had screamed out her name! Was she really able to communicate with Shira somehow? Could it be? Even now as they flew, Royce watched the back of his little sister. He could tell that Keli was talking to Shira, and by her reaction she was acknowledging her! She could understand Keli! Somehow she knew what Keli was saying, he was positive!

They sailed on and landed on a rock ledge that was very familiar to two of them. It was the same ledge that Royce had first faced Shira with the sword. They were back where they had been several days before. It was Shira's home, the rock ledge and the small cave. This is where the dragon had lived undetected for many years. This was due to the fact that it was nearly impossible to get to, from above or below. It had been a safe place for her, and for now, it was a safe place for them! In no more than an hour, she had gone as far as it took them days to go.

All slid off the dragon's back to the ground, except for Sherwin. He had such a death grip on her fins, that it took both Royce and Wyn to get him to the ground. Once there, he seemed to have difficulty walking.

"Whoa! The rocks are moving!"

Royce knew just how he felt. The solid rock felt strange to them now that they had been airborne for so long. Their adrenalin had been running high, their knees felt weak. It took a few minutes to get back to normal.

It would be getting dark soon. All were about starved. Royce was sure this place was remote enough to have a fire, even if it was overlooking the canyons. The only person that might possibly see the light would be Anoka and what if she did. He gathered a few pieces of wood left here and there, retrieved Wyn's fire starting mechanism from one of the supply packs, and went to work. As he concentrated on lighting the fire, he did not notice that Shira had taken an interest in his efforts. She slowly began to creep up behind him. For an animal as big as she, it was amazing how stealthily she could move. Before Royce knew it, the dragon had lowered her head right over his left shoulder. The startled boy jumped back in surprise. It was good that he did, for no quicker than he had, Shira blasted from her nostrils a ball of fire that totally engulfed the pile of sticks and leaves he had collected.

"Whoa!" Royce scrambled back and jumped to his feet.

Five seconds later, the huge dragon backed away, leaving a perfect little campfire fully ablaze. After recovering his poise and checking if he had any hair left, he looked at the fire and then smiled at Keli. Wyn and Sherwin stood speechless.

"That wasn't so hard this time, now was it?" Keli smiled back.

"Sherwin, meet your leviathan," Royce spoke slowly. "This is Shira."

"The fire of a thousand candles!" Sherwin said, thinking the same thing. "But they were just old stories told by some old knight that once hung around the castle."

"Maybe they were not just old stories," Keli said.

"The fire! The bridge! It all makes sense now! It was the dragon! The dragon set that bridge on fire!" Royce was ecstatic. "Keli, was it? Was it Shira that made the bridge go up in flames?"

Wyn looked stunned. "What are you asking her for?"

"Because, I think she is able to communicate with her somehow. I don't know how, but I think she is!"

"Royce, you are going mad." Wyn was thinking Royce was having a mental break down.

"No. I'm not!" he defended. "Keli, did you tell Shira to start the fire just now?"

All stared at Keli as they waited for her reply. She stared back at them with a look of deep thought and slowly turned her head to look at Shira.

"Listen to me Keli. When the wolves were after you, what did you do?"

"I ran."

"After that?"

"I climbed up on the rock. I fought off the wolves with a stick."

"Did you say anything?"

"I… I guess I was screaming something."

"When you were in the river, you were screaming for help! I heard you!"

"Anybody would," Wyn interjected. "Royce, keep your wits. Don't go mad on us *now*. We need you!"

"No… I'm not," he insisted. "Listen! Each time Keli cried for help, Shira came to her aid and saved her! When we were here, on this very ledge, Keli said she was hungry, and Shira left and returned with apples! When the highwaymen were chasing us this afternoon, Keli said 'We need Shira!' and she just appeared. How else would you explain it?"

Everyone was silent, staring at Royce.

"Keli, did you ask Shira to start the campfire?"

Keli looked back at the rest of the children and sheepishly nodded her head.

Wyn made a 'humph' sound, as if she did not believe her.

"Keli, this is amazing!" Royce exclaimed. "How did you know that she could do that?"

"I don't know, I just knew!"

"Keli, ask Shira to do something unusual, something that she would never just do on her own.

"Why don't you ask her to *waltz*?" Wyn joked.

"I'm serious!" Royce insisted.

"How would she know how to do a waltz?" Keli smiled and turned to Shira. "Shira, if you can understand me would you let us know?"

The huge dragon was near the back of the ledge moving some boulders around as if they were pebbles. When Keli said her name, she turned and looked right at her as she spoke. To Wyn's amazement, in fact to everyone's amazement, the dragon sat on her back legs and lifted her head high into the air. She let out a deafening roar just as she had done before. The children had to cover their ears. The sound lasted for several seconds and echoed off the canyon walls for several more seconds. Royce, Wyn and Sherwin were speechless.

Keli giggled and then made another request, "Fire, Shira!"

Shira then blasted a ball of fire into the sky that seemed to light the whole canyon. As far away as the children were, they still felt the heat on their faces. Then Keli whispered something that no one heard but Shira.

The dragon raised one of her back feet off the ground and then slowly raised the other one. She leaned back on her tail with all four feet in the air. Shira looked so strange in that position that Keli burst into a fit of laughter in which the others had to join in, except for Sherwin, of course.

"I always did like that dragon!" Royce said.

What about Father?

Royce laughed with the rest for a while, but his heart was not in it. His thoughts kept returning to his father. He felt he would have to tell his sisters of the burden he carried, or he would explode. So after they had eaten their evening meal, he told them the whole story of meeting the shopkeeper, how he had known him and the whole family, and how he had provided the supplies at no charge. When he had told of the news about their father being arrested, both sisters were in tears. Sherwin said nothing, but he listened to every word with great interest. By the time he had finished, the fire had begun to die.

Wyn asked, "Think he was telling you straight?"

"Yes, I think he was… I think."

"Oh, I can't stand the thought of Father in some cold, dark dungeon." Keli was crying.

"Don't cry, my lady. He would not be in the dungeons," Sherwin spoke again.

"He wouldn't?" Keli asked.

"Sherwin?" Royce asked. "What do you mean?"

"The dangerous prisoners are never kept in the palace dungeons."

"How do you know all this?" Royce glanced at Wyn.

"When one spends a lot of time in the king's castle, one just has to keep his ears open."

Now Sherwin had caught Wyn's attention. "Sherwin, if he is not in a dungeon, do you know *where* he would be?"

"Yes my la…" Sherwin caught himself this time, but only because he was looking directly at Wyn. "Yes. He would be in the Castle Delthyna, but not in a dungeon. There are no dungeons in the Castle Delthyna. That castle is built on the edge of Lake Elipse. Did you not know?" Sherwin spoke as if that must have been common knowledge. "They just put the dangerous prisoners in the east tower."

Royce was still confounded with the things that Sherwin had

knowledge of, if in fact he was a staff boy.

"Sherwin, do you know which one is the east tower?" Royce asked.

"Yes."

"Which one would that be?"

"The one on the east." Sherwin looked at him curiously.

Royce and Keli chuckled, but Wyn rolled her eyes.

"I want to go see Father," Wyn announced. "When can we leave?"

"How would we get there?" Sherwin asked. "Do you know what a distance that is?"

"Maybe we could fly," Keli suggested quietly.

"Now you're thinking," Royce agreed.

"Oh, dear." Sherwin was remembering the ride he had been taken on that evening. "You cannot just walk in and see him. He will be under heavy guard. They would never allow you in. Also, remember it is Devlin that is holding him, and it is Devlin that is after us! We would be in for trouble."

"Then what are we going to do?" Wyn replied.

"I have thought on that all evening…" Royce spoke determinedly. "I think I have it. It is a long shot, but I can't think of anything else!"

"What are you planning?" Wyn asked in a manner that told Royce that she already doubted his plan, and she had not heard it yet.

"Just hear me out," Royce begged.

"I'm listening."

"It is obvious our only way of travel is Shira, seeing we have lost the horses. We have Shira fly us out of here, not to the Castle Delthyna, but to the king's castle.

"What…" Wyn started.

"Just listen!" he defended. "She could put us down in the inner court, on the other side of the guards. We find the king and appeal to him on behalf of Father!"

"The king's castle?" Wyn exclaimed. "Do you know how dangerous that would be? How could you even consider a stunt like that? That would mean certain death."

"Yes, it would," Sherwin agreed.

Royce looked at Sherwin then looked back to Wyn. "Wyn," he said, never looking more serious in all of his fifteen years, "they have charged him with… with treason."

"No! Royce!" Wyn knew what that would mean. The punishment for treason was death by hanging.

"We have to do something. If we don't, we will lose Father... like we lost Mother. I will not hide out here in the woods and do nothing!" His face was turning red in anger. "Father is innocent, I know he is. I would never be able to live with myself if I didn't try. I have to do something."

"Well, riding right into the king's castle and getting yourself killed is not the something that's going to help Father. That would be suicide," Wyn cried.

"Yes, it would be." Sherwin agreed again.

Royce glared at Sherwin. "Would you be quiet?"

"Yes, my..." Wyn's glare stopped him in mid-sentence.

"Well, does anyone have any other ideas?"

"I just don't know," Wyn said sadly.

Keli shook her head.

"Sherwin?" Royce inquired.

"Yes, but I can't tell you."

"Why not?"

"You instructed me to be quiet."

"Okay, I'm sorry. You take everything too precisely. What can you tell us?"

"You cannot drop down in the inner court," Sherwin interjected.

"Why not?" Royce asked.

"There is no inner court in the king's castle...only the outer court." He paused a moment to gather his thoughts. "The king...he will have all castle guards on full alert. Anyone found to be there without the king's clearance would be executed immediately. They will defend first and inquire later."

"Full alert?" Wyn and Royce said together.

"When someone has done a great disservice to the king and the royal family, the whole castle will be in an uproar."

"Sherwin! How could you possibly know all this?" he spoke eagerly. "You are a... You are the heir! You are the king's son! Aren't you?"

"Royce!" Wyn called him down.

"Sherwin, if that is your *real* name, I want to know who you are and where did you come from?"

"No. I'm not the heir! Royce, I dwelt at the king's castle before coming in service for your father. My ears are always open. I listen to all, the advisors, the counselors, the knights, as they come and go. That is how I know these things."

"How was it that you left the service at the king's castle?"

"I... I had been threatened, by someone in the king's service. Your beloved Uncle Devlin to be exact."

"He is *not* our uncle!" Royce corrected again, trying to save face. At this point, he was feeling very foolish.

"I fled for fear of my life. Your father found me and helped me." Royce and Wyn said nothing, so Sherwin continued, "Your father is a good man. I will aid you in any way I can. I know the castles well, the palace and Delthyna. I will help you."

"Sherwin, I'm sorry. And we thank you for your offer, but I'm not sure what you will be able to do," Royce said meekly.

"I will help *you*, and in return, you will help me."

"Dear Sherwin, if you help us save our father, we will owe you a great debt. We will do anything in our power to help you. What is it that you need?" Wyn asked.

"You will know soon. First we must concentrate on saving your father. There may not be much time."

"Deal!" Royce extended his hand for a handshake, but Sherwin just looked at it, and then at Royce, then at Wyn, a puzzled look was on his face.

"You're supposed to shake—like this." She then took Royce's hand in her own and gave him a hardy shake.

"Sherwin, for someone who knows so much, you sure don't know very much!" Royce chuckled and gave him a pat on the back.

"And you say you have trouble understanding me?"

Sherwin then shook Royce's hand as he had seen Wyn do. A little smile almost crossed his face; quite possibly the first time they had ever seen him do so.

"You must see the king," Sherwin began again. "He is the only one that can stay an execution." He looked back and forth between Royce and Wyn. "I can get you in to see the king."

"How can you possibly do that, I thought you said the guards..." Royce did not get to finish.

"Guards will not be a problem! There are ways in that even the guards don't know about."

"What?" Wyn questioned.

"There are passages in the lower levels that will take you

almost anywhere in the castle. I have explored many of them. We can get in absolutely undetected."

"Hold on. Let's think this thing through. First, is Shira willing and able to take us there?" Royce turned to Keli. "Keli, can you ask her?"

"I will know in a minute," she replied.

Keli jumped up and ran to speak to Shira who had retreated deep into her cave. Wyn shook her head, still not totally convinced Keli could communicate with a dragon.

Royce continued, "Even if she is willing, we will have to travel by cover of darkness. A dragon in broad daylight would bring us attention we would not want."

"Right! The family on the road was quite disturbed by what they saw this morning," Wyn said.

"How far are we from the king's castle?" Sherwin asked

"Several days ride on horse back. But, I'm guessing two hours on dragon back!" Royce was beginning to put a bit of faith in Shira. He hoped it wasn't too much.

"If what you are saying is true, then we need to leave at once! We must ride tonight!" With a definite plan now emerging, Wyn was now ready to storm the king's castle.

***

Keli walked through the entrance of Shira's cave. Would she be willing to go to where people were? Keli wondered. Would she be willing to do that for them? Would she be willing to take them to the palace? In the flicker from the firelight, she saw something she had not seen before.

There on the cave wall was a crude sketch of a dragon done in a white chalky substance. Under the drawing was some letters that looked to have faded over the years.

"A...something...N...I...S," she read out loud. "Anni? Anni's Dragon. Anni was the girl Anoka spoke of. She has been here. She must have written Shira's name on the cave wall."

She pondered this as she searched deeper into the cave. She found Shira in one of the dark shadows at the far end of the cavern. As she approached the dragon, she raised her enormous head and acknowledged Keli.

"Shira, dear friend, what are you doing back here?" The dragon lowered her head slightly to the side. Keli noticed Shira was hovering over several round looking rocks, speckled black and gray in color. As she looked closer she realized that they were not rocks at all, they were eggs! Shira's eggs!

Keli's face lit up. "Eggs?" She looked at Shira. "Your babies! This is great! When will they hatch?"

The excitement left her when she looked into the sad eyes of the owner of the eggs. Immediately, Keli understood. She had been around enough animals to know that as long as there was not a male dragon, they would never hatch.

"Oh... they won't hatch will they?" Her heart went out to her new friend. She could see that she cared very much for her children, even though they would never be. "I am sorry."

The massive animal understood; she lowered her head to a level even with Keli's. Keli put her hand on one of the speckled eggs.

"I know what that is like." She caressed the egg, which was almost half as big as she was. "You will miss your children, just like I miss my mother. There is so much I need to know. So much I wish I could ask her."

The dragon looked at her so intently that Keli felt as if she understood every word.

"...And now I am afraid I am going to lose Father too. Shira, he has been locked up and... I have something to ask. Would you take us to our father? It would mean going where people are, and it may be dangerous. I know you have been avoiding people, but you came to us when we needed you, and we need you again... now more than ever."

Shira rose up straight and bowed her head low in answer to Keli. The little girl bowed herself in return.

"Thank you, Shira! Thank you!"

Father's plight

At the same time that the children were at Shira's cave planning the daring rescue of their father, high in the east tower of the Delthyna castle, Spencer Windmere sat on the floor of his cell.

The night the Ole Travelers Inn was attacked, Spencer Windmere had headed south, just as he planned. With the four horses, he left an obvious trail for the highwaymen to follow. A little too obvious, he soon realized. For four days, he led them back and forth across the whole of the southern part of the kingdom. The plan was to confuse them enough to allow him to circle back and head north without being followed, and eventually, rendezvous with his children at the chalet. Nevertheless, it was to no avail. In the end, he found himself fleeing from two squadrons of the king's most highly trained. He chose the best horse of the four and left the other three, hoping to out run them. Being greatly out-numbered and running out of countryside, they hemmed him in against the southern shores. He had nowhere to go but the sea, which did not seem too good of a plan, seeing that his horse could not swim. There they bound him and hauled him back to face Devlin. Left now, was only the hope that he had misguided the soldiers long enough to assure the safe passage of his dear children. He prayed that his children's attempts at eluding Devlin and his men had gone better than his own!

His spirits lifted when the first question Devlin asked him was, "Where are your children?"

Spencer told him nothing, so he had him locked up. His back was against the wall; his head propped on his arms which in turn where supported by his knees. The room was about ten foot square, built from large chisel-cut stones, left rough and jagged to the touch. There was no bed, no chair, and no furniture of any kind. At one end was a heavy wooden door that one had to duck to go through. Unfortunately, it was locked and bolted from the other side. In the opposite end wall was a small window, just a hole really, a gap in the stones left by the masons. It was left for ventilation purposes only.

For this he had been truly grateful, for every morning he would watch the sunrise. That simple joy was one thing that kept him sane.

He had checked the hinges on the door, the crack in the wall, the floor, the ceiling; he had searched every detail for the possibility of escape. For days he had exhausted every conceivable thought of breaking out, explored every option for the chance of freeing himself from this prison. Nothing had worked. He concentrated most on the small window. If he could just squeeze himself through that tiny opening, he could escape. It would be just a small drop of fifty feet to the water in the lake below, swim to shore, and he would be free!

But the opening was just small enough to prevent him from squeezing through, he knew well, for he had tried several times, but to no avail. During one of the failed attempts, he was sure that the guards were going to enter and find him stuck half in, half out, but after an hour or so, he managed to free himself and pull himself back in before they returned. He had decided to wait a few more days. By then he may have grown thin enough to try again, for the food (if you could call it food) was not worth eating any way.

This night, so-called suppertime came early, or so he thought. The sound of the latch bolt being pulled back and the door swinging open aroused Spencer. But the cook did not bring in a bowl of liquid acid as he usually did, in fact, it was not the cook at all, instead two soldiers entered and confronted him.

"Devlin has requested your presence," the first soldier spoke kindly to him.

Spencer looked up at the two clad in battle armor. "Thomas, are you still following that thieving Devlin? You know he does not have the king's interests in mind. He pursues his own agenda, not the king's will."

"Come now." The two did not reply to Spencer's words. For days, Spencer had preached to them at every opportunity. They had heard all that he had had to say and deep down, they knew he was right. They knew of Devlin and his treachery, they knew of his evil ambitions, but they were also deathly afraid of him. Devlin was a powerful man—a powerfully evil man. Anyone that crossed him could find himself in Spencer's position or worse.

"What about you, Mantis?" Spencer continued. "Are you going to keep serving such a traitor as Devlin? Can you imagine what the kingdom will come to if Devlin gets into power?"

All the way out of the cell and down the spiral stone steps,

Spencer preached to Devlin's two minions.

"Quiet now, Spencer, you will get us into trouble," the second soldier urged.

"I fear you have not known trouble as you are about to if Devlin has his way," Spencer said sadly.

As they left the tower and entered the courtyard, the sun was just beginning to touch the ground, marking the end of another day. Spencer was not taken to Devlin's office chamber as he had expected, but his two guards stopped him in the middle of the courtyard. Presently, Devlin approached him. He wore a long elegant robe, that of which one would expect to see the king wear. His eyes had that pious smirk that infuriated Spencer. He had clenched in his hand the reigns that were connected to two horses. He led them up and positioned them purposefully in front of Spencer.

"Ah, our guest has come out to watch the sunset. Take a good look; it may very well be your last. I trust your accommodations have been adequate?"

"Surprisingly so, considering who offered them."

Devlin motioned to the horses. "Do you recognize these?"

"Yes," Spencer replied, "they are horses."

Devlin was not amused at his joke. "Funny! Do you know who were riding them?"

Spencer had recognized the horses immediately; he knew the two animals well. He had saddled and bridled them the night of the attack on the inn; they were Ole Murdoch and Victor. A pain shot through him as he looked upon the two animals. If their horses were here, where were his children? Although his heart was full of grief, he did not lose his self-control. He would not give Devlin that satisfaction.

"Should I?" he answered Devlin's question with complete composure.

"You should! For a short time ago these horses carried your children. Now they are no more!" Devlin watched for Spencer's reaction before he continued. "Where were they headed, Spencer? What was it that you were having them do? Just who was it that they had with them?"

"Children, Devlin? Your own words condemn you. The man entrusted of the king to direct his highwaymen lets children get the best of him! Some fearless leader, hunting down innocent children! I will never tell you anything! If they are no more, show me their bodies, not these horses!" Spencer's anger was burning inside him. He wanted to fall upon Devlin with all that he had, with all the ferocity in his being.

"I will show you nothing!" Devlin's face was torn in rage.

"That's because you have nothing," Spencer defied. "You have no children. You have no dignity! You have no honor! And you have no respect!"

"Tomorrow, at sunrise, you will hang for the offences you have committed against the good King William Robinson and his kingdom!" Devlin shouted.

"The only offences I have committed have been against you… to keep you from your foul plans to overthrow the king and take the kingdom." Spencer replied in full composure.

There was a murmur among the soldiers. Devlin looked side to side at his armed men. "Silence! It is lies! … All lies!"

"Why don't you tell your men why you are searching so desperately for the children?"

"Silence!"

"He knows the truth about you! He knows what you are! And he can have you destroyed. If he makes it back to the king, it will mean your neck!"

"I said SILENCE!"

This unsettled the crowd of soldiers. They were now looking intensely at Devlin.

"This is not true! This traitor is trying to save his own skin. Gag him and return him to his cell!"

The soldiers hesitated.

"Do it now, or I will have you all for insubordination!"

The guards led the prisoner back to his cell, but they did not gag him.

Up until now, Spencer's determination had been strong, his will unbroken. For days he had been taken and threatened for information. Devlin wanted to know where the children were, and he would stop at nothing. Do what they may, but that information was not to cross his lips; he would not endanger the lives of his children, no matter what they did to him. He had stood firm. He had been a rock. He had been a mighty fortress. Nothing had fazed him, that is, until today, until he had seen those horses. They were in fact his horses. Where were his children?

Now, he began to slip into depression. The possibility that

Devlin may have found his children was too much for him to withstand. Ole Murdoch and Victor, two of the horses that had carried his beloved children, were now in Devlin's possession. Devlin's vicious lie could not possibly be the truth. He could not give up hope. He would not! If he was stripped of the only things he had left in this life, his will to resist would be destroyed. He would have to see it before he would believe it. Nevertheless, if it was true, and his children were in fact gone, then nothing mattered any longer. He was to die at first light. He would be ready.

A Visit to the King

Shira covered the twenty-seven leagues to the king's castle in less than two hours, very near what Royce had estimated. The dragon could fly when she had a mind to. Reaching speeds up to five or six times faster than any horse and straight as an arrow. The flight put to shame any type of ground travel.

It was fully dark by now, but the moon and stars were as bright as they had ever seen them.

Sherwin now rode behind Keli since he seemed to know more about where the palace should be. He carefully watched the ground for villages, roads, and landmarks. He gave Keli directions, who in turn, relayed them to Shira. Keli developed a method of steering as they went. She would gently tap Shira on whichever side she desired her to turn. This would bring her around in that direction. When speed was desired she would just holler for her to go. This she had done at the beginning of the flight, and Shira had well provided. Flying at top speed most of the trip, they reached the king's palace by midnight.

Near the end of the flight they passed over the richest farmland of the kingdom. Corn, wheat, and hay crops stretched for leagues in every direction. The king owned some, but most belonged to independent farmers.

The king lived in the very center of it all. His castle was high on a knoll, overlooking the great farming valley. This location had been chosen for the royal castle years earlier by a now ancient king. It proved a wise decision, for an approaching army could be spotted from one of the lofty lookouts hours before they arrived. The steep rocky cliffs on all sides made it easy to defend. This proved to be a well-planned foresight more times than can be recalled by the oldest of Arielana's citizens.

The castle itself was a tall structure that stretched three hundred spans above the plains. Its many spires gave it a majestic presence, looking down upon all the other buildings in the surrounding village. Royce, Wyn and Keli had never been to the palace, nor had they ever seen it. They had only been told of its beauty, so naturally they were slightly taken by its grandeur. Nevertheless, Sherwin paid little attention to it, for he had seen it many times.

Sherwin directed Keli to fly Shira in a large half circle to the backside of the castle. After a suitable landing spot had been pointed out away from the main village, Shira landed softy in a small clearing, below the steep rocky bluff supporting the castle's back wall.

"I hope we're not going to have to scale up the side of *that*!" Wyn complained.

"No, we will take the stairs." All chuckled at Sherwin words. He gave them a strange look. He had not made a joke; he was serious.

Shira allowed Royce, Wyn and Sherwin to climb down. Keli instructed her to find a place to hide in a small grove of trees near the base of the cliffs and to be most careful to keep herself out of sight. Then *she* slid down as well. The siblings, following Sherwin's lead, hiked up into a crevice between the stones. Finding a hole up under a large outcropping, Sherwin pulled himself up and crawled in on all fours. Royce, Wyn and Keli followed. Once inside, they found it impossible to see a thing. They had to feel their way along the side of the cave and follow the sound of Sherwin's voice. After what seemed like a long ways in the dark, Royce bumped into the back of Sherwin.

"Hold it here," Sherwin's voice echoed.

Royce could hear Sherwin working with something, but he could not tell what by only the sound. Directly, he heard what sounded like a rock hitting against another, and his eye caught a tiny flash of light. Then he heard the sound several times; each time he saw a tiny spark. Then suddenly a flame lit the inside of the cave. Sherwin had somehow lit a fire on a stick. He stood holding a torch that brightened the whole cavern, which was quite large.

"How did you do that?" Wyn asked, her voice echoing also.

"Flint! You can make it spark by hitting two pieces together. The spark ignites the oils on the torch."

"Clever, Sherwin," Keli said.

"I will have to try that some day, on a camp fire," Royce said, with a smile.

"It will work only with oil, not wood," Sherwin explained.

Once the torch was lit, the going became much easier. Sherwin led them through the dark passageway as if he was right at home. Each time another passage veered off, he would not pause to think but continued with confidence, occasionally urging the rest to stay close.

"Ouch!" Wyn bumped her head on the low hanging ceiling. "How do you know where you are going?"

"As I have said, I have been here before." Sherwin did not slow. "This way."

Eventually, the passage began to make its way up. Occasionally, the channel would narrow. In these places, the rock obviously had been chipped away, expanding the opening to allow a person to climb through. Stones had been placed for steps when the rises were too steep to ascend comfortably.

"Steps! These caves are not natural," Royce commented. "They look almost man made."

"Many places had to be dug out," Sherwin spoke as he

continued to climb. "One of the old king's, I'm not sure which one, had these tunnels dug to make a way of escape if ever the castle fell to an attack. No one knows of these caverns but the king. It is a knowledge that is handed only to a new king from his predecessors…" Sherwin now stopped and turned to the others. "You must never divulge this information to anyone! Ever!" A little fear showed in his eyes. "I need your word on this!"

There was a pause while the three siblings looked at each other, then back to Sherwin.

"Do I have it?" he asked again.

"Yes," Royce answered slowly.

"Good, let's go on."

As they ascended, the cave wall gave way to cut stones and mortar; the rugged floor became carefully laid cobbles. They realized they were now inside what appeared to be castle walls. Still, they ascended up several more dusty steps through cobwebbed passages, until Sherwin stopped. He snuffed out the torch and discarded it. All went dark except for a faint glow in front of him. He then proceeded to squeeze himself through a small square opening in the laid stones of the wall. Suddenly, he disappeared through and plopped down on the other side. His face popped back up in the opening.

"We are here!" he said in a loud whisper.

"Where is here?" Keli questioned, as she began to climb through the opening.

Royce helped her through, and as he proceeded to assist Wyn up and through, he heard Keli's voice from the other side of the wall.

"Oh, my!" she said it in a long, soft, drawn out sort of way.

"What is the matter with her?" Royce asked.

When Wyn had pulled herself through, Royce began to enter the opening. Before he was able to squeeze himself thru, he heard Wyn's voice speaking in the same slow, drawn out manner.

"Oh, dear!"

Royce pulled himself through the hole and dropped down into what appeared to be a fireplace.

"It is a good thing it is not cold. We would have…" he stopped when he had crawled onto the hearth and looked up. "Whoooaa!"

"Don't worry. It is not a real fireplace, just made to look as one."

They found they had stepped into a great hall, brightly lit by torches down each side. Walls of stone reached high to an arched ceiling. Lining the walls were statues and figures of great knights and famous people of the country's history. A huge double door centered in the opposite end of the room. It was large enough for a coachman to drive a carriage and a full barrage of horses between its posts. Above it was glass windows arranged to match the arch in the ceiling, some of which were stained in brilliant colors that reflected the torch light. To the right and to the left were magnificent staircases in half circles winding their way to the upper levels, beautifully and meticulously hand carved out of stone. The three stood in awe until Sherwin demanded their attention.

"Come on, this way!" he had to say it twice before they began to move. Nervously they followed.

He led them up one stairway and down a short hall. Then through a set of double doors, up another set of stairs then down another hall, none of which were quite as brightly lit as the main entrance, but all were just as carefully constructed.

"Sherwin, we are going to get caught!" Wyn worried. "Then we will be in so much trouble!"

"Only if we run into Abes," Sherwin replied. "But don't worry; he is probably fast asleep right now."

"Who?" Wyn asked.

Sherwin turned another corner of the hallway and bumped into someone. Thud! "Abes!" he hollered, looking up. "Oh! Neville, it's you. You scared me."

Royce's stomach went to his throat and he felt his heart beating wildly in his chest.

"Master Edwin?" Neville's face lit up. "Is it really you or is it your ghost?"

Edwin? Royce thought.

"Yes. It is I."

"How?" The face of the young man was white as if he were seeing a spirit.

"There is not time now, Neville!" Sherwin spoke in an authoritative voice. "We must see the king at once!"

"Who is with you?"

"Some of His Majesty's most faithful subjects that are in dire need!" he replied.

Neville paused to eye the three roughly dressed children. "Indeed, I can see that! For sure!"

Royce thought he detected a look of disgust on the young man's face, even in the dim light. He was sure they had gone as far as they were going to be allowed to go! This would be the end! He would holler for the guards, and they would be arrested and put in the dungeons!

"At once, Neville!" Sherwin repeated.

"Yes, Master Edwin." The young man whirled. "This way!"

He escorted Sherwin down the hall. Royce, Wyn and Keli nervously followed, not sure of what they had gotten into. What was Sherwin doing? They wondered greatly at the way Sherwin had ordered the castle servant, but more so at the way he had obeyed so readily. Had he mistaken Sherwin for this Edwin? Or had they mistaken this Edwin for Sherwin.

The young man led the four children through another set of doors that opened into a brightly lit chamber. He told them to wait here, exiting the room though another door, leaving it open.

The room was elegantly decorated. On the walls and around the windows hung brightly covered tapestries from floor to ceiling. All the furniture was hand carved of mahogany. The couch, the chairs, and the footstools were upholstered with purple and scarlet, in shimmering velvet. Each item was carefully crafted and meticulously placed. A huge crystal chandelier that hung from the center of the ceiling illuminated the whole room. It seemed as if it had a thousand candles all aglow. The room was perfectly spotless, not a single thing was out of place, except for the four children that stood frozen on the hearth in front of a magnificent stone fire place. They were covered with cobwebs and dirt from the climb up from the caverns.

On the walls were hand-painted portraits of important looking people. It was as if they stared back at the children indignantly, not approving. There was one of a lovely young woman with long flowing, dark hair. She was standing, holding a single rose, wearing a beautiful pink ball gown. There was still another of a small boy, approximately four or five years old, wearing blue, tight legged trousers, black boots and a white puffy shirt. His face seemed amazingly familiar to Royce. He was sure he had seem him somewhere before, but he could not think of where or when. There was one of a man seated on a horse, holding a shield and a sword raised high in the air. He had the sourest look on his face. Royce took a double take at the sword; it was the same sword he had strapped to his waist! The blade, the hilt, the scabbard, it was identical to the smallest detail!

"We shouldn't be here!" whispered Keli.

"Sherwin, where are we?" Wyn demanded.

"Oh, His Majesty's inner chambers," Sherwin answered, as if it was everyday one would find himself in the king's private chambers.

"Oh, oh! We are going to get caught!" Wyn was nervous. "We are taking such a risk."

"You have already said that, Wyn," Sherwin reminded her.

Suddenly, Wyn gasped so loudly that everyone jumped. Her eyes were wide; her face white, her expression was of total astonishment. She was staring at a painted portrait that hung on the far wall opposite the fireplace. The others quickly understood what made her act this way, for they saw it too, as soon as she had pointed. The subject was a little girl in a beautiful ball gown, which was not so unusual. What disturbed the children was that the girls face was Keli's; it looked just like her! Royce and Keli also gasped, their eyes widened, and their mouth dropped.

"The girl in the painting... She looks like Keli!" Royce said in a loud whisper.

Sherwin looked up at the portrait for a second. He shook his head. "I don't...I don't see it."

"Are you blind? It looks just like her! It could be her!" Royce stared at it still. "Who is she?"

Sherwin did not get a chance to answer.

"Who's there?" a voice shouted from the next room. "Who did you say? ... Listen here, young man, I'll have your head for idle words! How could it possibly be...?"

"It is I, Sir," Sherwin spoke out big and loud before anyone could stop him. He stared at the doorway leading to the next room. Then there was silence. There was a sound of a chair being pushed back, then footsteps of someone walking rather quickly.

Royce thought Sherwin had lost his mind, a sickening feeling rose from his stomach up into his throat. Wyn started to look for a place to escape. Keli backed up against the stone fireplace. All three were panic stricken.

"Sherwin! What are you doing?" Royce whispered as furiously as he could and still keep his voice low.

"You wanted an audience with the king, did you not?"

"Yes, but..."

"Tonight, you will have it." Sherwin gave them a serious look, so strange that Royce feared for a second that they had been double-crossed. "Don't worry. He will listen to…"

"Edwin!" The voice from the other room had now materialized into an old man standing in the doorway. He stood stone still with a strange look on his face. He was slightly bent over as a result of the years, but he retained all his wits. His face was in dire need of a shave. A dark green robe draped from his shoulders to the floor. His hair was gray and uncombed, his face slightly wrinkled, his eyes were red and puffy. It was obvious something of great importance weighted heavily on this man. Worry and sleeplessness were taking its toll. He hesitated for a second, and then he entered the room, faltering in his steps only slightly.

"Is it true! Edwin, is that you? My eyes aren't what they were!"

"Yes, it is!" he replied.

The old man quickly crossed the room and put his hand on Sherwin. "Edwin, how did you…? Where have you been? Your mother has just about gone mad with worry! Are you alright?"

"I'm fine, Sir."

The old man was now down on one knee checking the boy. "Have they hurt you?"

"No, Sir." Apparently the old man knew him well, but it was obvious Edwin was not used to getting such attention. As a matter of fact, he looked down right uncomfortable. The two beheld each other for a long moment. The three Windmere children just stood silently, trying to fit all the pieces together, feeling very much out of place.

"We thought you were dead." The old man looked at the boy. "We received word that you had been killed."

"Someone made a mistake," Sherwin, now known as Edwin, spoke in his usual, stiff, solemn Sherwin manner, even in front of the king.

"So they did! Praise be! You are back!" he said gleefully.

"Wow, they really think a lot of their servants around here." Keli whispered. Wyn shushed her.

The old man suddenly spotted Royce, Wyn and Keli. The three wanted desperately to run back out the way they had come.

Utterly aghast at finding three horribly dirty children standing in the spotless chamber (although Sherwin was just as dirty, yet he had not noticed that) he became very disturbed.

"Abes! Who are these...these children?" he spoke in somewhat of an angered tone.

Royce's heart skipped a beat. Surely this would be the end, all this way to be arrested! Three peasant children would not be thought of twice, but thrown out of the castle, or worse! All he had to do was summon the guards and it would be over! If this happened, any chance of saving their father would be lost!

Edwin, the former Sherwin, stepped in front of his ragged rescuers. "These are the three who are responsible for bringing me back, Sir. They and their father have kept me safe these two weeks. If it were not for the courage of these, I would be dead."

Would be dead? Royce stared at Sherwin or Edwin or whoever he was. The old man's gaze softened greatly. Edwin continued.

"This is Royce. ... This is his sister, Wyn. ... And this is also his sister, Keli." He laid his hand on each one's shoulder as he introduced them. Then he turned to the three. "This is King Robinson, King of Arielana."

For a second, Royce was dumbfounded. Suddenly realizing his place, he quickly found his manners and bowed himself on one knee. Wyn gasped and did the same. A few seconds later, when Keli realized what the others were doing, she too bowed herself.

"Oh, my!" Keli cried.

"Sire, forgive us!" Royce pleaded. "We did not realize!"

"On your feet. On your feet." The children obeyed and the king continued. "Of what family do you come from?"

The three were still so nervous that Edwin spoke for them. "Sir, these are the Windmere children."

"Windmere? ... Windmere." At first the king looked up as if he was deep in thought, then turned back to the children with great interest. "Who is your father?"

Royce had recovered enough to speak for the group, "Our father's name is Spencer, Sire."

"Windmere?" The king's face went blank.

At that point Royce just knew it was all over.

"Spencer Windmere," Wyn added.

"Spencer?" The king looked horrified. "Spencer Windmere!"

"Yes, our father!" Royce answered.

"Oh, my, could there be two of them?" the king questioned. Suddenly, a ghastly expression came over his face. He whirled around and hollered, "Abes!"

All wondered what that meant.

The king's mouth dropped. "Oh, dear!" He looked at all who were standing in the room. All noticed the horrid look on his face, but no one had a clue to what was bothering him.

Then he looked back at Royce, Wyn, and Keli. "Oh, dear! Oh, dear." The old man was almost horror stricken. "Children, forgive me, but I have to attend to something immediately! Abes! …Oh, that man is never around when you need him. Abes!" The king walked around the chair somewhat mumbling to himself, then he burst out louder than ever, "Abes!" Turning again to the children, he spoke a little softer, "You will excuse me… Where is that…?" The king whirled around and hollered once more. "Abes!" he yelled directly into the serious face of a tall thin man. He had appeared from the door leading to the outer chambers. Apparently this was Abes.

"Sire?" Abes addressed the king in a dry fashion, but his face lit up when he saw Edwin. "Prince Edwin!"

"Oh, good! You're here! Take these three. Get them unsoiled and get them a bit of nourishment." The king turned back to the three. "I will want an audience with them in my chambers as soon you can get them back." He turned to leave.

"Right away, Sire!" Abes replied.

"But first, have Neville meet me in the governing chamber immediately!" He looked at Abes determinedly then to Edwin. "Edwin! You go find your mother; she will not believe her eyes!" The king left the room speedily.

As soon as he was out of the room, all eyes fell upon Edwin. Abes had called him Prince Edwin! The three children felt very awkward. For days they had spoken with him as a friend, traveled with him as a companion, an equal, even at times, ordered him around as a servant. Now, after learning his true identity, the three siblings could not say a word to him. They had been traveling with the prince and had not known it.

Abes spoke kindly to the children, "This way, if you please."

"Go and refresh yourselves," Edwin said pleasantly. "We will speak when you return."

They obediently followed, still looking back as they left the room. Each was given a chamber supplied with soap and water. A change of clothing was also supplied. Royce declined, but Abes insisted. They seemed to fit him surprisingly well. It was a welcome change from his trousers. They had been ripped since the second day of traveling back on the cliffs. When he finished changing, he stepped out the door and waited for his sisters.

Presently, Abes returned escorting two young ladies dressed tidily in black and white dresses. Their hair was down, carefully brushed. They nearly stood in front of Royce before he recognized his sisters.

Wyn was absolutely joyful, and she was beaming, obviously delighted to be clean again. They were only uniforms that the young maid-servants wore while working in the castle, but to her it was a ball gown, for she never had owned such a dress of her own.

Keli did not at all seem happy. "They made us change into these." She rolled her eyes.

"Keli, you're going to meet the king. This is what you should wear for such an occasion," Wyn tried to explain to her the need for such attire. She nodded but still did not like it.

A server courteously showed them to the main dining hall. The room was huge with a domed ceiling and large glass windows along one side. The table and its chairs, made from dark mahogany, would have easily seated thirty. They seated Royce at the head, Wyn at his right, and Keli at his left. Royce felt completely out of place, a little embarrassed and very nervous.

They were given a bit of nourishment. A *bit* of nourishment? Royce had never seen so much food in all of his days, nor had he tasted of such cookery. Silver platters that were overflowing with just about every type of food imaginable covered the end of the table. The only sound heard was the tinkling of the utensils on the china echoing off the large room's stone walls. Only after the servants left them to themselves did they speak.

"So Sherwin is the heir, the heir that no one knew of his whereabouts! Remember what he said? He was speaking of himself," Wyn said.

"I knew it. Why would he say he was not?" Royce asked.

"He is Prince Edwin! And he is amazingly clever, he had to try and hide it from us so. Aren't we ashamed of the way we treated him now?" Wyn glared at Royce.

Royce's anger burned inside of him, knowing that she was right, she was *always* right! "Oh, oh! I ordered the prince to take care of my horse! I ordered him to fill water bottles! He *is* the heir! He could have us thrown in the dungeons!" Royce worried. The thought of how the prince may treat them now upset him terribly. "Why would he hide it from us?"

"Maybe he was too ashamed of our behavior."

Royce thought out loud, giving Wyn a worried look, "I have really put us in a fix, now. What do you think he will do with us? What do you think the king will do?"

"Well, the king would not have given us such a welcome if he were not going to at least listen to our plea. They have fed us, look how lavishly!"

"A last supper!" Royce interjected.

Wyn frowned and then continued, "If he thinks we are sincere in our request for Father, he will help us. We will be honest, we will tell him the truth, in that we did not know who Sherwin was. On the other hand, if he learns how we ordered him around...it's hard to say. But until then, we should enjoy what we have been offered and keep the faith, for we have never been treated in such a manner as this!"

"I want to leave!" Keli interrupted.

The other two stared at their sister, a tear in her eye.

"I don't like it here," Keli said quietly.

"What is it, Keli?" Wyn asked. "They have treated us kindly so far."

"Yes, but it's... so... it is just ... so sad..." Keli put her fork down. "And Father is still..."

The two others knew exactly what she was feeling.

"She is right!" Wyn agreed. "It is not right. Father is in some cell, going through who knows what, while we sit here in..."

"I will tell them we have finished," Royce stood to find the server and request to be taken back to the king.

Sherwin's Flight

Minutes later, they were in the great hall standing once again in front of the huge stone fireplace and the colorful tapestries. Edwin entered, now dressed in more suitable attire for a prince. Now, clean and groomed, he looked nothing like the staff boy they had been traveling with for days. With him was a lady of elegance. She was much older than he and she wore a long gown of velvet green and white lace. Her eyes were red and puffy and looked as if she had been crying. The three were greatly embarrassed and bowed themselves on one knee once more.

Edwin sensed the awkward situation; looking somewhat embarrassed himself. He began to speak, "Mother, this is Royce, Wyn and Keli Windmere. Royce, Wyn, Keli, this is my mother, Clarice."

"Very pleased, Your Majesty." Each one of them bowed and greeted her in the humblest manner they knew.

She burst into tears and gave each one a hug. "You wonderful sweet children, we owe you a great debt. You brought Edwin back. We thought he was dead." She started to cry again. She hugged her son.

"Mother, I told you I'm fine." He was embarrassed by the way his mother was doting over him. He looked at the three and shrugged. "I'm… sorry! I wanted to tell you, but I could not … for your sakes. At first I was not sure I could trust you, and then I was not sure you trusted me. It was better that way. In case one of us had been captured, they would not have been able to...well, you wouldn't have…it is just that you could not pass on what you had no knowledge of."

Finally, Wyn mustered the courage to speak, "Prince Edwin, please forgive our ill treatment of you. Had we known…"

"Would you please get up?" Edwin motioned with his hands at the three still bowed on the stone hearth. "Sit down and I will tell you all."

When they had settled on the couch, Edwin started his story.

"Wyn, my la… my lady, it was because of your very own words that first day that I chose to stay with you and your brother and sister. For I must admit, I had planned to take one of the horses and return to the castle at my first opportunity. I would have except for the fact that I feared Devlin. But I felt I was safe with you. You treated me as a companion, as an equal. And I will expect you to continue to treat me as you always have. I consider you all friends. And I count myself lucky to have found such *good* friends as you came to be."

"Thank you, but you told us you were not the king's son."

"My lady, I told you no untruth. For I am not."

"No? I don't understand. Are you not a prince?" Wyn asked the question that all were wondering; still she was the only one who had enough courage to speak.

"Yes, I am. The queen is my mother, but the king is not my father. My mother and the king were only married five years ago.

"How did you end up at the inn with us?" Keli asked.

"More than two weeks ago, I left the palace to go to my annual training for knighthood. Each year, the king sends me south to the training ground of the knights to learn what I will need to know, when, as he says, I become of age. Because of all the raids and unrest going on in the kingdom, this trip I was escorted by none other than your beloved uncle, Devlin, supposedly for my protection. He is the king's most trusted advisor you know… err… was. He, a squadron of his most faithful followers and I set out on the two day ride to go to Owertaubec Training Grounds."

"When we camped that night, they thought I was asleep, but I was not. I overheard Devlin talking to one of his men. I heard one say to throw me over the ocean cliffs at Calanor Pass the next day as we passed by the inlet. Another man said not to kill me, but that they should take me to Port Baudwren and sell me to a slave trader. Then I heard Devlin say that he needed to keep me around long enough for him to get the king to see things his way. After that, they could do with me what they would. I was terrified. I lay quiet for hours, until I was sure that they were all asleep, and then I eased out of camp. I wandered for several days in the woods, nearly starved and exhausted."

"I was found by your father. He recognized me at once, I'm not sure how. When he found out that Devlin and all the highwaymen were searching for me, he realized that it would not be safe taking me to the castle. Knowing how dangerous Devlin was, he took me to the inn. He had me change into common clothes so I could fit in with the common folk. I started acting as a commoner. Remember, I used to be one."

"When I disappeared from the camp that night, Devlin searched for me throughout the kingdom. When he did not find me, he reported to the king that I had been kidnapped. Anyone I was found with would be arrested. A decree had been sent out from the palace for all the highwaymen, the soldiers, and any in the service of the king to search the country for me. If I was found, those with me were to be taken, no questions asked, if they resisted, then they were authorized to use whatever means necessary."

"This put your father in grave danger. Your father managed to send a message to the king. He said I was fine and that he would take me to the old chalet for my protection, from there he would arrange a safe way to get me back. In the message, he told of the treacheries of Devlin, he was not to be trusted. He told how he has been the rebel leader. He told the king that he had been the cause of all the unrest in the kingdom, the cause of all the attacks, the one responsible for all the raids on the villages. I do not know if the king ever received the message. The night before we were to leave for the chalet, your father received word that the inn, your home, was to be attacked. I am sure Devlin must have found out that I was there. Immediately, Mr. Windmere devised a plan to get me safely away and to lead the highwaymen astray. I was to travel with you."

"That is why Father sent us through the Black Forest!" Royce said.

"The rest of the story you know," Edwin finished.

"We must tell the king!" Royce insisted.

"He knows. I have just told him everything."

"You did?" Royce shot a glance at Wyn and Keli.

"Oh, Sher…Edwin. I can't imagine what you have been through," Keli said. She and Wyn were on the verge of tears.

"When I heard that your father had been arrested, I knew it would have been without the knowledge of the king. Therefore, I brought you straight here… err… or more correctly you brought me."

"Yes! … Father!" Royce suddenly remembered why they had come to the castle. "Will the king…will he…?"

Presently, the old king swept back into the room.

"Can you imagine, asleep at three o'clock in the morning! What servants I have!" The king went straight to Edwin, his mother, and his three friends. "Clarice, would you stop smothering the boy."

"I can't help it," she replied.

"Windmere children!" the king cried. "You have done your country a great service. Devlin reported that Edwin had died in a fire at the old chalet."

"Your Majesty, you can *not* trust Devlin!" Royce spoke without thinking.

"I have heard all I want to hear about Devlin, my trusted advisor!" the anger in the king's voice made everyone feel uneasy.

"Oh, sorry, my lord. Permission to speak, Your Majesty?" Royce felt as if he was treading on thin ice.

"Yes. We must speak. It is very urgent. Of course, my boy, speak on." King Robinson still looked upset.

"Sire, if I may. Our father has been arrested." Royce had now gained a little courage. "Arrested by... Devlin!"

There was silence while the king hesitated.

"Your father..." The king's face paled again as he looked seriously at the three children. "Children, listen to me carefully. A tragedy has occurred... I just signed the execution order yesterday, by Devlin's direction. He said he had apprehended the man responsible for the death of Edwin. He had been found with the evidence... I didn't even read the order completely, I just signed it, I was so angry... I believed Devlin... It is by my order—Spencer Windmere is to be hanged at dawn."

Orders from the King

"No!" Wyn cried when she heard of the execution order against her father.

"Your Majesty, please, you have to stop the order. Our father is innocent!" Wyn said boldly, stepping forward. "He has fought against the ones raiding the villages, the ones harassing the people, the *one* who has rebelled against the king! The one who has rebelled against you, Sire! Against Devlin! Sire, if there was anyone most faithful to the kingdom, it would have to be our father!"

"William, you have got to stop this," Clarice cried.

"If there is any way to save your father, child, it would be done! I have already dispatched my fastest horse and rider with a stay of execution."

"Sir, it is a full five hours hard ride from here to the Castle Delthyna. The fastest horse could never make it before sunrise," Edwin said.

"No!" Wyn screamed again. "This can't be!"

Edwin calculated. "A horse could not but…" He glanced over to Keli's direction.

"Shira could," Keli said quietly between sobs and behind streaming tears.

Royce brightened. "Sire, if we could deliver the order for the stay of execution, would you rewrite another one and seal it? Would you allow us to carry it?"

"Of course! Of course! But son, I am truly sorry, there is no way humanly possible you can get to the Castle Delthyna before sunrise."

"Sir!" Edwin stepped forward. "These three can do it!"

"What!" The king looked hard at the boy.

"I have been with these three for many days. These are not your ordinary children. I have seen Royce fight off the panther in the Black Forest…"

"Edwin! You have been in the Black Forest?" the queen cried.

She was unnerved to hear of this news.

"Yes Mother. Sir, these have fought the wolves, conquered raging rivers, they have avoided … no, outsmarted the highwaymen! Keli can communicate with animals! Wyn can use a bow like no one else in the kingdom! They have taken me through the Black Forest, across the Forbidden Canyon, to Mount Hestia and back! All since the last time I stood before you!"

"No one could have done all that." The king looked shocked. "They would have to be enchanters."

"No, Sir. They are just God's favored." Edwin stood his ground. "Please give them the order and let them try to save their father. We owe them this much."

The king thought on the request. "Very well, fetch me parchment, a quill, and my seal from my governing chambers."

"Oh, thank you, Sire." Before she realized it, Wyn was giving the king a hug in front of everyone. Suddenly she backed away, looking very embarrassed. "Oh, forgive me."

"No need! That's quite alright, my dear."

"Thank you, Sire," Royce offered his gratitude, also bowing in the process. "Keli, can you call Shira?"

"Yes!" She turned to go back the way she had entered the castle when someone took a hold of her hand.

"This way my lady, it will be faster," Edwin said.

He took her out through the door the king had entered. They crossed another room that was just as magnificently adorned, then out a set of double doors that opened to a large balcony overlooking the village below. Not a single light was visible in the whole kingdom, but the nighttime sky was brilliant with stars. The landscape was bright with detail in the silvery moonlight.

"Can you call Shira from here?" Edwin asked.

"I think so," she answered.

"Have her land here. There is more than enough room here on the balcony."

Keli nodded. "Shira, we need you!" Keli hollered up into the night sky. Her voice carried on the wind to the ears of the waiting dragon far below in the valley. Then Keli turned back to face Edwin.

"That is it?" he asked. "Are you sure she heard you?"

"Yes, she is coming."

Edwin just shook his head. "I hope you find your father safe." he said.

"Sher... I mean, Edwin, are you coming?"

"I must stay here, but my heart goes with you. I bid you God speed!"

Keli realized Edwin was still holding her hand. "Thank you for all that you have done." She gave him a kiss on the cheek. "We shall never forget it."

The prince could not say anything. He was so taken by her display of affection; all he could do was stand there. He looked completely embarrassed, but he was smiling! She had done it; he *was* smiling!

Edwin looked away just in time to see Shira rising out of the forest below. He pulled Keli to one side giving the dragon the whole balcony to land. When she had folded her wings over her back, Keli stepped forward to meet her dear friend. Edwin backed away, having never gotten used to the great animal. The animal took nearly the whole balcony to maneuver, but she managed to rotate herself, giving them room to get around her.

"Shira, are you ready to fly? We need you to fly faster than you have ever flown before. We must save Father—tonight!"

Shira gave a roar of excitement.

Royce and Wyn hearing the sound from inside the castle soon arrived on the balcony, followed by Clarice and Abes. When the queen saw the dragon she went shrieking back into the castle. Abes did not know whether to follow her or freeze, so he just fainted.

Keli was atop Shira in no time. Wyn climbed up behind her. When Royce started up Edwin pulled him to the side.

"Listen. The king is going to give you a stay of execution. When you get to Delthyna, I am not sure who you should deliver it to, certainly not Devlin. I know not which officer is still faithful to the king, if any!" Edwin looked more serious than ever. "Here, take this. I think you are going to need this too."

King Robinson ran out onto the balcony. Edwin quickly shoved a piece of rolled parchment in Royce's hand and backed away.

"Here my boy. Ugh! ... A dragon... you have a dragon!"

Shira whirled her head around to see the king, who immediately scrambled back quicker than any would have thought possible of him.

"Yes, Your Highness," Royce answered.

"Trying to kill the king are you! Prepare an old man!"

"Yes, Sire. I mean, no, Sire. I mean...I'm very sorry, Your

Majesty. This is Shira…. Shira this is King Robinson."

Shira bowed her head in the king's direction.

"Err…ah… How do …err… you do?" Shira shook her head slightly and turned back around.

"She says she does very well, thank you!" Keli giggled from atop Shira.

After seeing Wyn and Keli on the back of the dragon, a look of amazement crossed his face. "And she allows you to ride her? This is extraordinary! This is unheard of! This is…!" He did not take his eyes off of the scaly beast. "Why, if my grandfather were here, I would have to make amends. He told me of stories of great flying dragons from years ago. Why, I thought it was just idle tales. You know when I was a lad…"

"Sire," Royce interrupted, "The time is short."

The king knew what he meant. "Yes, of course. Here is the order demanding a stay of execution along with a full pardon, all sealed with the royal seal. Now go and may God be with you!"

"Thank you, Sire!" Royce bowed. "We will forever be in your service." He turned to go.

"Royce!" the king called after him. "When you find your father, you must bring him here. I need to see him. Do not fail me, my boy! It is gravely important."

"*We* will not fail, Sire!" He then mounted along with his sisters. Shira unfolded her wings and took to the sky.

Almost instantly, the crowded balcony was emptied, leaving only the king, his son, and Clarice who was peeking back out the door, as her curiosity was getting the best of her. Abes came to in just enough time to see Shira lift off. He fainted again.

In no time, the huge dragon became just a tiny speck in the huge night sky.

"They will never make it by first light," the king spoke wearily.

"Sire," said Edwin, stepping up beside the king. "I know they will."

The king put a hand on the boy's shoulder. "If they don't, I will never be able to live with the consequences."

Queen Clarice, who had ventured back out onto the balcony after Shira had departed, gave him a concerned look.

The Castle on the Lake

T he countryside glowed of a misty shade of blue as it moved far below the dragon in flight. Occasionally, the reflection of the moonlight would sparkle on a lake or stream causing little flashes of light on the landscape below. Small patches of fog filled in the low-lying areas giving the appearance of a mysterious sea among the rising hills.

Royce was not sure how the dragon knew where to go, she just went, and she never seemed to struggle to find her way. The pleasant flight gave him the chance rethink all that had just happened. They had come from the far side of the Black Forest, sneaked into the royal palace, and pleaded his father's case before the king! Now they were on their way to the Castle Delthyna with sealed orders of the king that were going to free his father! All in one night! It was more than the mind could fathom. Indeed, they were truly favored.

He pondered the sealed orders hidden in his cloak! Who would he give them to? He knew Edwin was right. He could not hand them to Devlin. After all that he had learned of his father's old friend, that would be a worthless proposition. He was sure that if he did, all would be lost. Maybe he could give them to someone else, but who did he know that was still faithful to the king. A great dilemma, what would they do upon arrival at Delthyna?

Royce then remembered the parchment that Edwin had handed him. *What did he mean when he said he was going to need this,* Royce thought as he pulled it from his cloak and unrolled it? He struggled to read it in the moonlight. It was a drawing! Hurriedly sketched, but rather detailed, it was a map, a floor plan of Castle Delthyna. On the left side of the layout was an 'X' drawn in very dark. Under the 'X' were the words, 'The east tower, your father will be here!'

At that moment, Royce figured just what he had to do! Edwin had known before they left the royal palace. Now he knew too; find his father! He would not find Devlin when they got to the castle on the lake. He would not seek anyone, except his father.

In the hour flight between the king's castle and Delthyna, Royce, Wyn, and Keli had put together a plan.

Before one could know another by the first light from the eastern sky, the children made their approach on the castle. The cool night air and the warm lake water had formed a mist that covered the entire lake with a blanket of fog. Shira cleared the last ridge and descended into the valley. She flew right down into the mist. Unable to see in the thick haze, the children had no idea where they were going, but Shira knew. She had eyes of a cat. She could see in the night just as well as the day and now it seemed she could see just as well in fog too. Shira had descended so low that Royce could sense they were near the lake's surface. The clammy, humid smell of water was strong in his nostrils. Shira skimmed across the lake's surface like a sled on ice.

Shira suddenly pulled up hard. The rock walls of Delthyna Castle loomed directly in front of her. The force pressed Royce down hard against the dragon's back. Wyn almost screamed out, but caught herself. In seconds, they had reached the top of the wall. Before Royce realized what was happening, Shira did a u-turn in the air and with the tip of her wing knocked one of the guards over the edge of the wall. The man hollered out in surprise and was not silenced until he hit the water with a splash. Shira disappeared back down over the edge of the wall and into the cover of the fog.

***

Jake, one of the night guards, heard the wail and splash, but saw nothing in the thick mist. All was quiet again.

"Argas?" he hollered to his companion.

"Yeah!" Argas answered back.

"What was that?"

"I think Ruel jumped in the lake."

"What would he do that for?"

"Wanted to go for a swim, I guess. I don't know!"

"Reckon one of us ought to go down and to check on him?"

"Yeah. I guess we ought to. I'll go."

There was a scuffling sound, a thud, followed a few seconds later by another splash.

"Argas?"

There was no answer.

"ARGAS?"

***

After taking out the second guard, Shira climbed high above the level of the fog and made a big sweeping circle of the castle. Delthyna's spires were the only visible parts above the thick blanket of mist. There were several, all of differing heights and sizes. Each of their lower supporting structures was completely hidden by the fog, making them seem to float in the mist. Above the highest, center-most spire was a pole extending high into the air. On this pole flew the ensign of the kingdom. Royce wondered how loyal the occupants of this castle were to those colors.

As Shira circled and dived for another approach, Royce tried to identify the east tower, the dragon's flight had disoriented him so, he was having trouble. Before Shira dived completely back into the mist, Royce noted a slight glow in the sky; that had to be east. The east tower would be on the east, as simple as that, according to Edwin and his map.

Now that the attack had begun, they knew it would not be long before the whole castle would be alerted to their presence. They would have only a few minutes to get in, locate their father and get out, particularly if one of the guards were to sound the alarm.

Shira had accomplished half of the first objective, taking out two of the night watchmen. There were six guards that were stationed around the clock. Shira could spot them as if they were lighted torches. There was one that patrolled each of the four walls on the topside and two on the ground to secure the main gate. The two on the ground would not pose much of a threat, but the two remaining on the topside would have to go.

Shira landed softly on the northeast wall where the first guard had been knocked from his post. Royce and Wyn slid off Shira's back and ducked down behind the edging stones that lined the walkway atop the wall. Shira then lifted off again with Keli still on board.

"What is she doing?" Royce whispered to Wyn.

"Staying out of sight, I hope," she answered.

***

Keli and Shira had more plans than to just stay out of sight, unbeknown to Royce, they went to take out the two remaining guards on the topside. They would then have free air space over the castle.

Jake peered hard in the direction of his comrade, listening hard for any sound, his head was still but his eyes darted back and forth, he saw nothing. Suddenly, he heard another thud and a splash. This time it was from his left. "Jonas! Please tell me you didn't! Jonas?" his voice cracked. "A swim? In the middle of the night?" It then occurred to Jake to sound the alarm. He began to run.

The same fate had been planned for Jake, until Keli realized that if they knocked him over the wall, he would not land in the lake. Directly below him were jagged rocks rising out of the water at the castle's base. So instead, Shira swooped around to his side of the castle, and before Jake knew anything, he was dangling in the claws of a dragon, rising above his assigned station. The attack had come so quickly that his spear was knocked out of his hand and he had not the wits about him to use his sword. He just hung for dear sweet life, much the same way Keli had done when plucked from the river.

"Oh, Shira, don't harm him!" Keli urged.

Easy to say, but that also posed a problem; what to do with him so that he would be of no trouble. When Keli saw the tallest spire that flew the flag, she then knew just what to do.

***

Royce and Wyn concentrated on finding their father. From the top of the wall, they tried to enter the door to the section of the castle that hopefully led to the east tower. It was locked. They searched the area around the east tower for a way in but found none from the wall on which they stood. The only option was a window on the towers base, of which the shutter had been left open.

An ell-shape section of roof directly below the window also passed directly below where they were standing. One could easily climb over the wall and down about four feet, walk along this roof, making his way to the other roof, climb along it and enter the open window. Royce did not give it a second thought; he quickly, but quietly climbed down.

Halfway across to the tower's base, he froze. He heard voices. Below, on the second level walkway, two men were talking directly under him. Back on the wall, Wyn made a motion to him as if to say, 'What's wrong?' Royce put his hand up to his mouth to let her know to be quiet for a moment while he listened.

"What if the children don't show, will he hang the man anyway?" Royce did not recognize the first voice. "What if the old shopkeeper didn't even deliver the message? Or what if he did and they still don't come for their father?"

"They will come. I am almost certain. Ras, I know this

family well. I doubt there is another family in this kingdom that is more dedicated to one another," another man said. The second voice Royce did recognize, but he could not place it.

"I don't know what good that will do them," Ras said sourly.

"I also know Spencer Windmere has been a thorn in Devlin's side for a long time," the second voice continued. "Now that the king believes him to be an enemy to the kingdom, Devlin will not let this opportunity pass."

"The boy's clothes were found in his inn! He knows more than he is telling us," the first voice spoke again.

"Spencer is innocent! You know he is! He has hidden the boy to protect him from Devlin!" the second voice continued. "Ras, we can't let him kill Windmere, it is just not right. He is in that cell only because he dared to stand against Devlin!"

"It is not wise to cross Devlin either, Marcus. I have learned that the hard way! If we do, we will be facing the gallows."

Royce was sure he heard two sets of footsteps walk away, one in each direction. Marcus! That name struck a memory. Father had often spoken of a Marcus. Royce ran the words of the man back through his mind. Had the shopkeeper been part of a setup, a trap to get him to come to his father's aide? If so, he had taken the bait. Well, he was here now. What was he to do? They had come this far and had not been discovered *yet*; they were too close to their father to turn back now!

He waited for another minute; all was quiet so he continued. The old shakes on the roof rattled under his feet. It was difficult to be as quiet as he needed to. He reached the corner and started across the other roof. A couple of steps out, he had a real problem. This roof pitch was much steeper than the first. Because of the slope and the fact that the fog had caused a heavy dew to collect on the wooden shakes, his boots no longer had the traction that he needed. He was slipping. Down the slope he was sliding. He put his hands and his knees down to try to gain a little more traction, it helped a little, but not enough. Digging his fingernails in to try to stop himself, still he slid. He was going to slide off the edge of the roof, slowly but surely—slide off the roof! He glanced behind him; it was a good twenty feet to the ground, too far to fall and not acquire some serious injury. Scratching and clawing he tried to get some kind of grip. It was too slippery. Closer to the edge he slipped. Suddenly, he heard a sound—a sound he knew well. Twang—it was the sound of an arrow embedding into the wooden shakes. Someone was shooting arrows at him! Some one was trying to kill him!

Cloud of Fire

The arrow hit just below his right foot and buried deep into the shake. Not only did he have to worry about falling off of the roof, now he also had to deal with someone trying to kill him. He tried to see where the arrow had come from; he saw no guard, no soldier, no one anywhere in the dim torch light! He slid down until his foot rested on top of the arrow. It gave just enough resistance to stop him from sliding any farther down the slope. Then he heard the sound again. Another arrow buried into the shake a few feet to the right of the first. Royce thought he was a sitting duck out here on the roof with no defense. Again, he tried to see where the shots were coming from. Then another arrow buried into the roof a couple of feet farther over from the second one.

"Luckily for me, this guy is a terrible shot!" he thought out loud.

Then still another arrow stuck into the roof yet farther over from the last. Only then did he look behind him far enough to see Wyn standing, still on the top of the wall, aiming her bow at him. His first thought was, *What is she doing? She is trying to kill me.* Then he realized she was supplying the arrows to keep him from sliding off the roof. She was creating steppingstones up the steep slope of the roof. Feeling very foolish, he gave Wyn a grateful nod. Shifting his weight from one arrow to another, he made his way safely across the roof. He waited for the next one. Thud, another arrow embedded itself into the roof not far from his face. That one was too close! He gave her a look that would let her know it. She replied by motioning him to look up. The shutter that hung open was directly above him. He now used that last arrow that had once angered him, to propel himself to the base of the windowsill. He pulled himself up and through the open window. He hoped the room was empty—it was. He took a moment to collect his wits, grateful for the flat, level surface.

Wyn waited at the door for Royce to unlock it. When she

heard the sound of the latch being undone, the thought that it might be someone else caused her to hide in the shadows.

The door opened, it was Royce. He whispered, "Wyn?"

"Here," she answered.

"That was awesome! I thought you were trying to kill me! I love the way your mind works," Royce praised.

"Thanks…I think. Unfortunately, I only have three arrows left."

"It will be enough!" he assured. "Come on."

Once inside, they found a lighted torch, removed it from its perch, crossed the room, and climbed the winding stairs up into the east tower. As they neared the top, Royce stopped. In front of a heavy wooden door was the jailor. He was sitting on a bench. His back was against the wall with his feet sprawled halfway across the hallway. The two children eased up the rest of the steps, tip-toed across the room and stood on each side of the sleeping man. Wyn set an arrow on the string of the bow and tightened the string. When she was ready, she gave him a nod. Royce grabbed the sword from the man's scabbard and quickly pitched it down the stairwell. The noise startled the jailor. He jumped as he tried to figure what was going on.

"Don't move!" Royce spoke as loud, deep and as rough as he could make his voice.

The jailor was not impressed. He lunged for Royce. Wyn instantly released the bow. The arrow pierced through the sleeve of his heavy mantle, pinning his right hand to the back of the bench. Wyn, with the speed of lightning pulled another arrow from the quiver and reloaded the bow.

"I don't want to hurt you. Now, just sit still!" Wyn demanded.

"Well, you're going to have to hurt me, you little tart." The jailor reached down with his left hand and began to pull a dagger from a sheath that was strapped to his leg below the knee. In the dim light, Royce had not seen that he had another weapon. As he brought the short knife up, Wyn fired her bow again. This time the arrow pierced the mantle of his left sleeve, pinning his left arm to the seat of the bench.

He dropped the dagger and hollered, "You got me with that one!"

"Please, don't do that again! This arrow will not be through your sleeve." In a fraction of a second, Wyn had loaded her last arrow, only then realizing what she would have to do if the jailor did not obey.

"I would do what she says. I have never seen her miss!" Royce said to the man calmly.

Wyn still held the bow tightly, the arrow pointed at his chest. At this, the jailor decided to stay put. She was greatly relieved.

"Keep him there. I'm going after Father." When Royce was sure that they would have no more trouble out of him, he picked up the dagger. He crossed the room, unlatched the cell door and labored to push it open.

Spencer had been listening to the scuffle from behind the solid wood door and knew something was not normal. Still, he was unprepared to see his own son standing there when the door opened. "Royce?" Spencer Windmere jumped to his feet; a renewed strength filled him despite the weakness the hunger had caused.

"Father!"

"Royce!" He grabbed his son and hugged him. "I thought I had lost you!"

"Father, we thought we had lost you too!" Royce hugged his father as he had never hugged him before. "But we have to go now and we must hurry!"

He pulled loose from his father's hug and ran for the door. Spencer was thoroughly confused, but he followed. Outside the cell door he was in for another shock. There was the jailor, a man of forty, trained to be a soldier, being held at bay by Wyn, his daughter of thirteen. She had not moved a muscle, but still held the arrow trained at his chest.

"Wyn? You're alive!" He would have hugged her too, but then he realized what she was doing.

While his father freed the man by working the arrows out of the back and the seat of the bench, Royce collected them and put them back in Wyn's quiver.

Wyn then saw a little spot of blood on the jailor's sleeve. "Oh, dear, sir, you're bleeding pretty badly! I am very sorry about that!"

Spencer checked the man's arm. "Don't worry, Wyn, it is just a scratch. He will be fine."

"I guess she does miss every now and then," Royce said to the jailor.

He gave him a snide grunt as they shuffled him into the cell and bolted the door. Once the door was locked, Wyn lowered the bow and removed the arrow.

"Oh, Gwendolyn, you are becoming just like your mother!" Spencer cried. The weapon was put to the side and he gave his daughter a hug. Then he turned on the both of them. "Now, what in under the sun are you doing here? It is not safe here! You were supposed to be at the chalet! And where's Keli?"

"She's fine! She is waiting for us outside!"

At that point the jailor began hollering for help out the tiny cell window. It would not take him long to wake the whole castle.

"We must go now, before he tells the rest of the castle we're here!" Royce urged and started for the stairs.

"You got all the way up *here* and the only one that knows you're here is the jailor?"

"Well, not the only one. There are a few guards that may have a pretty good idea that something's up."

"What did you do, *fly* in?" Spencer said with much more truth than he realized.

They bounded down the stairs as quickly as they could go. Spencer picked up the jailor's sword as he went. At the bottom, Royce ran smack into someone. He bounced back and fell to the floor. The man took the bump as a stone wall. He did not move, but he *was* a bit surprised. He, brawny and muscular, made Royce look like a sapling.

"What?" The man was not sure what had bounced off of him, but the first person he saw was Spencer. "Spencer! What are you doing?"

"Marcus! You gave me a scare. I thought you were one of the guards!" Spencer already had the sword up in front of him before he recognized his old friend. "I am getting out of here!" He lowered the weapon.

"Who are these children?"

"They are mine, Royce and Wyn."

"Oh, no! Oh, dear! This is not good! Spencer, they should not have come here! This is just what Devlin wanted."

"I know. That's why I am getting them out of here, *now*!"

"How? If Devlin catches them, they too will be in grave danger!" Marcus spied nervously out the open window. "Even if you do get out of the castle, Devlin will just have you arrested again."

"I have something for Devlin!" Royce remembered the orders from the king, and he pulled them from his cloak.

"What?" His father looked confused.

"I have here a signed order from the king for your release, Father," Royce had been waiting all night to say that.

"What?" his father repeated.

"It is true, Father," Wyn added.

"You have been to see the king?" Spencer questioned in amazement. "Where is Sherwin?"

"He is safe," Wyn assured him, "safe with the king. Father, we know who Sherwin is."

A wave of relief crossed over Spencer as he realized what she was saying. "Thank the Father above."

Marcus took the package from Royce and looked it over. "This *is* the king's seal! You *have* been to the palace!"

"That is a stay of execution and a full pardon. Open it and see," Royce told Marcus.

"Son, you don't understand. This packet is addressed to Devlin. I have no authority to open a sealed letter from the king. I could lose my life." He looked worried. "The *only* one here that has the authority to open this...is Devlin."

They looked at each other grimly; they all knew what this would mean. Royce had not thought this through. In his haste, the king had addressed the stay of execution to Devlin. No one else could legally open the order. If that was so, what good had he accomplished? Devlin would just delay opening the letter and act as if he received it too late, or not at all, and their efforts would be wasted. Royce knew there was only one thing to do, get out and get out quick. "Father, we have to get you out of here!"

Marcus apparently agreed, "There is only one way out of the castle and that's the front gate."

This was true. Sneaking into the castle would have been extremely hard, if not impossible, had they not had the help of Shira. There were no secret, underground passages. Castle Delthyna was on an island of rock at the edge of the Lake Elipse. The designers had built a stone bridge that stretched almost from the mainland to the castle gate. The last section of the crossover was a drawbridge. When pulled up, it formed an impenetrable gate on the front of the castle and a huge gap in the roadway. This bridge was always drawn up at sunset and lowered after sunrise.

Marcus continued, "I can help you down the back stairs, but I don't know how we will ever get through the main gate without being…"

"No!" Royce hollered. "We have to go up! To the top of the wall!"

"What?" Marcus questioned. "That's no good. That is going to lead you farther away from…"

"No! We got in undetected. We can get out the same way," Royce insisted.

"Just how *did* you get in here, son? How did you get past the guards without sounding the alarm?"

Royce did not want to speak of Shira in front of Marcus. "From the top of the wall."

"You scaled the wall? That's seventy spans, child. You're talking mad!" Marcus was not helping.

"Son, if Devlin catches us it is over," Spencer added.

"Trust me."

"Son, I…"

"Father, you will just have to trust *me* this time. We have a plan."

"It is true Father, we must hurry!" Wyn urged.

His father looked at his son sternly. "Okay. Royce. you keep that letter. We may still need it yet." He waited for him to tuck it away. "Let's go."

Marcus smiled weakly. "Very well. God speed my friend!"

The two men hugged briefly and the Windmeres headed out the door to the castle wall.

The jailor's wailing had not gone unheeded, for outside the door a man confronted them with a sword drawn. It was Devlin. He was a tall thin man, dressed all in black except for a breastplate of chain woven armor that was polished to a shine.

As quick as lightning Spencer brandished the jailor's sword, bringing it up to the ready, he stepped in front of his children. Royce did likewise stepping to the right of his father. Wyn readied the bow and stood on her father's left.

"One side, Devlin, you traitorous snake," Spencer ordered.

"Where are you going, Spencer?" Devlin had a soft, but deep voice. He spoke slowly and precisely, and he emphasized the end of Spencer's name, obviously showing his disdain for him. "Checking out so soon?"

"Step aside, Devlin. I am taking these children to safety." Spencer, on the other hand spoke with a voice of determination, without fear, as one in authority.

"But you haven't allowed me to fulfill the king's order yet," Devlin said coolly. "Spence, I don't want to fight you."

"No, you don't. You would lose. I was once an Elite, remember."

"Ha!" he tried to laugh it away. "I will make a deal with you. Tell me where the other child is and you can go free."

"Not going to happen, Devlin."

"Don't be a fool, Spence, I'm offering you your freedom. Take it!"

"In case you haven't noticed, I'm no longer your prisoner."

"Free? Huh! You're not going anywhere." He looked at Royce who held his sword at the ready.

At that point Spencer lunged forward. The swords clashed again and again. Only to be seen was the reflection of the torch light on the polished surfaces of the blades. Their father attacked with such force, Devlin could only retreat backward in defense. One particular hard blow sent Devlin reeling back onto the stone surface.

"You're out of shape, old man," Spencer commented. To see the two together, one would think Devlin had to be twenty years older, but in reality they were almost the same age.

Devlin chuckled, and then hollered an order at the top of his lungs. Soldiers began to appear from several directions at the same time. It was as if they had been on stand by, waiting for the order to be given. It was true, the whole thing had been a setup, a trick, a lure, and he had fallen for it. He had brought the whole family right to Devlin; Father had been the bait. And now, Royce had sprung Devlin's trap.

Spencer backed up to stand with his children, sword still in his hand. The men were coming at them from each end of the wall and coming up the stairs that led to the lower court. There was no escape. When the soldiers saw the children, they hesitated. They seemed puzzled. *This* was the threat to the kingdom, two children?

Devlin got up off the floor and dusted himself off. He began to laugh. "Spencer, you had your chance. Poor, foolish Spence, did you think you were free?"

One of the soldiers recognized Royce and started shouting, "Stay back! He's the one! He's the boy with the sword, the one from the bridge!"

Another soldier agreed with the first. "It *is* him."

Royce did not know what that meant. He had heard nothing of the tales the highwaymen had brought back to Devlin.

"So, is this the little sorcerer?" Devlin smirked. "Let's see some magic, little sorcerer.

Royce said nothing. He just stared at him, his anger burning within.

"What's wrong? Your fire gone out?"

Royce put two and two together. A thought came to him on a whim and he decided to use it.

"Royce, don't!" said Spencer. Royce had stepped out and around his father.

"How do you think I got in here, Devlin?"

"What?" Devlin looked uneasy. Spencer looked puzzled.

"Check the gate. It has not been opened. Where are your trusted sentries? Where are your trusted guards? Ask them."

Devlin was quite uncomfortable now. Could it be that he was just as superstitious as his men?

"Brave little sorcerer," Devlin mocked. "Let's see some fire, little sorcerer!"

"Fire?" Royce questioned rather loudly. "You want fire?"

Royce took another step forward and raised his sword into the air, acting as if he was staring at it. The men that had recognized him started backing away. Many of those who had not, began to follow their lead and did also. Devlin looked uneasily at his men.

"You cowards, it's just a boy!" Devlin derided his men.

"Son, what are you doing?" Spencer whispered, barely moving his lips.

"Devlin has asked for fire," Royce said with a grin. "I think we can give him some fire."

Royce stalled for just a moment longer. Actually he had not been looking at his sword, he was looking past it. For he and he alone had noticed Shira and Keli easing forward on the roof just above and behind the group of soldiers. The two were only just visible in the dim torch light and the thick haze.

Suddenly, Spencer also caught sight of the dragon. He dropped his sword to his side and backed up. A look of terror swept over his face.

This completely disquieted Devlin. He looked at Spencer in dismay.

Unless Keli understood what Royce wanted her to do, this was going to make him look as if he was completely out his mind. He hoped she did and that he was not.

Keli made a motion with her hand. The dragon and the little girl lifted off. The crowd of men felt the whoosh of wind that was forced down upon them. They turned to look, but they saw nothing. Fear gripped their hearts.

Royce brought his sword down. "Now, Shira! Now!"

At that very moment, Shira released a ball of fire that lit the whole cloud of mist above the castle.

She flew far over their heads, unseen because of the fog, but the fire's eerie glow was brilliant. For a few short seconds it illuminated the entire castle, walls, arches, spires, and all. Devlin stared up in amazement.

Spencer looked at his son in extreme anxiety. "Son?"

"Yes, Father! Here comes the plan now!" Royce motioned up toward the sky.

Devlin ordered the soldiers to seize the man and his children, but the men hesitated. Murmurs were heard amongst the armed fighters about fire, scorched clothes, and singed beards. Devlin shouted the order again, much louder this time.

As he did, a ball of fire lit the whole inner court of the castle as bright day. This time it was not up in the sky, it was right down among the whole group of men. The soldiers scrambled in every direction. The skilled men had been trained in every type of battle known of the day, but none of them had been prepared for this. All they could do was recoil from the dragon's vicious attack. Some attempted to protect themselves from the intense heat by hiding behind their shields. Nevertheless, the flame was more than they could stand. They withdrew. Shira just missed Spencer's head by a few spans as she flew over; she turned and blasted another flame at the men advancing from the other wall. They too could do nothing but retreat. One more blast and the whole of the army were running for their lives. The dragon had just cleared the entire hoard in less than half a minute. Even Devlin scrambled to get away from the huge beast. Shira settled precariously on the narrow wall.

"Father!" Keli hollered from the back of Shira.

"Oh, my... my daughter's on a...!" Spencer was completely amazed at what he was seeing, his youngest child sitting on the back of a ferocious dragon. He stared, almost in a state of shock.

"Hurry Father, mount up! We haven't much time," Royce

said urgently. "Before the soldiers come back. They will not stay away long."

Spencer stared at the huge animal, not believing what he was seeing. Royce helped Wyn up onto the back of the dragon from the tail, for there was not room for her to lower her head onto the narrow walkway. Then he climbed aboard.

"Don't let them get away! Attack! Attack!" Devlin was hollering orders, though he had placed himself safely out of danger.

The soldiers regrouped once the flame died, for there was nothing combustible for it to continue, all was made of stone.

The men continued to advance on Spencer and the children slowly, for they were not sure of what to expect.

"They are coming again!" Keli cried aloud. "We must go now!"

Shira, upon hearing this, stretched her wings wide, knocking a couple more men over the edge of the wall in the process.

"Father, get on!" Wyn cried. "Get on!"

Shira started her wings in motion to lift off. Spencer, realizing his children were leaving on the back of the dragon, and he was about to be left, had to make a quick decision. Climb on with his children on a fearsome looking beast that could devour him in one bite or be left to stay with Devlin and deal with his subordinates. He chose the dragon. Throwing himself onto Shira's tail, he wrapped his arms around and held on with all his might.

"Keli, can she carry us all?" Royce hollered. "Father is much bigger than Sherwin!"

"Now is a fine time to ask that!" Wyn hollered.

"I don't KNOOOWWW!"

As Keli answered, Shira threw herself over the wall and nosed straight down. Several screams were heard from the four riders, including Spencer. Using gravity as a source of acceleration, she pulled out of the power dive just in time to skim across the water's surface. Royce's stomach was in the back of his throat. Keli squealed out with laughter. Wyn looked as if she was going to be sick; her face was as white as a sheet. Spencer had not moved. He had a death grip on Shira's tail. He was being given a wild ride as Shira mindlessly swung her pointy tail back and forth as she flew.

"Father, climb up here on the back!" Royce had to holler to overcome the wind in his ears.

Spencer did not dare move.

"Let go and climb up here!" he urged his father.

"Let go!" Spencer cried. "Are you mad?"

As they flew from the castle, the morning light was beginning to glow red, orange, and purple in the eastern sky. Soon she began to gain altitude, rising up out of the fog, her huge wings flapping mightily. In the distance, one could still see the ensign hanging from the pole above the tallest spire of the Castle Delthyna. Dangling from the pole was Jake the guard, clinging to it for dear life.

Seize Him!

A ll was quiet when Devlin entered the king's palace by noon the following day. He had ridden hard to get from Delthyna Castle to the king' palace in what would have been record time, unless you count travel on the back of a dragon. Devlin was desperate, but these were times that called for desperate measures. He demanded that the attendant see to his horse immediately as he dismounted in front of the palace in the outer courtyard. He hurried up the steps and into the front entry. Abes met him just inside the door and greeted him in his normal somber manner.

"I must see King Robinson immediately!" Devlin began to pace back and forth. "It is a matter of utmost consequence."

"I will announce you at once, Sir." Abes dipped his chin slightly and turned to go. "Wait here please."

Presently, he returned to a very impatient Devlin.

"King Robinson will see you in the royal governing chamber."

Devlin started to walk by Abes when he stepped in front him. "Forgetting something are we?" the old butler said.

Devlin stared angrily at Abes. "I think I shall keep it this time!"

"Palace policy has not changed, Sir."

Two of the door guards began to walk towards them.

"Alright! Here!" He handed his sword over to the two guards.

"This way, Sir." Abes began to show him to the chamber.

"I know where it is! One side, old man!" Devlin grumbled.

He stormed up the steps and down the hall, bursting into the room where the king awaited him. The king was seated behind an elegant table that was placed back just slightly from the center of the chamber.

"Devlin, my trusted advisor, enter. I really was thinking I would not see you for some time."

"Your Majesty! I bring news of a very serious nature."

"You have found Edwin?"

"No, Sire." Devlin wanted to avoid that topic. "There is a new threat to your realm. A matter that must be attended to immediately! There is a dragon in our kingdom, on our own soil!"

"A dragon, Devlin?"

"Yes, Your Majesty! A dragon! An ugly, ferocious creature, enormous in size! This beast will do irreparable damage to your kingdom! I purpose that…"

"Have you seen…this…this dragon?"

"Yes, Sire, it attacked the Castle Delthyna early this morning."

"Did it, now?" the king spoke calmly. "I have never heard of a dragon of such behavior. Such creatures usually avoid men at all costs. Why would it do that?"

"I cannot say, Your Majesty, but it must be hunted down and destroyed. It wreaked havoc on the castle! Nearly wiped out the entire guard patrol!"

"Kill them?" the king inquired. "How many?"

"Well, I haven't accounted for everyone yet. But…" Devlin was sure the king did not believe him. "Sire! We must give this matter our immediate attention! We need to pursue…"

"Devlin… you have been my advisor for many years. I have always listened to what you had to say because I trusted you. You proved yourself to be very reliable and trustworthy over the years past. I have treated you well, have I not?"

"Yes, Sire, you have."

"Then why do you come to me with such a fool hardy story, thinking I would believe it?"

"Sire, I…"

"Devlin, I haven't time for such wild tales! At the present, I have much more pressing concerns! … I agree with you, Devlin. There is a new threat to the kingdom. It is just as you said. There is a creature that can do irreparable damage to my realm."

"Exactly, Sire!"

"But it is not a dragon." The king told Devlin to sit, and then he continued, "You tell me you caught the one that abducted Edwin?"

"Yes, the black heart!"

Have you taken care of him then?"

"Yes, Your Majesty. I…"

"That's funny. I heard that you let him escape," the king's speech slowed and his face went extremely serious.

"Es...escape?" Devlin's words faltered and his face paled.

"Yes, escape. I am told that you allowed him to get away." The king stared hard at his trusted advisor.

"Where... Who told you this, Sire?"

"The black heart himself. In fact, he is here in the palace as we speak."

"So you have him in custody?" Devlin's voice trembled slightly.

"You could say that," the king smiled.

"Good work, Sire." Devlin flattered.

"Hello, Devlin." the voice was Spencer's. He had entered the room behind Devlin, along with several armed castle guards.

Devlin whirled around. "Good work, Sire! Now we will find out where your Edwin is!"

"Where Edwin is? He perished in a fire at the old chalet. Or have you forgotten what you told me?" the king demanded.

"Turn him over to me and I will get the truth out of him!"

"I have already saved you the trouble," the king's voice suddenly became very solemn.

"Sire. I..."

"Devlin, do you recognize this man?"

"Yes! ... Yes, this is the man who took the boy! We have the evidence! We found Edwin's things in his house!"

Edwin stepped through a door directly behind where the king was seated. If it were possible for a man to turn as white as flour, he did it.

"Devlin, what is his name?" the king asked sternly.

Devlin was ghostly silent.

The king turned to his faithful servant, "Abes, bring out the rest of the children."

Royce, Wyn, and Keli stepped through the same door that Edwin had.

The king turned back to Devlin. "What about these three children? Do you recognize *them*?"

Devlin still did not say anything. Perspiration appeared on his face as he slowly began to shake his head no.

"SEIZE HIM!" the king ordered.

Devlin panicked. He ran across the room. The sound of shattering glass filled the chamber as colorful shards scattered in all directions. He disappeared out and down to the courtyard below.

Spencer, Royce, and several of the guards ran to the window, half expecting to see Devlin lying dead on the cobble pavement. That is not what they saw. Unbelievably, he had escaped serious injury. He ran with only a slight limp across the yard. Attacking an unsuspecting rider that had just entered the court, he pulled the man off his horse, took his animal, mounted up, and spurred it on through the gates before anyone could think to close them.

"Detain him!" a guard hollered down from the window to some of his comrades in the courtyard below. Urgently, they mounted up and rode after him. The criminal had a good head start as he led them through the village and out across the farming plain. Over the rise, he disappeared like a fox on the run, from the hounds on the hunt.

Sadly, the guards watching from the window turned back to the king. "Sire, it looks as if he got away."

"I want him arrested! Not a man in this kingdom will rest until we have him in chains! Put every highwayman, every guard, and every soldier on it! Where are the Elite?"

"Sire," Keli said. "You will not have to do that." She was smiling from ear to ear.

"Why not, Keli?" The king looked at her peculiarly.

"Look!" The ten-year-old girl pointed out of the broken window.

Every eye saw it at the same time, a speck in the morning sky. It was the shape of a dragon rising up from a cornfield, flapping her mighty wings in flight, growing ever larger. As it came closer, they could see that she was carrying something. In her claws, Devlin dangled, hanging by one leg. As she neared the castle, they heard screaming. He was squirming as an animal picked up from the ground by a bird of prey.

Never Again!

By the king's order, the guards rushed out to attend the returning Devlin, though they would be very wary of Shira once she arrived. Nevertheless, they went. The rest stood watching through the broken window as Shira approached the castle, all that is, except the king. He just sat at the table staring at the three Windmere children. For the longest time, he did not say any thing, only stared. Finally he seemed to gather his thoughts.

"So, these are Alaina's children?" the king slowly asked.

"Yes," Spencer answered.

When Keli heard the king speak of her mother she turned to him. "Sire, did you know our mother?"

The king laughed out big and hardy, but as he looked at Keli, who thought he was acting strange, his smile faded. Sadness came over him like a dark cloud covering the blue sky. "Child...that is about the saddest thing I have ever heard. ... Spencer, do they not know? ... Did you never...tell them?"

Spencer Windmere walked over to the table and took a seat in one of the chairs placed at the side of the table. "Sire, the last time we spoke, do you remember what you said to Alaina and me?"

The king nodded his head, but did not speak. A severe pain shot through his heart as he remembered. It was not a physical pain, but that of heartbreak. His mind began to spin, his memories flooded to nineteen years earlier...

***

...It was the same room. It was the same table. It was the same man seated at the same table, but he was much younger. Very little gray was in his hair and far less wrinkles had encroached upon his face. His left hand held some documents as his right held a quill, he was writing in a book that lay open before him. He did not look up when a beautiful young woman entered the chamber, nor did he when she approached his table, but he purposely continued to study the parchments, ignoring her.

The young lady's eyes, and her nose, were a perfect replica of Keli's, her chin and cheeks pronounced and slender, the same as Royce's. Her hair, dark and flowing over her shoulders, waved gently as she crossed the floor. It was the precise color of Wyn's. She walked straight up in front of the king and waited. When the man did not acknowledge her, she spoke.

"Father."

"Whatever it is, it can wait!" he snapped angrily.

"Father, this is what you said yesterday, and the day before! It can not wait any longer."

The man said nothing.

"Father, we want your blessing! We need your blessing!" The woman's eyes were red and teary.

"I'll not give it!" He hit his fist down hard against the table and slammed the book shut. "My daughter will never marry a commoner! A... A peasant! Of all the young gentlemen in the kingdom, all the lord's and lady's sons, *this* is the man? Alaina, you could have had any man you chose!"

"Spencer *is* the man I have chosen! Why can you not accept that?"

The king glared hard at a young man of twenty that had appeared in the doorway. "Daughter, you shame yourself... and me!" Anger flashed in his eyes. "What kind of life do you think he can give you?" he asked angrily, motioning in the young man's direction.

"A lifetime of love and happiness! A life where one truly cares for another. Where one does not look down upon another because he has or has not... money! Away from all this hatred and bitterness! Away from all this loneliness! I love him... and he loves me!"

"Hah! That will put food on your table!"

The young man mustered up enough courage to speak, but he did not approach the king's table. "I do not have a lot, but what I have will be hers. I love her! And she loves me! I do fear you have no knowledge of what that is. We *will* be together and *will* be married, with or without your consent."

In a fit of rage the king hammered both fists down on the table and stood. "Get out! Get out now!"

"If he leaves, I leave!" Thinking only with her heart, the beautiful young woman had proclaimed her ultimatum, but she was not sorry nor would she ever be. It only pained her that her father did not approve.

The king stiffened. "If you go, you will be my daughter no more!"

"Father, don't do this," she said, backing away.

"Aliana!" The king trembled as the anger built up as a cauldron about to boil over. "If you leave, don't ever come back." The king stared into his daughter's eyes.

The woman backed to the door, tears were streaming down her face. "I'm sorry Father. I love you. I always will. But I love Spencer and I am going to be his wife."

The king was so angry his fist tightened and his knuckles paled as he watched his daughter and the man join hands. They both looked back at him only once. With a sad expression, an expression of pity, not of anger or malice, they were gone.

"You will never see my face again! Do you hear?" he shouted after them. "Never again!" ...

***

... The old King Robinson now sat in the same chair at the same table. It was the same king, but not the same man. With a lost look on his face, he stared straight ahead.

"Yes, I know exactly what I said. Little did I know that those words would be fulfilled precisely." The king stared blankly. "I never saw her again."

"She loved you. She always did. ... She never stopped." Spencer tried to comfort the grieving old man.

"Her mother never regarded me the same again." The king wiped his eye. "She did not live long after that, after I said that to Alaina. I suppose she lived maybe two years after. I think she died of a broken heart, a heart I broke!"

There was a long awkward silence before he spoke again.

"Spencer, tell me, I pray you, what happened to Aliana?"

"Do you not know?"

"At the time I refused to hear it, but..." The king took a deep breath. "Now, I need to know."

Spencer also took a deep breath. This was going to be hard for him. "A year ago June... when the skirmish broke out between Arielana and the Norgerbecs, do you remember?"

The king nodded slightly.

"You sent a delegation by ship to Norgerby to ensue for peace. When Alaina heard that you refused to go, she attached herself to that delegation."

"That was not her place!" the king said indignantly.

"No, Sire… it was yours," Spencer said calmly.

The king withheld his reply, though he was quite angry.

"She may have been no longer your daughter, but you were always her father. I heard that she was instrumental in achieving a settlement." Spencer paused for a long moment before he continued. "On the return voyage, her ship… never made the voyage back across the Alasheron Sea.

"Dear God, have mercy on my soul!"

The children, hearing the retelling of this heartbreaking story, were all in tears, even Edwin. They all slowly edged closer to the table.

After hearing this, the king's eyes were red with tears. "Spencer, you have every right to be angry at me."

"I am not angry… I have a good life. So did Alaina."

"And I… I have had… I lost my daughter! I lost my wife. I lost out on my grandchildren! And I lost my self-respect! Only in the last few years have I begun to understand."

"Understand?" Spencer questioned.

"Yes, understand what love Alaina must have for you."

"How could you…?"

"Clarice is not of royal blood." The king's face softened a little. "She was a peasant! She was working in a cabbage field the very first time I saw her! For ten years after Gwenn died I sank to the depths of despair. I was miserable and bitter. I was angry with her for dying, angry with Alaina for leaving, and with you for taking her! Oh, was I angry with you! I was angry at the world. But mostly I was angry with myself! It was not until I met Clarice that… well, she helped me to see that I have been wrong. We have been married five years. And now, I know some of what you must have felt for Alaina."

The king looked up. Royce, Wyn and Keli were staring at him in complete dismay.

"So, Sher… Edwin is…" Wyn began to say.

"My stepson," the king finished for her. "If I had only known Alaina had had children, I would have…!"

"I would have sent you word if I had only known that you…" Spencer defended.

"Was a fool!" the king burst out. "My grandchildren stand here before me nearly grown and I never knew them! And they don't know me!"

"Grandchildren?" Wyn's mouth dropped open as the thought finally sank in and landed on her heart. She lowered down into a chair. Reality hit them like a boulder. Royce and Keli looked at each other stunned, finally realizing who they really are.

"Yes, grandchildren, I…I am your grandfather." The old man rose up and rounded the table. He knelt down in front of the three. His eyes were full of pain and joy at the same time, glistening with tears. Looking from one to another of his grandchildren, he said, "Can you find it in your hearts to forgive a stupid, selfish, old man?"

The king stared at Royce, most likely expecting him to speak for the three, he being the oldest. Royce's mind was racing with every imaginable thought, but his tongue was completely empty. He looked at Keli first. She was smiling, being her happy, normal self. Then he looked at Wyn. She was still confused and bewildered. She shrugged her shoulders. Royce looked back to the king, still not sure what to say, but some words did find their way to his lips.

"We never… We could… I don't …"

The king looked a little puzzled.

Wyn tried to help. "It is difficult for us to forgive when we never knew we had been wronged to begin with."

"I'll understand if you hate me," the king said sadly

"We don't hate you," Wyn said slowly. "We don't know you."

"But we would like to. You seem really nice!" Keli added.

"And I want to get to know you too!" the king cried.

He reached out, desperately wanting to give them all a hug. Royce was not sure what to do. He felt very strange. To think, all these years, he was the grandson of the king and never knew it! The look on Wyn's face told him that she felt just as awkward.

"You do know what this means, don't you?" The king now had a twinkle in his eye from more than just the tears.

"What?" Wyn wondered.

"I know!" Keli grinned from ear to ear.

"What do you know, Kelina?" He leaned closer.

"I am a princess!" she squealed.

"Right you are, Kelina!" The king turned to Wyn with a smile. "And so are you, my dear Gwendolyn."

Wyn and Keli stared at the king in amazement. "How would you know our true names?"

"Believe it or not, I knew my daughter well enough to know one thing. Those were her favorite names. They were also the names of her mother and her grandmother. Gwendolyn was my first queen and Kelina was her mother's name."

Then he turned to Royce. "And you, my boy, this means… you are the next heir to the throne, you will be the next king of Arielana."

Royce could not believe what he was hearing. This frightened him. "Me! But what about Edwin?"

"Edwin is the son of Clarice, but not my son. Edwin was five when we were married. You are the heir, my grandson by blood, the rightful heir to the throne."

"But Devlin chased us over the whole country trying to get Sherwin, I mean… Edwin." Royce was sure he had figured it right.

"Yes, Royce, he was," Spencer interjected. "Edwin was the only one who knew what Devlin really was and he could put a stop to him by telling the king. But Devlin was also after you… you and your sisters. He knew who you were. He knew you were the heirs. So he went after you also. When he attacked the inn, he was looking for Edwin, but he was after you as well. He chased you over the whole country. And every time, you slipped right through his fingers."

"It was fate," the king added.

"You did everything that I asked you to. Even greater than I thought possible." Spencer said.

"But what good would it have done Devlin to get rid of us?" Wyn asked.

"Sadly, Devlin is my second cousin. He is my closest living relative. With no heir to precede me, he would have been next in line to receive the crown. The records would have confirmed it. So he tried to do away with the three of you. But you outsmarted him!"

"You knew," Royce's mind was racing as he searched his fathers face. "All these years, you knew and you never told us? Mother was the king's daughter and you never told us?"

"Knowing the truth would have served you no purpose. It would have just caused bitterness. We told you what you needed to know, your mother and I. That is what has made you who you are today."

"And who am I?"

"You are the same Royce Windmere that you have always

been, you are my son and I am very proud of you. You just happen to be the one and only grandson of the king." He hugged his son. "And you!" He then pulled Wyn into the embrace. "You and Keli are the king's only two granddaughters!" Looking for Keli he pulled her in, adding her to the group too.

Presently, Keli pulled loose from the group, extended her hand to the king and pulled him into the cluster also.

He began to sob.

There was a sound of someone clearing his throat.

The king looked up. "Oh, dear!" The king pulled loose and straightened himself. "Announce yourself when you enter a room, Abes!"

"Very sorry, Sire," the butler said uncomfortably. "Shall I go out and come back in again?"

"Oh, no. Never mind, what is it?"

"I interrupted to let you know that they have Devlin, Sire."

"Good! Where?"

"In the main courtyard, Sire."

"I will be there at once!"

The king straightened up, adjusted his robe and left the chamber wiping his eyes in the process. Royce, Wyn, and Keli ran for the balcony to see what was to become of Devlin. Shira had dropped him in the outer court where several soldiers had been waiting and then she had lifted off, coming to rest on the balcony. She was waiting for them when they got there.

An Abundant Friend

Unhand me, you barbarians!" Devlin struggled to free himself from the clutches of two rather large soldiers who kept him anchored to the spot. "I give the orders around here!"

"Sorry, Devlin, you did—not any more," one soldier of some rank spoke, facing the besieged man. "The king does not like the orders you have been giving." Several of the soldiers laughed out.

"He'll be giving his own orders from now on," another soldier said.

Several more laughs were heard. Then suddenly, all quieted rather abruptly, for the king had stepped out of the arched double-door entry. He made his way down the steps, across the courtyard and up to Devlin.

"Devlin Rekaso, you are charged with high treason against the country of Arielana, the attempted kidnapping of a royal member of the king's family, the attempted murder of one Spencer Windmere by deception and the attempted murder of my three grandchildren! How do you plead?"

When the king said the word 'grandchildren', a murmur shot through the crowd.

"I did what I did for the country of Arielana!"

"You did what you did for Devlin!" he spoke slowly and steadily, the anger still obvious in his voice. "I trusted you, Devlin! You could have had anything you wanted, up to the half of the kingdom. You knew the three Windmere children were my grandchildren and yet you tried to destroy them. Why?"

"You are weak old man! This country has no place for a weak king."

The king turned to the head officer. "Permit him to speak no more. He will have his chance at the trial."

"Robinson!" Devlin shouted "This is not..." He stopped in mid-sentence when the officer touched him with the end of his spear.

"What you have mistaken for weakness was mercy!

Something you will see very little of from here on!" King Robinson turned to the officer. "Take him away! Lock him up, and I want you to treat him in exactly the same manner that he had you treat Spencer Windmere!" The king turned to the head officer again. "Is that understood?"

"Yes, Sire, completely!" The officer nodded.

"That is my final word!" With that, he turned and swept back into the palace.

***

"What shall we do now?" Wyn asked her brother and sister, when the commotion died down in the outer court.

"What do you mean?" asked Keli. She had crawled up on Shira. Shira turned and nudged her and she rubbed her on top of the head. "I just want to go home!"

"Do you think the king will allow us to?" Royce wondered out loud.

"Why would we want to? Don't you see, we could have anything we ever wanted right here!" Wyn eyes lighted. "We are the king's grandchildren. We are princesses. We could have the most excellent dresses, eat the best food, and wear the finest jewelry."

"What?" Keli asked.

"We would have servants to do our bidding. No more chores! No more cooking for strangers and cleaning up after them. We would not have to want for anything!"

"Really?" Keli asked suspiciously.

"Yes, and we could live in this beautiful castle in safety and do whatever we wanted!" Wyn would have continued, but the sad look of Royce and Keli caused her to stop.

Royce listened with mixed emotions. Was this Wyn, his sister, saying all these things?

"Live in the *castle*?" Keli questioned.

"Yes!" interrupted Edwin, as he appeared on the balcony. "And be told what you can eat and what you cannot eat, what you can wear and what you cannot! And you will be told where you will go and when you will go there! You will be told whom you can talk to and whom you can play with! You will see your old friends no more. And you will be sent away to schools where you have no friends. You will be sent to be trained as a soldier. You will be instructed to act like a prince or a princess and not as a child. And... you will see very little of your father."

It was enough to remove the sparkle from Wyn's eyes, particularly when he mentioned her father.

"Oh, Sher...I mean Edwin. This is what has happened to you isn't it?" Keli wrinkled her nose. "It sounds like a prison!"

"Edwin is right! Where would Father fit into this new life?" Royce thought out loud.

"I want to go home," Keli said again.

Wyn now had a blank expression as she looked out over the far stretching lands of the kingdom.

"Yes, I do too," she said longingly.

"So do I!" Royce said, extending his hand to Edwin. This time he knew what to do with it. "Thank you, Edwin. I have learned so much from you."

Edwin gave Royce a good hardy handshake. "And I from you! You have given me something I will remember forever. Thank you!"

The handshake reminded Royce of something. "Oh, our agreement! We are still in debt to you. What was it that you needed us to help you with?

"You have already done it!" Edwin smiled a big smile.

"Ah, I knew you could smile, Sher...I mean Edwin!" Keli grinned.

"Please, Keli, if it is all the same to you, would you please call me Sherwin, all three of you. Your father chose that name to hide my identity. I think I like it."

"Okay, Sherwin!" Keli agreed. "That is so much easier to say anyway. I wonder what it means?"

"It means abundant... friend," Sherwin smiled.

"I knew you would know that!" she said. "And it is a perfect name for you,"

"Please come and see me often!" he pleaded.

"We will!" Wyn stepped up. "Thank you, Sherwin or Edwin, or whoever you are! We would not have been able to save Father if it had not been for you. We shall forever be in your debt."

"No, you have saved me, my lady." He gave her a purposeful smile, and she did not correct him. "I would not have escaped Devlin if it had not been for you three!"

Keli slid off Shira and now stood before Sherwin. "I will miss you." She hugged him.

"And I, you, Keli!" he replied, pulling away quite

embarrassed. "And you too, Shira!"

He started to touch the great dragon on the snout. Shira gave a little snort, and a small puff of smoke rose from her nostrils in his direction. Edwin jumped back.

"What was that?" he said.

"She says she likes you too!" Keli giggled.

The three Windmere children had just climbed upon the back of Shira when their father returned alongside of the king and his queen, Clarice.

"Children, there you are. Oh! Now come down at once. There is much to do, many arrangements to be made. From now on you will live with me. We must see to your new chambers, and we will have some new clothing made for you, and you will..."

He stopped short when Shira dropped her head in his direction and gave a little puff of smoke, which did *not* mean that she liked him. The king jumped back. When he noticed that the children did not move, he became a little indignant.

"Come down here at once!" the king insisted. "Children, did you hear me?"

Royce glanced at Sherwin. Sherwin gave him an acknowledging smile.

"Yes, Sire," Royce said somewhat sadly. "We did."

"So, do you know what it means to be a prince and princesses?"

"Yes, Sire. We think we do," Wyn replied.

"Well then, get down from that... that dragon this instant!" King Robinson was beginning to become somewhat angry.

The children glanced at each other nervously, but still, they had not moved.

"Sire." Spencer stepped close to the king. "If I may, you will not be able to force them to stay any more than you were able to force Alaina."

"Now, see here!" the king stated indignantly.

"They are their mother's children," he said.

"But...but...!" The old man's expression softened.

"Don't you want to be a prince?" The king stared right at Royce. "Don't you want to be a princess?" He looked at Wyn and Keli.

Royce glanced at Wyn and Keli. The look they gave him, told him all he needed. Then glancing at Sherwin, he smiled with a look of recognition. Royce knew that only *he* would understand.

"We will have to get back with you on that... Sire." Royce nodded to his little sister. Shira began to spread her wings.

"Bye, Grandfather!" Keli said, waving sweetly.

"Wait!" The king looked disturbed at the children and then at Spencer, who stood smiling at his children. "Spencer, stop them! Put some sense into your children!"

"I have been doing that all their life, Sire. Seems to me that just maybe, they are beginning to use some of it." Spencer's smile widened.

Shira lifted from the balcony floor and took to the skies once again. She circled the castle once then turned to the beckoning call of a great expansive world. All the while, the king hollered after them to return. The dragon soon became just a speck in the western sky, carrying the three Windmere children in search of their next great adventure!

About the Author

Don Clayton was born and raised by a farming family in south-central Kentucky, USA. He lives there still, with his sweet wife and three wonderful children. For much of his life, he worked in the construction industry building houses. He currently works as a CNC programmer in a family owned machining business. He began writing stories in 2006 because he felt that children today need to have stories with moral values and good solid heroes that they could look up to. *Shira's Children (2009)* is his first published work. He gets much of his inspiration from his own children. He is currently working on several other stories, including the second book in the *Shira's Children Series*.

Check out this and many other great stories at lulu.com.

To purchase a copy of this book go to:
http://stores.lulu.com/donclaytonbooks

www.ingramcontent.com/pod-product-compliance
Lightning Source LLC
Chambersburg PA
CBHW020955180626
46814CB00003B/1101